SIDE EFFECTS

A FOOTLOOSE JOURNEY TO THE APOCALYPSE

D1158669

GUERNICA WORLD EDITIONS 29

SIDE EFFECTS

A FOOTLOOSE JOURNEY TO THE APOCALYPSE

S. MONTANA KATZ

GUERNICA
World
EDITIONS

TORONTO—CHICAGO—BUFFALO—LANCASTER (U.K.)
2020

Michael Mirolla, general editor
Keith Garebian, editor
Cover design: Allen Jomoc Jr.
Interior layout: Jill Ronsley, suneditwrite.com
Guernica Editions Inc.
287 Templemead Drive, Hamilton (ON), Canada L8W 2W4
2250 Military Road, Tonawanda, N.Y. 14150-6000 U.S.A.
www.guernicaeditions.com

Distributors:
Independent Publishers Group (IPG)
600 North Pulaski Road, Chicago IL 60624
University of Toronto Press Distribution,
5201 Dufferin Street, Toronto (ON), Canada M3H 5T8
Gazelle Book Services, White Cross Mills
High Town, Lancaster LA1 4XS U.K.

First edition.
Printed in Canada.

Legal Deposit—Third Quarter
Library of Congress Catalog Card Number: 2019949207
Library and Archives Canada Cataloguing in Publication
Title: Side effects : a footloose journey to the apocalypse / S. Montana Katz.
Names: Katz, Montana, author.
Description: Series statement: Guernica world editions ; 29
Identifiers: Canadiana (print) 20190173580 | Canadiana (ebook)
20190173769 | ISBN 9781771835503
(softcover) | ISBN 9781771835510 (EPUB) | ISBN 9781771835527 (Kindle)
Classification: LCC PS3611.A8458 S53 2020 | DDC 813/.6—dc23

THEIR BEGINNING

W HEN THEY ARRIVED AT THE San Francisco Bay the vista unfolded before their eyes. They leapt in unison off their blue rusted out coated with dead bugs motorcycle and let it fall to the ground with a thud so taken with the scene neither noticed. Side by side they stood for a moment in silence looking out and dropped to their knees.

It was a perfect clear blue-sky day with sunshine toasting their faces. They knew they had arrived at Mecca and knew they'd never ever leave.

That was their real beginning together, there on a precipice viewing the Bay, the Golden Gate and the lushness of Northern California in the afternoon sun in the middle of July. Eventually she mustered the nerve to look straight into his eyes and say, "This is it, we're here" to which he looking back into hers said, "Yes."

They stayed a full two weeks crashing in cabins sleeping in their flannel camping bags in Tilden Park in the East Bay, a park fragrant with eucalyptus trees and shocks of magenta manzanita bushes giving way to wide open panoramas of the Bay, a heaven neither had known before. They somehow managed an overnight in Golden Gate Park under a statue, a feat that shocked even them with all of the camp-out antics they scored along their cross-country trek.

When they felt they just had to swing it there was the occasional crash in a motel, the sort with glaring neon green and pink lights flashing into their room all night like the one they had a great time in on Grove Street in the Berkeley flats. Once inside they hung all sorts of trophies from the road on the walls to make it festive and feel like it was theirs at least for the night. The beat-up Nevada license plate they found went over the medicine cabinet in the bathroom the rattle snake skin hung from the upper window frame some deep red earth from the Navajo reservation in Arizona poured in a leather pouch on the bedside table and an arrowhead they found out in the California desert was placed prominently on the only chair in the room. They cherished every second laughing warm laughs and sharing hugs together. This was the culmination of the expedition before they were forced to acknowledge that their vehicle wasn't going another revolution of the wheels farther and so they mustered their courage and got on a bus to start back to their home in Columbus, Ohio. Along the return they recounted segments of their trip, what led them to go and their big shiny plans for the future.

They had to switch buses a couple of times en route. By the third leg the sky was the main stage on the horizon. The vast open majestic sky is where the action is on the plains. The plain states of the US of A. They kept watching out the bus windows as if in a theater holding hands while it kept on changing its dramatic clouds and hues of blue. The land was bright and gigantic. The colors of the earth out there are no match for the sky, the light browns and creams with dots of green tufts and the endless fields and fields of crops on and on and on. They had never seen anything like it and thought it was mesmerizingly beautiful. Saw it in transit now and had it smack in their faces on the way West cruising the open road exposed on all sides to the wind the sun the cloud storms the crop pollen flying about all of it they loved every bit every scene every change.

He from East Germany that he fled of course long before the East-West divide, his family too. She from Sheepshead Bay Brooklyn and had barely ever left the neighborhood let alone the borough save a jaunt into the city meaning Manhattan with her older and much-admired sister until at eighteen she got herself a reprieve from the rabbi and her parents from kosher food and orthodox rituals to go all the way to Poughkeepsie for Vassar College and the unknown that was waiting there for her. Soon to be Editor-in-Chief of the *Vassar Miscellany News* during the days of McCarthy. Quite a time. Always pretty radical this experience stretched her further and sustained her political spirit for the rest of her life. She had barely graduated when they hopped on the motorcycle bought with some of their wedding money to the chagrin of her parents. They zoomed off from Avenue X across the Manhattan Bridge on through and out of the city heading for Niagara Falls and points west. Or anyway thought they were zooming on a rather beaten down version of a vehicle that they ended up having to nurse at mechanics at this service station and that dotted all across clear to California. Neither had a clue how to fix even the simple things. But the pit stops at gas stations and truck stops for assistance to get it moving again were fun for the pair, they took the opportunity to speak with people from all parts of the route from one end of the country to the other, people they did not meet in Poughkeepsie or Columbus, that's for sure. And they did a nationwide sampling and taste test challenge of oatmeals at every diner they were stranded at waiting for repairs to be performed. That was to become their signature meal of choice for years and was one of their closely guarded secrets. Neither of their mothers would have approved and that was of course part of the attraction.

A bit more about them, he's a sociology professor, yes, that is how they met, she in his class. The only male sociologist in the department, her major for a stint. But anyway, the two fell in love, matched up his brother with his wife to be another Vassar student, matched her brother with his wife, another pick from Vassar and off they went the two of them on an eyes wide open odyssey across to the other side of the continent, to paradise as they found it.

That is what they both thought when they got to the other coast and still felt it deep in their bones on the bus back they had found nirvana and swore to come back to live forever and ever under the palm trees the green blue gorgeous pounding Pacific Ocean and the low stucco bungalow homes with flowering vines adorning the entries. Everything was perfect there and far away from families and their constrictions. He wearing his leather belt coffee with a splash of milk colored trousers short sleeved brown and rust checked shirt with a beige background and she in a fitted top with a bright red skirt that flowed out from a tight waist and ended just below her knees definitely not all the way to mid-calf black pumps with a not too high but not too close to flat heel and red as in bright red lipstick. That's not what she wore on the motorcycle across the plains and into Colorado Utah Arizona Nevada of course before making it all the way over to the San Francisco Bay. She did though driving for the first time over the orange eternally being painted Golden Gate into Sausalito to mark how special that maiden voyage was and now she had it on again riding back on the bus. Neither could bring much given their mode of transport not to mention their skimpy funds. It was heaven heaven heaven. They toasted at sunset on the marina there in Marin and swore to go back East for only the most briefest time possible. He had to finish the year out in Columbus teaching and she was going to begin a graduate program never to be finished it would have flabbergasted her to know cruising there on the bus.

They were fresh off on the trip from their wedding at the Pierre Hotel in midtown, something no one could really afford but there it was and they did it both families pitching in some and so did he from his rather too small salary especially for her father's taste. "A professor's salary," her father would say over and over shaking his head to anyone who was listening, "what can you buy with that?" But that was before the wedding, he stopped at a decent point in advance of the event. Big ballroom with chandeliers and heavy drapes high ceilings with ornate plaster molding accented with gold all around in a grand style. And the long banquet table with the newlywed couple in the center and fanning out from them on either side their parents, maid of honor and bridesmaids and the best man and so forth, the central table. Lots of cigars and cigarettes in engraved silver holders matchbooks with the couple's name and the wedding date embossed in gold on the face ashtrays for the taking home with the same etched in the glass. Round tables set for eight places ringing the circumference of the room with the dance floor in the middle. The band, a live band with a crooner, off to one side but where all could have a good view. There was even an MC of sorts and he was funny as he should be for this crowd, so happy they were to be successful such as they were and to the extent they were to be making it in the US of A and to be free. I mean not that they had huge illusions but relatively speaking they were in the land of the free and in the post-war years of limitless possibilities like the trek across the country the options wide open for the asking. Men could walk into establishments, companies, universities and get jobs be a professor be a manager own a business and earn a living wage, a family wage as it was called. The guys could get that or anyway a certain segment of them. It was a land of immigrants who could have and reach dreams. Not saying everyone was so easily accepted and not that there weren't battles prejudice racism and turf wars but even with all of that for a large chunk of the population some version of the American Dream felt attainable. Right in Sheepshead Bay not to say that the Italians the Jews and the Irish didn't have their territorial wars and fist fights but her father who came from Lithuania alone at fourteen made his way to Canada Pennsylvania New York and Brooklyn worked in schmatas for a while and now owned a juke box rental business. Rough business it was but he did it and supported his family of six from it and any other relatives or refugees who needed help. Certainly nothing lavish but they were stable. One son served in the war to come back and finish law and engineering degrees and invent the living bra the molded soft cup kind without points another at Princeton a son of course and Nobel laureate to be and the oldest a daughter who had already married twice the second and last time to a war hero from Denmark working as an architect and taking them to such far flung and unimaginable places as Indonesia. The bride was the youngest of the four a surprise baby as it happened. The night before the wedding while attending to last minute details for the event her mother let her in on the secret until that moment, that she had considered an abortion illegal for sure in those early thirties and imagined herself leaving behind three small children having bled out from a botched procedure all too common in those days.

One of the bride's uncles was a prize fighter who already had cauliflower ear another a cat burglar and so many aunts hard to count them and cousins. She grew up in a very tiny two story two family home with three cousins an aunt and uncle upstairs everyone watching out for everyone else in a good way that often felt merciless and constricting to her. The other aunts and uncles cousins and such all lived within a one block radius so there were eyes and ears everywhere. Sonny Fox and Ruth Bader lived close by as did others. All attending the same schools from beginning to end. And the postal delivery man lived nearby who had a breakdown during the war, just couldn't keep delivering the death notices and went on permanent disability. The war wasn't talked about much in her house they didn't think the kids should know about that kind of evil.

He in his tux and she in a long, flowing white satin gown with pearls stitched in and a long veil and the pictures and her parents his parents and siblings and cousins and aunts and uncles and so many many people all having a wonderful time wonderful food in honor of this wonderful and very attractive couple. Most of the men in tuxes most of the women in gowns really done up fifties style with the little hats that they wore indoors the little purses to hold a lipstick and a compact for powder and the taffetas the silks the laces. Of course she was very young and the expression on her face in the photos is radiant but a bit off, a bit confused or not knowing what she is getting into while she thought she did. He was older and had survived hell in Germany as did the family members who were out and mostly in New York, some never got out to anywhere but some did thanks to his father, a business man who would take people one at a time posing them as his assistant or secretary back and forth across the border he went each time with someone else who didn't return with him. Must have taken a lot of bribing. His wife was detained for a day but somehow got out and eventually the family made it to Ellis Island.

This was the honeymoon, the motorcycle, the trip. An adventure the likes of which neither had ever had but only fantasized about and had no idea what they were to find along the way and once they got there. I mean, they saw pictures on postcards and such but remember no internet in those days no homogenization of urban areas like now and not such a monopoly of big chain stores. Sears but none of the megastore chains we have now so they really didn't know what to expect or what they were going to see. A lot of travel by ship and train, planes even little ones weren't a common method of transport. That was going to take a few more years. Did I forget to say we're in the middle of the 1950s on this trip with them to the golden state?

Imagine what they saw. This country with all its variety and there weren't mega highways yet either or even freeways as they call them in California the free part reinforcing the myth of everything being perfect out there. They went through Niagara Falls and the Great Lakes the Plains the Rockies some desert a long romantic stay on the Navajo reservation near Window Rock and then on to the oasis of palms and bougainvilleas and roses and lemon trees and grape vines and wilderness and ocean and all under the great big warm sun shining down every single day. Irresistible, especially to these two as they were embarking on the rest of their lives. They were definitely going for their version of the American Dream including a healthy or more dose of idealism for the world. Ethics and politics and struggle and open discussion and equality and equity were all going to work together to sweep the world into a wonderful place for all.

In the meantime the tract housing and the building of the suburban dream was well underway. Young couples could take out mortgages and buy a ranch house to hold their growing family of two parents two kids and a dog on a freshly minted circular road holding many such identical or slightly different homes some split level, those were really cool. With appliances people didn't dream of before, their own washer and dryer set electric ovens and stove tops vacuum cleaners so many things that made life so much easier. And cleaner. And more time for leisure. So many swimming pools in California. People owned them privately in their own backyards even. And car ports or garages and station wagons. And lawns that could be sparklingly green and fragrantly fresh cut into an even soft carpet. There were enormous side effects to the post war palliation going on as it turns out, we'll get to those shortly.

Back in Columbus, arms wrapped over shoulders sitting on their second hand couch in their quite small starter apartment looking out on a lot of concrete and a small diner across the way with a blue and white striped awning whose oatmeal was pretty bland they spent a lot of time thinking back on their brush with destiny. They plotted and planned their way back with a job for him and a graduate program transfer for her. She was studying political science in a Master's program to help her figure out how to change the world. One evening after the particularly heated study group discussion on ethics, Freud, and German re-education that met in their apartment once a month with a small handful of colleagues and friends, they decided to make a move to fulfill their historic proclamation upon their first glimpse of the San Fran environs panorama.

"Look," she said sitting on the couch in her Peter Pan collared short sleeved shirt she had sewn with green calico fabric atop indigo blue slacks, "just put your name in for the job at Berkeley, it's a research position, why wouldn't they want you, you're overqualified. Of course they will."

"But," he wearing another checked short sleeved button-down cotton shirt this one with blue and green lines, the brown slacks and brown leather shoes, continued the thinking, "we'll need more money than that. We need to hold out for a teaching position there or maybe Stanford."

"No, the money will work out, I'll be in school but I can get a job too."

"Doing what?"

That question didn't sit so well including the fact that she didn't have an answer and the conversation ended at that point. A gnawing feeling persisted in the pit of her belly for a while over that one. She wasn't upset with him but with herself tumbling the question over and over in her head, how could she have gotten this far and have no saleable practical skills? Only later it occurred to her that maybe she could work on a newspaper after all she had just been doing that for four years in school. Her stomach settled after that.

He did apply and did get the research job beginning in the winter and they began to make plans to go. In the meantime they each had almost a semester's worth of work to do. She was taking more than a full course load trying to rack up credits towards her MA faster than usual. Their study groups taught her more than the university courses but still she was learning and had a goal. Policy or politics or both, but something effective in the world. She had already embarked on many political projects most of them communist leaning while in college and had even received a grant to go to Russia. It was the days of McCarthy as I've already told you and the college wouldn't allow it citing one lame excuse after another until it was too late. She kept jumping the hurdles but to no avail in the end and she never forgot it.

They had a full life in Columbus with a good group of colleagues and friends and very busy academic schedules taking courses and teaching courses. Almost like bouncing kangaroos their exuberance seemed to emanate from their pores and rub off in all their endeavors. Separately and together they moved from one activity to another day in and day out well into the evenings. They didn't let anything bog them down it was always full steam ahead between the two of them and they loved each other for it and really felt they were made from different cloths that melded together into a perfect fit.

His assistant professor salary covered the rent on their small apartment and their frugal expenses but that was about it. Neither was sure how they were going to afford the move West but it didn't seem to worry either of them. It was the era of limitless possibility as I've mentioned what you may have already known and they both implicitly bought the ideology of the time. The details would work out, they didn't need to worry. Or to put it differently and more accurately they didn't think of or about details just the over-all that they were going to sunny California and not coming back anytime soon. In their minds they were really already there. She'd wake up and breathe in the scent of lemon trees in that twilight time between sleep and waking he'd envision strutting about the UC Berkeley campus he the émigré who persevered and landed in heaven on earth out of the bowels of war and destruction.

Midway into the semester she started to feel sick and didn't know what was happening. It wasn't so bad though that she gave it a lot of thought. A while later the vomiting began and cravings. She did ordinarily have cravings indulging in all the things she couldn't eat growing up. Ham and eggs milkshakes together with a burger or hotdog candy bars and on and on and none of it kosher and not so healthy either. The opposite. But she had more hankerings and by the time they figured it out and she went to a doctor she was showing pretty clearly, tall and athletic as she was it probably took a little longer than most the little bit of a mound to emerge visibly on the front of her belly. Inside that mound held a lot of future for the two of them but especially for me, I was in there growing by the day, cell upon cell.

She was getting tired and walking to and staying in her classes was becoming more and more difficult. She would lie on their bed feet on the floor knees hooking over the edge feeling like a beached whale and wondering what she had done. I mean of course she wanted this, this was the normal thing to do once you get married and they did it both getting married and having sex but somehow it was unexpected and she was shocked. Women usually are even if they understand how procreation works which she barely did. Somehow no one had explained it to her and she had never thought to be curious about it either. Well over a decade later when she tried to explain things like menstruation to me there were a lot of gaps in detail and confusion about essential body parts like whether you pee from the same place the menstrual blood comes out not to mention a baby and such.

He was delighted and head over heels already with the baby that was barely a concept at that point. Kind of chutzpah to be as crazy in love with a baby that wasn't born yet but he was and with the whole idea of it that they were going to have a family be a family really really really.

He pranced around their little living room when she told him the news. Jumping around, he made up a little song, "We did it, we're doing it, you're going to have a baby, we're going to be three!" As he sang he grabbed her hands and tried to entice her to join him.

She did get up feeling happy with his happiness, kind of drunk on it they both were, and she gave him a huge sloppy hug and kiss. In an embrace, she said in a soft voice, "I know when it happened, do you?"

"Of course! On our journey West, a fateful trip in so many ways that we're still discovering them."

"Yes, of course on our trip," she said affectionately. "But when on our trip, do you know when the magic revealed itself?"

He took a pace back thinking. And thinking some more trying to calculate what he didn't have enough info to figure. "Right at the beginning I think, Niagara?"

"No! It was in Arizona, I know it, I'm sure. On the reservation. We stayed there a while, remember, it was so beautiful, the orange vistas, the huge sky so deep with stars at night, that was our place."

They both did love that part of the trip which is why they lingered there longer than anywhere else on the way. In college she had been very deep into studying the Indian tribes as they were called then including the indignities they suffered at the hands of the invading white people. She didn't know so much about what had taken place on that reservation nor what was happening right under their feet planted on the rust colored earth as they were there and ongoing into the decades ahead. Not a metaphor I'm making here but literally right under their feet, the insides of the sacred grounds being scratched and clawed at or worse dynamited deep into the understructure of the mud and log dwellings animal pastures weaveries and civilization as the Navajo had constructed it there against the unforgiving but breathtaking backdrop of the area. The mining for one of course, caused plenty of side effects of all the progress right there on the res. The uranium and coal mining gas and oil drilling the water restrictions lack of enforcement of safety and environmental regs and the toxic waste from all of it left right there on and in the land that was so sacred to the Navajo and other native tribes. So many resulting diseases and deaths and only a small fraction studied or recorded. Mine the one I got there and then still hiding out in utero in the early days and weeks before I was a known confirmed thing wasn't recorded like so many others still haven't been. I'll tell you about it later.

"Our bag of sand! We still have it, that was the omen, right there in that pouch we have kept above our bed. What an apt symbol!" My father went rushing into the bedroom pointing over the headboard.

My mother went scooting after him exclaiming, "Yes, even if you don't believe in omens being the pragmatist you are," she said gently teasing and affectionately placing a hand around the side of his neck under his shirt collar and dabbing his nose with the index finger on her other hand.

The two continued on with their reminiscences of the conception. Then in a flash they shifted to thinking about the future. My father almost jumped back causing my mother's hands to go into a free fall, "We'll need a car! With seats and doors and windows even!"

"Yes," my mother responded in unison without missing a beat, "we've got to ditch the motorcycle concept forever! Wow," she said wistfully.

Eventually they got a four door Studebaker station wagon, blue with wood paneling on the side and were so proud. That was later another baby or two later. She was pregnant for ten long months during which they debated back and forth and eventually decided to stay in Columbus the full academic year and wait for a better job in the Golden State of eagles grizzly bears monarch butterflies poppies and clear skies and just everything good. In the end they concluded that they wanted to wait for the baby to be born somewhere they knew and were settled in for the moment. And they did get to California and they did have a bouncing smiling happy baby and I'm going to tell you about the whole story as it unfolds after a bit of an interlude with the present as we are now bumps warts and side effects as I've been calling them all stemming from those booming years of plenty. So fast forward for a bit but they will come back baby in tow I absolutely promise.

THE BOOMING LEGACY

G ETTING FROM 1955 TO THE here and now requires flying over huge and I mean macro changes in every which way. Some inversions that we'll talk about too, you and I. Think about it, back in their beginning no cell phones, not even cordless in home phones, no skinny laptops or personal computers of any sort no watches that can do so many things most owners of them only use a small fraction of the functions and so much more we totally take for granted, none of that in the fifties not even as an idea not even on the Jetsons a bit later. But what there was in the fifties was unlimited possibility as I've said a couple of times already as in the sky's the limit kind of thing, idealism that now (then) the world could be made into a better place, evil could be conquered once people had seen its face in the war. All the energy and money that went into the war could be turned back to society, to building homes and businesses and places of learning and in the US of A the American Dream wasn't just a dream but emerging reality.

Now, and here comes an inversion, we're in a different place the opposite the inside out of the boom. On these pages I'm going to take you on a journey from the fifties then to our now visiting enough sights. Maybe it'll incite you to action or maybe to depressive lethargy or hopeless apathy (the latter two things I hope you'll see aren't good options in case my saying that makes any difference whatsoever). I'll try to keep my cool but I'm sure I'll become mighty angry at times, I'm feeling it right now. That's another thing we'll discover along the way, with whom to be angry I mean it's important to know that, right? We'll together see how all that American Dream stuff had some major undersides not restricted to out on reservations but everywhere nationwide and worldwide and was only for some people and even if the US of A was sold as a melting pot or a salad bowl or whatever the metaphor we (have to locate the proper set for this "we" at some point in this story sooner rather than later because it is necessarily exclusionary and might as well fess up to it) did it on the backs of massacre and mass extinction of existing ways of life for plants and animals on this continent not to mention that the dream was only accessible to a segment of that pot/bowl. We'll catch sight of that and also that the possibilities are no longer wide open in fact they're dwindling to a shriveled crumb as we speak and breathe (something not everyone everywhere can do anymore without serious filtration masks on), we've got twenty years max more likely maybe only eleven according to scientists and environmentalists to totally reverse climate change *by cooperation of the whole, entire world*. When has that happened for anything is the reality so the fact is we've all got Damocles' sword hanging over our heads. What's bound to come first and is really already underway in so many corners of the earth, mass genocides of the weakest and most vulnerable and then second of us all though some think they'll survive in their Ralph Lauren luxury bunkers. Who would want to is what I wonder and I also wonder if they realize they would need to "save" a lot of service and professional workers to make the bunker survival viable. So here we are plunk in the middle of a reversal of the mentality the zeitgeist if you want to call it that of the fifties and pretty much every aspect is different from the expansion to the shrinkage of options in all walks of life and including how we even talk and think and imagine and hope and fear.

Right, I mean we don't even have innermost thoughts like we used to keeping things inside the contours of our mind/bodies, now they're out on social media of all sorts before the thought has even ripened into something formulatable into words just out it goes. Somehow it isn't an experience if it isn't shared worldwide today this instant before I've even had a chance to experience it let alone think about it. People have come to speak in a radically altered way nowadays if you think about it, something akin to hysterical screaming along with all the exaggeration that goes with it, something they didn't need to do in the fifties with all the security of abundance and promise of a fairy book future people could just talk in soft tones of voice at low decibels of course people weren't as deaf then either from the blasting of music straight into our ears with the ear buds jammed in deep and such. Just an example: "This is extreme—like capital letters extreme, exclamation point extreme," and these particular words were spoken by a scientist. Point being that even those of us trained and used to stating things clearly, methodically, maybe even factually if one still believes in facts, these days shouts, overdoes it. Sounds undereducated in the process too, don't you agree? And we all do it at least sometimes it's how things go now, I mean, haven't you found yourself overstating and too loudly sometimes like the commercials that we're exposed to everywhere even on our phones! Unthinkable in the fifties when phones were heavy objects that had dials on them and the zero dial actually got you a real live person to talk to who connected your call and for that matter who would know who you were going to speak with and could listen in and stuff like that not to mention party lines but anyway they didn't have advertisements shrieking at us on or in them. Scientists back in the fifties would've been more dignified and measured, had conversations, debates but always sounded factual at the right scale. They didn't need the wild fanfare. They felt more secure. Not so media driven and soundbitey as we are today. Funding structures were different back then I must say and that's a big part of the point the funding and what its willing to pay for.

In this world that we're in today music doesn't play, it blares out of headphones so crazy loud the whole D line subway car headed out to the far reaches of Brooklyn can hear every nuance, we are deaf unless the decibel level is beyond high high high, blind without a billboard, and so on, without complete, total overemphasis of

everything—this is the best ..., the worst absolute worst ..., I hate
... I love ...—I know you get the *idea* but the reality of it has so
inundated us, so soaked into every fiber of our perception that it's
difficult to discern or notice even. We're so trained in numbing hy-
perbole the climate change facts go whipping by without sustained
alarm. Even calling it that (down from global warming which really
wasn't bad except for the idiots who'd say when it's cold out, "see,
there's no warming!") it sounds like we're saying something like
it's going to rain later, nothing catastrophic just a change in the
weather pattern. Have no fear in case you're scratching you head
right about now not getting where I am taking you, our journey
is going to counterbalance the complacence lack of action lack of
the registration of panic in the bones and mind of each and every
one of us in other words it will inject some glaring reality along the
path of how we got here from that glorious boom to its underside.
That is how I see it, we're all presently dwelling in an underside in
the aftershocks the side effects as I've been calling them so far.

Along our journey here together I am going to try hard to keep
things judiciously put, to keep things in a low enough register to
put them back into proper perspective. Some things are very very
big and require our immediate attention and other matters not so
much. Maybe that'll help you ponder and think and feel even about
the details. So, don't expect hand wringing, bold emphases all over
the place or slap you in the face realism unless I feel I really really
really have to. Just to say, I'm sure though that I will become angry
to a boiling point here and there but I'm imagining that you will also
maybe not at the exact same points and maybe that'll be good, we
can motivate each other, but we'll see as we go along. On the whole
I am going to try to just tell it, nuanced and not overly spiced up,
volume set at a reasonable transmission level. Sounds like I'm old,
right? I am but you know that already since I was conceived back
there in fifty-five on the reservation out in the middle of the splendid
romantic auburn hued desert. From the little egg and sperm back in
Arizona to the embryo in Columbus. Sixty-three to be clear and
precise enough, but you probably already did the math. Not so old

I should be dying even with life expectancy on the decrease in the US of A but mostly it seems from deaths of despair—aren't we all or shouldn't we all be despairing? I mean really I'm asking—and not so old my experience reaches back to something really really different like World War I style battles or leaving people hand written notes in their mail box to communicate or selling eggs individually on the subway and in the streets. Yet, pretty different as I've already said. Like I remember as a young adult there being nothing very very fast like fax machines (people barely bother with those anymore) or fiber optics or snapping and sending a digital image *from your phone.* Like the double helix—1953—was still news people were getting their heads around when I was growing up. The Salk polio vaccine—the very first vaccine against polio, and the safe one, the one I insisted upon for my kids much much later. The Sabin caused some polio cases and I know some of them—had just become available, we're talking 1955 again here. Party lines on the telephone, old wonderful Bakelite heavy black phones, pink princess phones all wired into a wall. In order to talk people were tethered to cords in a way young people can't imagine now. Cars that even I could look under the hood and figure out what was going on (not even I because I'm female but even I because I don't know anything about car mechanics plain and simple). Computers that you can wear on your wrist and not to mention no longer need a deck of long cream-colored cards with weird holes punched in them that had to be read through a garage sized machine to run a program. Any young people reading at this point I'm guessing you have no idea what I'm referring to here. Can't imagine what computers were like and how careful one had to be to not drop that large deck of paper cards if one wanted to run a program and don't spill coffee on them either or muck up any of the little holes in them. And if you wanted to communicate with someone you most likely hand wrote words on a piece of paper maybe with a pencil that you hand sharpened if you wanted to be able to erase and correct and sealed it in an envelope stamped and mailed it through the USPS system. It could take a week to get to the person, maybe faster maybe slower and maybe never. Copying on a ditto machine, filing paper—lots of it—in color coded light weight cardboard files in actual, physical, metal and wood file cabinets that took up lots of space. So many differences, but I'm getting ahead here. I want to get back to the beginning, my beginning with all the lousy nooks and crannies underneath all that gloss.

Yeah, born in 1956 to my exuberant parents in Columbus. We lived in that little apartment they had until we got the go ahead to move. No beeline to sunny wonderful California but we did get there my parents did not forget being bowled over on that motorcycle trip west when they hit the Golden State. They saw so much on that trip but what stuck them straight in the heart both hearts struck together was that gleaming bay the Golden Gate Mount Tam and the whole surround there, they were going to get back whatever it eventually took. So far as we are in the story now, there we were once I was born planted in the Midwest in the middle of the post-World War II baby boom. Not out ahead, not in the tail, smack dab in the middle.

Let's see if we can together understand any of this divide this reversal of fortune really between then and now, see if you think I'm making any sense. Not so much for them back then as for us, us as in everyone on earth now and in the future. I'll try to get us through this the nightmare of what's happened from the years of plenty to the years of neglect famine drought employing a documentary style without biased commentary. Right, if you buy that one as if that were *ever* possible I have a bridge to sell you too! Not even possible in astrophysics. If you still cling to the idea that lack of bias anywhere is even in theory possible note that the Observer Effect was identified quite a long while ago. Yet we love to hang onto the ideas of Objectivity Truth Knowledge Science. Let me know those of you who cling to objectivity what's left by the time we're done here. Objectivity truth foundations facts are outdated discredited terms and interactivity inter-personality contextualism these are what is in now. Onwards, journalism style, as I mockingly said, here we go back to the Midwest to my parents and even to me now that I've been born, here we go.

A THREESOME
IN THE MIDWEST

THERE THEY WERE IN THAT a bit college student-ish apartment even though neither of them was that anymore by a long shot. I think they saw it as a reflection of their bohemian outlook and maybe it was and I'm being too hard on them I mean the other junior faculty member's homes were outfitted more predictably for the mid-fifties more square as it used to be called. Given what was in the works—me!—they made an effort to massage the place into an adult home with curtains regular furniture and all but now with a very bulging belly on her and the maternity wear she really really needed some of it friends and neighbors gave her and some she sewed along with the curtains they started and never completed making it more of a recognizably family home. Not that they were overly concerned with such material details so overjoyed they were together doing what they were doing with huge dreams for the future, mine and theirs.

Got a plaid cloth bassinette from a professor's wife down the street and started to nest. He was continuously thrilled dancing around the apartment holding up the baby stuff and maternity clothes as he pranced and she was a touch disoriented having stopped attending or even thinking about classes there in her third and very tired trimester just couldn't do it anymore so she got busy with the baby prep. So much anticipation about the genius they were going to have oy! that's me and the expectations were high let me tell you but is it worse and I'm really asking you this here to have low or no expectations of you? I don't think so or even "realistic" ones whatever that is I mean how can you know? Better to think and hope for the best of the best, right? The fantasies were soaring emanating from both of them and they were pretty darned happy together in this shared thing going on. They even named one of their oatmeal concoctions the Pregnancy yup you guessed it had a bit of everything in it definitely pickles definitely ice cream and salted pretzels.

One morning at the table while she was practically inhaling her portion he set his spoon down and asked in a mournful tone, "Did you add sardines to the formula now?"

Keeping her gaze down and fixed on her bowl she just slowly nodded with a bit of a grin breaking out from under.

Relatives in New York were pleased too and telephoned often with advice offerings and general excitement. There they were lapping it all in with everything different and the same all at once. The monthly reading/discussion groups continued the idealism continued they were still going to make the world better and now not just for the whole wide wide world but specifically for their perfect baby they didn't yet have a name for, or two names since there was no determining sex in those days. If you think about it there's no real determining it now what with all the gender/sex self-identifying options that need not be anchored in biological sex categories the latter of which remain to be properly catalogued there being so many more than just the two we officially recognize. The biological ones I mean there are lots of those a spectrum of them like so much else that we lazily put into binary categories, we humans just somehow never really committed to the documented reality of a downright plethora of biological sex classifications. Finally just now admitting that there may be more than two legit sex categories and that's not even talking about gender where the range is infinite. In their fantasies I guess I was a boy since the name they had until I was born was Alexander. Came up with mine on the spot when they needed it. In retrospect the Alexander name would have been apt also. Anyway, following tradition I had to be named for someone dead and there were quite a lot of post-war choices after all.

He was teaching two courses, advising and doing all the duties that come with being a professor while on the lookout for posts in California and the necessary contacts to smooth it all into place. He was learning how to make the perfect martini when they could spring for the alcohol and olives on their tight budget learning to do it with just the right amount of swirling and so forth for the cocktail parties that come with and need to be hosted and anyway it's just plain fun to hobnob with people doing interesting sorts of research and get to talk about your own as part of the academic life that was unfolding for them in front of their eyes. I mean as a family and her for the time being as a faculty wife which is of course what the women for the most part were then but she was sure sure sure she would complete school and have her own slice of it just a bit later. Three children later? What was she thinking? I mean she did do it eventually but it wasn't exactly easy not like it was for him. For now she was eating all the chocolate cake and whatever else she wanted or as her still thriving cravings dictated. She generally did that anyway being tall and athletic female friends would notice that she could and did eat like a guy even in her non-gestating state.

They were almost or at least getting close to being ready when I was born—a month late by OB statistical norms but no one including the doctor paid any attention to such things in those days. Liability was such a different ball of wax then compared with now. The OB was a calm elderly guy and he didn't get too bustled about rules and norms. He had been delivering babies—that is what was done in those days and even now still, delivering I mean rather than the mother and baby in their own birthing process that the birthing couple drives—for a long time. She felt safe with this doctor and believed that everything was going to be all right, which it was as far as the birth went and as far as my having all the requisite number of fingers and toes she counted immediately and proportions and such and I fed well.

I was finally born and named and settling nicely into the rhythm of the hospital routine where we were for a while that for me of course was an eternity since it was the whole of my air borne life to date. Me who is still here now to tell it. And, as I've been saying so many, many others all getting born in droves. Before, during and after my birthday. Maternity wards were bustling all over the country.

Boom's on!

The big event happened at Mount Carmel, a Catholic hospital, nurses all nuns, statues of Mary. A huge one standing there greeting people at the entrance. A few years later, not too many, I came to love Mary. A coincidence, maybe. I had the most beautiful, putty colored plastic rendition of her in a little case I could open and close with a click click, and I did so a lot.

And, by the way, what does the Catholic or any other church do with its money? Do they serve the poor? Tend to the sick? I don't know but if the trend in Catholic hospitals today is any indicator the answers are no, they are for-profit without in the US of A needing to pay taxes like a for-profit. As L. Ron Hubbard said, the best way to make a million (and this was a long time ago when a million was still a million meaning practically like a billion today) is to start a religion. As Lou Reed belted out, getting ahead, way ahead to the late eighties, go to church if its real estate you want to buy.

Not meaning to single out religions here, I just suspect we have to look at them and all that missionary for example activity that set about changing indigenous ways of life and the treatment of soil water air people and other animals across the globe in terms of our health poison and the earth like we do other corporations and the people in them. Some of my best friends. Well, maybe not *my* best friends, none of them, but someone I once married (wow! something I was never, ever going to do: another *what happened* kind of out of body experience—not giving myself excuses just describing the experience—almost physical—of it) is certainly part of this gang. And we are all co-conspirators and can't get off easy to get straight to the who to be angry at theme. How many snickers bars aerosol cans weed killer Drano take-out in Styrofoam gadgets you didn't need or maybe even ever use how much just junk did you buy consume by using or eating or snorting? We all have done plenty of it. How many batteries have been just tossed to the landfill and how many have you personally chucked into the garbage can? how many electric cars—really good I guess too good cars—were made and then trashed in the eighties? If you haven't, watch *What Ever Happened to the Electric Car?* It's edifying. How much perfectly good food clothing milk merchandise just gets tossed to a landfill by grocery stores supermarkets restaurants and each and every one of us? Perfectly good edible fresh even food?

Pause, rewind, let's get back to Mount Carmel and maternity wards. Not to mention maternity itself, pregnancy pathologized it was. Seemed good at the time safer cleaner more scientific less animal better. Medicalized, made into a high-risk condition in need of treatment, intervention, tools and toys. Did you know, back in the days of the 1950s, pregnant women were offered *cigarettes* cigarettes! as a relaxant? Replete with all the smoke and its 4,000 (I didn't make that number up!) chemicals, forty-three carcinogens, four hundred toxins including by the way carbon monoxide formaldehyde cyanide benzene arsenic DDT and acetone—wow! and that's not a full list but it's enough to make any of you readers out there who are still smoking want to quit isn't it? Alcohol too of course. Pre- and post-partum, *in the hospital.* Glyphosate its finally been admitted this very week is readily detected in wines and beers. Of course it is it's used on crops everywhere, right?

Mothers puffing away as the newborns were fed watching the feedings through a glass window or not watching at all. Never would have gone over in 1988 when I had my first. Maternity wards had to change up some, I know and okay getting ahead of myself again, dial back to a bit before my birth, 1951. It was the first year that baby formula was reformulated into a concentrated liquid instead of a powder product.

Powder needed to be mixed of course. Could be messy. Annoying to be doing that both for nurses in a busy hospital and for moms at home. It was the era of no muss no fuss easy living. Liquid was ready to serve in baby bottles (Bakelite, plastic, leaching stuff, more later on this) with nipples (ditto). Similac—did you ever wonder where that name came from, how about "similar to lactation." And what was similar you might now ask? Not the contents (Karo syrup??) not the nipple not the skin on skin contact of mother and baby—none of that happening in Mount Carmel or other hospitals of the boom era—and certainly not the gaze that flows from the nursing position—been credited, that gaze to and from, as the birth of language! The birth of metaphor this means, the capacity itself for metaphoric thinking. That's huge! What allegedly makes us human although I don't buy that seems to be going a step too far with the presumptions about human superiority, just the reverse if you ask me and being pretty sure other animals have their own metaphoric-linguistic capacity we just don't have the ability to ask them. Not smart enough I guess.

Easy for the nurses to administer in the nurseries where all the babies were. Pop pop pop one little bottle in every newborn's mouth easy easy easy. New mothers anesthetized were in their rooms, sometimes with their breasts tightly bound so the milk wouldn't come in and ruin the woman's cleavage. Or taking those dry-up pills.

Oy! Who dreams these things up? I wish I could say it was a mystery. Mothers and babies would stay in the hospital about five days. Often the mother would only see her baby at feeding times and then through that glass window I mentioned already. I think we call this breeding. Wouldn't you if it were a different animal? It was the booming fifties after all. Something had to replace all that war time activity, all that war time money manufacture jobs. Products! 1950s products! Cars! Housing developments! Cul-de-sacs en masse. Strollers pacifiers baby bottle nipples bottle warmers disposable stuff even Johnson & Johnson Baby Powder full of asbestos and still is with 11,700 plaintiffs suing as I write! Laundry soaps in so many options washers dryers *dishwashers* automatic lawn sprinkler systems and all the weed killer you can cart away.

Or better yet have someone else go near the stuff for you if you can swing it. It was all there for the taking or at least the buying, so one had to be able to buy first of all. But so many could, mobility upward financial mobility family wage for the guys maternity sets for the gals. Sell those electric can openers in the newfangled modern designed shapes and colors—all sorts. You might want—dare we say need?—more than one.

Okay, enough facts for now, back to me and *my* story.

Father of newborn (me): a Holocaust survivor from Germany which I know I've pointed out already. Zwickau. He was sent alone to Basel to finish Gymnasium leaving his middle brother as the sole Jew at the local Gymnasium in the thirties. Citizenship revoked for the whole family and a trek to Ellis Island. Way more about this later I'm sure. A traumatized psyche with visceral as he called them migraines, lots. Often when driving. I think he meant visual. Maybe both? so you can see that when he arrived in California with his new, young, beautiful, smart and smart-mouthed bride on that rusty old motorcycle he felt he was saved that the nightmares the anxiety the headaches could end once they put down stakes in this astonishing land of plenty. He was going to be able to be happy content secure stable with his family research writing in a place he could not have conjured up in his wildest of thoughts. He would stop tensing every fiber of his body in sweat-soaked sleep. It was going to be okay.

Mother: Already said she was raised orthodox Jewish in Sheepshead Bay Brooklyn, NY. Yes, as in the famous James Madison High School and my mother, uncles (including of the Nobel Laureate clan and living bras), aunts, cousins all went there—its notables include Bernie Sanders Ruth Bader Judge Judy Martin Landau Sonny Fox—oh! The Sonny Fox show *Wonderama*, any of you remember that? my sister Debbie did a Hawaiian Punch commercial for him, kept drinking for the whole minute it was so yummy. Chris Rock Carole King Sandra Feldman. Speaking of Bernie yes with the 2016 primaries way long over and the next ones whipping by, one on the list of the really truly deeply upsetting primary years. We had a shot at something a lot better and much more thoughtful to happen in the White House. Really needless to say given what we got. Okay, so now you have a sense of my politics, not at all the subject of this quest. Not at all, but I'm sure it will find its way to creep in here and there so you might as well have the divisive basics up front. Well, maybe it is part of the subject at hand, Democrats and Independents seem to do a lot better on the environment—Bernie Jerry Brown Jimmy Carter and on health care—Bernie, Bloomberg—yes! Bloomberg has done a lot and with his own money for health care and internationally, and for those in greater need—Bernie again, Jimmy Carter for sure. What modern day Republicans can we point to for any of this? Or churches or mosques or synagogues besides on the edges. Maybe I'm wrong here, maybe. Point is anyway, we're all guilty and we've all got it coming as Clint Eastwood told us long enough ago. Someone who would be on my list, Clint that is, along with Bernie and Jimmy while I've got all three here in one paragraph, for not being justifiably accusable of sexual harassment or misconduct. I hope I'm right. Hope the current #MeToo movement leads us somewhere good. There was a lot of hope for change after Anita Hill's testimony. More later.

Funny they ended up in a Catholic hospital. My parents, that is, getting ready for their first child to be born. Followed the doctor she loved straight into that hospital. I wonder what my grandmother would have thought. Did she know? She sure didn't like my plastic Mary (she didn't like the crucifix over my bed much either) came panting out of my room there in Menlo Park to get way ahead for a moment with horses racing on her chest as she said and my mother had to support her from a fainting fall. But there they were there we were with holy trinity and Madonna and child images swirling around us since I had just been born in the hospital staffed with nuns in the middle of the country and they we were going to be so happy. They already were so happy with so many high expectations for the future and loving every minute of the present. I don't even know what they noticed about the hospital so focused they were on each other and me the rest faded away.

One morning my father brought in some fixings for the watery mush they called oatmeal in the hospital. My father was proud to be able to help her in any way while she was recouping. That day he bounded in, bag in hand, "Guess what I've got here? Just one guess!" He waved the bag back and forth in front of my mother.

She giggled and exclaimed, "I can't, what is it? A deck of cards poker chips, the game's coming here tonight?"

"Nope and nope. Wrong twice be careful with your last chance before you strike out!" My father was grinning and dangling the bag, "I promise you want this!"

"I give up I don't want to strike out!"

"I know, I know how competitive you are! Okay," with that my father rotated the tray over her bed and began unpacking the bag. "Raisins, walnuts, banana, a chocolate bar," he raised each item as he said its name. "Your favorite oatmeal dream come true unfolding before your eyes. Where's that mush now that we're armed and ready for it?"

My mother was thrilled as they shared their breakfast ritual together.

We were in the hospital for days not that I remember but we were. And she was happy about getting to rest up for a few days and be fed and have her baby fed for her and even held if she that's me mind you cried or needed a fresh diaper and what not. Seemed too good to be true. And the formula thing, seemed like yet another modern miracle to her and to so many people pre-mixed and ready to go. Took a lot of samples home with her when the day came and my father showed up round face beaming with borrowed jangling car keys in his hand.

In between the—my! birth and going home my father would visit and go to work and got a lot of congratulations all around the department. It's what people were doing the young faculty and he was doing it in particular. He already had a contract to go back to Vassar the following year to teach and that would be a good stepping stone to their real destination. Our destination even though obviously I couldn't have a say yet if I could have I would have said

"Hell yes get us to California!" I did have some sort of say though developing what was called colic by my mother and pediatricians back in the day. Cried and cried so much was inconsolable although not sure what was tried to fix it but it broke my mother. Temporarily of course. She couldn't handle it and didn't know what to do. I mean she had never even held a baby before hadn't been near too many either. My father's mother came out from New York, living uptown in Washington Heights then. My Omi. She would help, cooking and she was pretty good at that, diapering holding rocking. I think I was a little quieter with her I think I could probably smell my mother's fear and Omi's lack of it. But the colic did end at least audibly although I kept up the digestive disturbances really my whole life kind of like my father had actually. But more on the sequelae of that later. I'll get us there soon enough.

They were exultant or were going to be they were sure of that. My mother when she had time was knitting me a little brown coat so cute I still have it. Fit me when I was about two or three my own daughter wore it too not to mention one of my nieces. Light fifties sort of pukey brown you know the color with dark brown buttons down the front fitted with such an adorable squared-off collar. Very very fifties colors and style, started my fashion sense right there at the very beginning. She started sewing my clothes at some point too probably a little later. She sewed ties for him and dresses for herself. She was his fashion consultant and picked out his suits and other clothes except the checked shirts that he insisted on and she opposed. He didn't have too many suits with their still miniscule budget but he had to have some if he was to advance up the academic ladder and each one was lovingly picked on a shopping expedition that they treated like a fun vacation. They'd go back and forth, "What do you think about this one with the green lines in it?"

"No the one with the darker brown looks more dignified more tenure-ish."

"Go with the solid cream shirt."

"But I like the checks," and he remained partial to checks his whole life.

They'd go on like that having a great time the purchase was almost secondary to the experience of selecting. I'm pretty sure I was with Omi or a neighbor when they'd do stuff like that and the rare dinner out or maybe a party with other faculty couples. The study groups were steadily continuing at our house though, that was a given. Little dishes placed around of salted peanuts fresh coffee made. These gatherings were too serious for alcohol. Fragrant pipe bowls of tobacco smoked cigarettes lots of coffee.

He would go to work early after their oatmeal breakfast together, still inventing new ways to make it different with add-ins that by this point they could've written the book on oatmeal. They'd joke that Quaker Oats should hire them. Once she even wrote a letter to the company offering her services as recipe consultant. When she got no response she reached out to cookbook publishers also to no avail. Finally in the last leg of this money making scheme seeing dollar signs floating in front of her thinking their breakfast expertise would bring them some cash she looked into opening a small diner that would advertise dozens of oatmeal flavors. Even went across the street to see if they'd sell the business to her or at least hire her to design their breakfast recipes. The manager just kind of stared at her until he just said "No." These endeavors were the precursors to the get rich schemes that became a theme for my mother later on. My father didn't discourage her thinking it was kind of amusing and he'd tease her a bit but also didn't participate in any of it either.

When she got to the diner phase he'd joke moving around the kitchen striking poses "What are you going to serve, oats with a side of communism? Cranberry oatmeal a la liberation? Will you paint the inside red?"

"These are all good ideas! Food for thought," she'd jab back with a smile but also thinking they actually were interesting possibilities.

Every day he'd come home for lunch and she having dropped out of school when it became too much as I said already in her third trimester which went on very very long but in those days they didn't induce they'd—that is, the OBs—would just assume the little woman got her dates wrong which according to that thought process my mother got wrong three times, not so likely, right? So anyway she had plenty of time to ponder these and other business plans—I'll tell you about the Gilly strap later in its proper time and place—while she and I were home. We'd go for walks her in a fashionable swing three-quarter length coat that her height could carry me in the navy baby carriage and they were big and bulky in those days sometimes to see friends especially those that had babies too, no lack of them there on the campus environs. It wasn't quite yet but it was seeming great they—we—were getting there and it was all so wonderfully normal. Even the oatmeal continued to feel like an adventure to them, they'd clink spoons and kiss each other and me between spoonfuls.

Omi was happy too she loved me and loved caring for a baby again. I was to be maybe already was her favorite grandchild especially since my father was clearly the favored child of her three boys. Not a ton of competition when I was born, having just two identical twin boys ahead of me. They developed into boy monsters of a sort, climbing all over her furniture, Omi's that is, and hitting at things in her apartment and generally wreaking havoc. Sadly though one died just weeks after passing out in a track meet turned out he had a huge mass on a testicle at the age of 21. Not the first cancer death in the family of many but certainly the youngest. But of course no one knew what was going to befall him back in my infancy days and Omi was having a great time holding feeding even diapering and definitely clothing me in those first weeks and she got to cook for my father and mother and made his favorites like brisket over noodles *tzimmis* with apricots and plums kugels and best of all the traditional jam filled donuts he so craved from his childhood in Germany. A throwback to the days when things seemed good over there. Not too much later he wouldn't go near the language or anything about the country swallowed whole except its reeducation. Omi stayed a few weeks past when she thought she'd leave and really could have stayed forever had it not been Columbus and she had an apartment and life waiting for her to return in New

York not to mention two other sons and their budding families in the New York area. So eventually back she went leaving a little tin box full of recipes she handwrote on index cards in the kitchen as a surprise for my mother to find. It was a shock especially for my mother when she left even with the instant baby formula and a diaper service. She was suddenly really on her own and with me this helpless full of constant needs baby whose hair wasn't up to the standards of my other grandmother. My mother's family had a lot of hair and so do my kids but I didn't again getting the inheritance from my father's side. Not no hair hardly but not thick gobs of it either. That grandmother thought maybe something was wrong. Thought maybe I was sick certainly malformed. I wonder if she thought I had a goyish biological father through an affair or something, maybe. Never thought of that before just came to me now. I did look a lot like my dad though. Anyway Omi gone and my mother went into a bit of a dip I think. She tried not to but she not only wasn't in school anymore but put her political and other plans on hold and was deep in diapers and mashed food and a mess and a really really happy but unrealistic husband or maybe he was realistic that his job was to go to work and advance and make a life for them. I think given the day that was realistic but my mother's friends from college did not get married and certainly did not as in never ever have children except the two who married her and his brothers. Her female friends on the whole were in graduate schools or out in the world doing things in far flung places.

My mother's dream was to go study an egalitarian peaceful culture somewhere and bring back all kinds of fresh ideas about how to re-shape our society, how to make it just and rich and fun and full of life for everyone and she really did mean everyone. She had this vision of being out in the field with me in tow, it would be a great adventure great for me to grow up in the midst of such a culture learn a different language and way of life and great for her to do something real concrete substantial for the world, she'd not only write up what we found but would figure out how to inject our culture with the seeds of equality nonviolence and the social-political structures that made those possible in the land of this far-off peoples we met and culture we became immersed in. She saw us, she and baby me, accepted and integrated into this foreign land. We'd work alongside the people we'd eat with them live amongst them play when they played. She wasn't leaving my father out of it at all, no she saw him joining us on his summer and winter breaks, that he'd bring in goods that the people needed or would be interested in. We'd have things to teach them also she figured that it would be a two-way street not just us taking taking taking.

In the meantime she occupied herself trying some experiments at home. Like proper nutrition didn't mean sticking the right balance of baby foods down my throat. No, once I could sit up maybe before the idea was to put an array of foods out in front of me on my high-chair tray and let me pick. Unhampered and unadulterated from dictates about what I should want I would naturally instinctively so she conjectured pick a good balance of foods. I never heard about how that went later like if she was paying attention to the choices to learn something about a balanced baby diet or about instinct or something I just heard about the experimental design. Some flaws in it if you ask me like I had already had months of baby formula and such under my belt so I wasn't exactly choosing *ex nihilo*. There were other investigations along the way and he had a few of them also we'll get to them I'm sure. In retrospect and as you'll see I was highly monitored for these ongoing experimental questions while at the same time completely unsupervised. Funny contradiction, no?

They were hardly alone and they knew that and reveled in other young families' company. Everyone was doing it as I've said now a few times, it's the fifties and time for expansion big and small. Having babies building homes making families roads cars the whole damned country in a growth spurt! Sex after marriage in their twin beds somehow. On tv anyway. Not the sex part of course. Did married couples actually have real live twin bed sets? I don't remember anyone's parents or my own having twin bed sets. But maybe they did. I mean furniture companies did make the other sizes not the California King yet but the others. Every tv show had those bed sets, think about it if you are old enough, you know, from the baby boom yourself. The *Dick van Dyke Show* had twin sets. *Father Knows Best*? I don't remember seeing the parents' bedroom on that show, but maybe. *I Love Lucy*? I'm pretty sure we saw a twin bed set there, Lucy making up the beds or cleaning or maybe hiding something she didn't want Ricky to see under a mattress. *Leave It to Beaver*, did we see their beds, Ward and June Cleaver? I doubt it, but might check on that later since I can kind of see Ward in his boxy pjs. Maybe that was some Xmas morning episode, robe, slippers. But maybe he already had those slacks of his on, shirt, vest over it, you know it, a fifties/sixties version of the Mr. Rogers look but tidier, fuller, solid, more antiseptic. And the do's, on the men, but also think of June's or Donna Reid's or Lucy and Ethel. Ethyl Eichelberger didn't have to imagine a thing, did he? Okay, okay, already skipping ahead to the eighties but he had to have all that floating in his head somewhere too, we boomers all do.

Nevertheless, everyone really was definitely doing it, having babies, in droves. More than two per. Streets full of kids in bunches. Stick ball, kick the can. Kool Aid before it became "drink the Kool Aid." Juice in frozen concentrate—remember that bright orange cylinder that would come out of the metal and cardboard freezer can with the super concentrated and weird taste you'd just mix with water?—powders that could make juices all colors all flavors. Anita Bryant and Florida oranges. Remember the blue popsicles? They were the best I loved them, especially the blue flavor. It wasn't blueberry it wasn't like anything that actually grows it was just blue an almost icy cerulean blue. Kids chewing Bazooka day and night and reading the comic on the wrapper and the little fortune at the bottom in teensy weensy print that in those days I could read. I used to challenge myself to see how many days I could keep chewing the same wad. I remember sticking it somewhere like on a window sill when I was going to sleep otherwise I might not be here to tell you about it having choked on the damn thing in my sleep. Why was chewing the same piece day after day a thing to do? Weird kid but kids are weird.

Grow the population, that's what was happening. "Stop at Two" was later, lots and lots of babies later. Couples had three or four or even five and not only the Catholics or Orthodox Jews. Children. Seas of them. Maternity sets, brand spanking new baby formula. Heat it up in the sterilized bottle, dab a bit on the inside of your wrist for temperature testing, and let the happy baby chug it down. No embarrassing baring of breasts (which was still illegal if you can believe it when I had my first in '88 a woman was actually arrested that year for nursing in public! Arrested for feeding her baby, wow), no need to sequester the feeding mom, just give it to the baby— anywhere! Full of corn syrup, we were all addicted young to sugars, no question.

And then those mass manufactured jars of baby food, all pre-mashed up. Yams, bananas, apples. Is it really so difficult to apply a fork to these soft things and mash away for a minute? Gerber babies. Happy round beautiful well fed in the case of the Gerber baby white too. Very. Little wisp of hair so cute really. The convenience inventions of the fifties and sixties were boons to so many. To the inventors, the manufacturers, the stores, and maybe the moms who bought all the new stuff. Maybe maybe we'll delve into this question later. And, the babies? Not sure there either yet, more later, depends on where the balance swings to ease or to the side effects. So many modern miracles (think Swanson, Sara Lee, Tater Tots, and don't forget the frozen fish sticks! the best part was dipping them in gobs of mayo if you ask me). Automats like Horn & Hardart—remember that one? Put in coins and get a sandwich out, just like that. A room full of food machines like the Jetsons but not pills, better. Something you could chew. Washing machines dryers (even in hot, dry climates that could dry a load hung out in practically minutes, faster than any dryer and think! fossil fuel free to boot) dishwashers (yes, I do like mine a lot) but electric can openers? what's that for? are they really better, faster, easier, or do they just consume electricity for fun? because they can? electric carving knives, heating and cooling in areas where minimally thoughtful building construction could take care of the bulk of it? Yeah, what were we thinking and what are we thinking now? Styrofoam take-out, plastic beads in soaps that scrub our skin clean clean clean while choking sea animals down the pike micro plastics in the stomachs of sea turtles in ninety percent of table salt and eighty three percent of tap water worldwide (higher in the US of A) and end up in our own bellies and in all human stool samples tested *all*, up the food chain, the food chain is real. The food chain isn't going anywhere until we've suffocated starved or poisoned all the links that come before us and then what? Oy! there is no end to this list, so I'm going to move on now. But just to say here once and for all we got to our current dire portrait somehow. I'm going to take us through bits and snatches and wonder a tad about the why of it. Today we'd say money, dummy, but I don't know. I don't "buy" that explanation. Money wasn't always money not like it is today. Today we live and breathe money and its acquisition, it is the Holy Grail. When we talk about what someone is worth we're talking dollars, that's odd isn't it? I mean that's not what I think of when I think of someone, how much money she/he has, do you? Maybe you do, I mean that's what the common parlance says, it's an equation X person = $. It jars me every time I hear it. Money has become our identity for God's sake! Wasn't always the case that that's all that was on most people's minds. Other goals and interests were more prominent then. Right and Wrong, Black and White (literally, right there on people's skin mashed all together with cold war mongering—think Boris and Natasha and Dudley Do-Right morals ideals nuclear families peace time and reparation. Next, sex was the It (not IT, we're back in the fifties here) thing, that took up a lot of time and energy and not just the actual sex part. We sure have mangled that one what with power mixing in, it became a violent thing like so many other pastimes. Then sports became the It thing, drove me crazy and was scary with all that frenetic crowd shrieking drinking stuff. No, there's got to be more to it can't just be money and a dash of because-we-can-ism (I think I hope that there is more to it I mean just for starters some of it was in the pursuit of progress in a naïve optimistic way wasn't it?).

This is all getting a bit ahead. Don't want to sound a negative tone here yet or really ever but it will seem like that's exactly what I am doing at times. Probably sound a bit bitter or sarcastic but that just seeps out around the edges, not the point at all. Really here and talking looking into things just to clarify to understand. Maybe we can still use it for some greater good or fix what we broke. Some seem to think we still can here and now. Would take a lot of coordination of all of us or by far most anyway. When does that ever happen? for anything? Just asking once more, I mean will you change the way you do things? Will you even turn off lights TVs computers when you're not using them? compost your food scraps especially those of you where your town or city will give you those nice brown countertop bins and put larger bins out at the curb and collect it all for you and collect your leaves in the fall, will you even participate in those things or is it too icky? These are pretty low-level changes to make we've got much bigger ones coming if we are to turn the tide in any meaningful way let's face it but you could start composting using less products electricity fossil fuels today start now as a beginning and start demanding with your pocket-books and voices and votes that corporations do the same.

So Europe is trying to ban single use plastic now, or at least some of it (why not all?? If banning plastic in most applications is too radical we're done for). Here near my own home town, Great Barrington Massachusetts voted to ban plastic water bottles a while ago. Yay! I and others were so happy and proud, the third town in the country to do so (why is it taking so long for such a simple obvious move?). Only to have a repeal movement spring up before the ink was dry. Well the repeal people lost but then implementation was set for a year hence and that's already been pushed back another year because there aren't enough water bottle filling stations in the town! What? like people can't fill their own bottles before they leave home like restaurants town halls grocery stores offices schools and wherever else people find themselves in that town, they don't have running water? What's wrong with people, I don't know. They really need to be sucking in those BPAs, PCBs or whatever else is leaching out of that miserable plastic to then toss it for animals or the ocean or somewhere to absorb the rest of its toxins while it never ever ever decomposes? Bought those green supposedly dissolving made out of corn like everything else compost bags once and a year later they hadn't decomposed an iota, watched them in my compost bin until I decided to fish them out empty their contents and put them in the landfill pile. Oh well, I hear they're still selling 'em. If you fill 'em with compost material and toss it in an urban compost bin, well good that you're at least doing that, but also you'll never see that they don't decompose. I'm telling you here and now they don't. So imagine those plastic bottles. I have a policy now to check over my shopping cart before getting to the checkout counter to make sure I haven't bought anything in plastic packaging unless it seems absolutely essential (an elastic concept in itself but I'm trying to be increasingly stringent which I measure by how much longer or not it is taking my recycling bin to fill up).

I know I know I am moving in between being rather vague and even a tad fluffy to overly specific with the electric can openers and corn bags but that will change, I promise. I'll get consistently focused and more and more specific as I review things from circa 1956 (really a bit before too as you've already seen) till now or till a stopping point when we've all had enough and get it maybe exhausted maybe exhilarated by the task at hand the hand we've dealt. I think I like that metaphor, we're all dealers and players every single day every one of us. With the now shifting the here and now keeps moving we keep saying we have time to put the cards down and clean up the house but time keeps on going and we keep saying it. The now as it were is still ever more literally minute by minute limited as I keep writing. Like stuff going through a funnel less and less can fit from flared top to small bottom tube. Like the Bay Area sinking and drowning not a pretty picture and far away different from the one my parents saw there at the end of their motorcycle jaunt. Not so picture perfect anymore and in so many ways.

Well now the scientists say we've got eleven very short years to fix things a hair over a decade is a pretty quick blip. Especially the

US of A needs to get a jump on mending things in every corner going to come from the states and industry and business certainly not from the presidential team in this go around need to wait and see what happens going forward. The Wheeler EPA hearings put chills down my spine, maybe yours too if you were listening. Still not at all clear what global leaders will bring us administratively environmentally education social justice criminal reform all those policy and practical decisions hanging out on a limb. Hopefully enough of us can drop everything extraneous and make things right. Not count on futuristic yet to be discovered solutions or even the existing but fraught carbon capture type of ideas or that the US of A population is on the decrease so that will slow carbon emissions oy! not enough we need a real plan. And we need to stop the bickering the stupid jealous cousin kind of backbiting like arguing that the plastic capture contraption being tested in the Pacific shouldn't get funding because we have to stop the proliferation of plastic, get to the roots of the problem to then get the retort, yes but there are tons and tons and tons of plastic in the ocean and we need to get that out too, and on and on. I mean both are for the most part on the same side, stop the nonsense and let's get to it! Bloomberg said he'd insist on the Dems those in the primary having a detailed climate change plan, what happened with that, with the Dems trying to forbid discussion of climate catastrophe—I mean, the environment to keep it polite.

No, not a pretty picture and not so fun to know what is going to kill you and from the vantage point of this moment maybe extinguish the whole world population segment by segment. I mean, we all do know even if we act like we don't that each and every one of us is going to die somehow. Extreme cryotherapy notwithstanding or even with it if we continue to do not much certainly not enough about climate change none of anything else will matter. Certain portions of the world population will go first but we'll all eventually go if we don't make maximal remedial use of these next eleven years. Every day of every one of them and the countdown is already on. I'll just tell you right now at the outset, well you've been reading a while already but close to the get-go I'm sick from all this climate change and pollution poisoning psychically and otherwise. One way or another we've all been doused in the poisons but us from the baby boom got hit the hardest. Side effects side effects unintended consequences perhaps but nevertheless we boomers were drenched in toxins from before the confluence of the egg and sperm and ongoing cell by contaminated altered cell. Only the mice hornets Lyme ticks are going to survive it not you and I. If mobilization en masse doesn't coalesce pronto no one need perseverate much about the future any human future. Some are already doomed from all the poisoning of the earth. Think of all the lead poisonings mercury toxicities radiation contagion and so many cancers. The people sick whose time is even more limited than the general population who one by one are becoming ill from the boom years fun. The general population which had two decades worth of warnings to say the least much much more half a century in fact if you even just go back to *Silent Spring* to watch the world and each of us in it doing nothing or anyway surely not enough. What is Earth Day really about anyway? Do we just pay attention one day a year and then feel good?

Can we stop and think about what we actually want? isn't doing not enough mass genocide? I mean not only is starvation already a huge problem but it's one that's going to get lots worse as all the climate change exponentially accelerates and also we've caused so many diseases some we know about even if we don't understand them or how to stop them like all the cancers especially those nasty impenetrable solid tumors but some we haven't identified yet even though probably lots of people have already contracted them. We and here I mean physicians scientists and so forth just aren't seeing them yet for what they are. As usual we see only what we already know the new takes time to come into focus. Like a revolution as Kuhn would have us believe I've never been particularly partial to that way of looking at things but it doesn't matter there's lots on the human disease front that we have not yet identified let alone tried to tackle. It'll be an uphill battle let's face it unless and even if we do something about all of our pernicious consumption. All that ingestion of toxins by breathing eating sleeping by just living for sure causes all kinds of cancers and we undeniably know about lots of them but what else are all the boom time developments causing have already caused and will cause in the future? Imagine all these sick people going about dying and nevertheless walk talk and act alive when they're not really still alive I mean, they are but not really with a foot and a half out the door. Yes they and we—remember we've all got it coming one way or another—can hope for a cure or some kind of solution to be invented but there's a lot of politics and money placed on not finding cures all the while the cancer rhetoric is the Search for the Cure. Chanted everywhere. You see people wearing buttons and T-shirts for that all the time, races to raise money and awareness and so on. But then there are the money interests that dictate there being not a lot of separation between investors and science if there's any at all. Here is what one Goldman Sachs VP of the Research Division Salveen Richter had to say about cancer research: "*The potential to deliver 'one shot cures' is one of the most attractive aspects of gene therapy. However, such treatments offer a very different outlook with regard to recurring revenue versus chronic therapies. While this proposition carries tremendous value for patients and society, it could represent a challenge for genome medicine developers looking for sustained cash flow.*" You couldn't make stuff up creepier than that. Anyway, it's one thing to know you're going to die sometime even if it's going to be from droughts rising seas pestilence starvation and another to know you are going to die a sometime much sooner than statistical averages and of a specific cause unless one gets hit by a truck or struck by lightning sooner or some such other freak type of incident.

Well, too many people have been sickened and died at indecently young ages. Some unavoidable, but the others? That's part of my question. The why of it. In case we don't know enough about the chemical dousing we from the boom years got from before day one in the uterine sack. Those days surely count, but that's verging on another hot topic. To be clear and up front about it right away,

I believe in a woman's right to choose everything about herself including her body and all its parts. But and it isn't really a but I also believe that the pre-natal life of the fetus (which, again, is part of a woman's body and reign at that point) counts for future development health et cetera and being soaked in chemicals at least so far has not been a good way to go. Think about seeds for plants or domesticated animals—the antibiotics a chicken gets on day one affect the rest of its life and contributes to the antibiotic resistant strains of disease for us. Again, the food chain is real and we do many of us still eat these chickens. And GMO seeds giving rise to GMO drift over fields and fields for miles and miles. Why should the human seed ova fetus be any different? Probably worse really if that's possible. Part of why my days are more limited at the moment than some others'—but less others than you'd think—of my birth era cohort.

The question so many people are asking *Why me?* prompted this story I'm telling you. You might've asked it in which case you're a bit ahead of the game here, maybe have something to add to the story. It's a question that's been tossed around before and for all kinds of reasons but in my generation—again, remember, in case I haven't stressed it enough this is the post WWII baby boom I'm talking about—the reason is pretty common. The question of the multitudes of us boomers and voices of the past present and as far as the eye can see—no, way beyond that surely—marching multitudes of the future so far as it goes for us earthlings. Ghosts in some limbo of exile before they are ghosts but they can keep on marching towards death asking the question. The question that is not going to go away softly.

Ghosts before we're dead. How many doctors in consultation look at each and every one of these multiple boomer cancer patients as if she were already dead and a great subject for study. Put her on a trial that is virtually sure to kill faster than the disease but she's dying anyway what's the diff? they say or think or think they know. It's for science after all to save so many others. And slap her with PET and CT scans—so much radiation!—because it doesn't matter and even though as the nurse at a radiology unit who has been doing this a while and who is one of the only people I trust there said CTs wouldn't even barely exist anymore if MRIs weren't nixed by insurance companies for being too expensive yeah and no radiation in them either can't make much on future diseases they don't hasten or cause can they? Yeah anyway back to the doctors' looks and what they'd say like you can hope to live long enough and not be too sick by the time something new is discovered something to really pin hopes on isn't it the rapid movement of science to the extent that medicine not to mention medication involves science as people usually think of it as rock-solid based in apolitical facts and so on. I already launched my debunking of that a few pages back if you remember.

What about the treatment though for all these boomers made sick by the side effects of their happy go lucky upbringing? We heap on more side effects this time from the drugs to not cure but only treat as in prolong life. The life made ill from side effects will be prolonged to endure a different class of horrific side effects. And the whole wide world endures side effects of the new side effects not just the individual. The individual is nauseous tired jaundiced immune compromised but the world is sopping up the drugs. Every cancer patient a singular walking toxic site. Moving about in the world spreading bits of poison where ere she goes, in this toilet, then that. Down this sewer system and another. Are all of them living walking breathing groaning brownfields? Yes, I think so.

In the treatment rooms filled with human toxic sites tethered to sacks of hazardous waste streaming into their veins through ports below their shoulders. Ports sticking out beyond even the person's victims? Adam's apple most spend the day attached to these tubes to sacks on poles, bald too. Head to toe bald that is. Maybe it isn't worth treating all these people. I mean that's a legitimate question even though it sounds horrible. Is it good globally to be treating all these people with toxic chemicals that then get poured into and onto the world? Treatment rooms are eerie sites, all these people tethered as I said from port to tube to plastic sack (a shortage of them now, many made in Puerto Rico and with what isn't happening there still so long after hurricane Maria in terms of restoring basic electricity, I don't think that industry is going to be up and running any time soon) of toxic medications hooked up to a post on wheels. Wheels so patients can wheel themselves with the drip drip drip to the bathroom to the consultation room to the front desk and back to their chairs. Hazardous waste in the bags in their bodies in the yellow hazmat disposal bins (where do those contents go?) all wheeling around back and forth, forth and back. Trying to zone out in a sea of those populated brownfield chairs not so easy even with reading music from headphones phone calls knitting.

Think about it, to try to save the victims of boom year and beyond toxic poisoning in the form of one cancer or another, each one, and there are so many, all over every city, each state, the country and the world, and those being treated are the lucky ones, all are mini-hazardous waste dumps. When a bag of fluid that is being pumped into someone is empty it goes into the yellow waste bin with the severe looking hazard logo on it and disposed of at hazardous waste sites. But now the stuff is in the patient, and then she pees or shits or sweats. Maybe in her home, maybe at the treatment center, maybe in a restaurant or a park or a movie theater—anywhere. Imagine all the dumpings and sploshings created wherever she goes of toxicity that gets into water systems land the air—everywhere. And now multiply by all the people being treated with this stuff.

Okay, good, if you sort of have that in mind now add in all the Viagra the Xanax Prozac Ambien Oxycodone OxyContin Tylenol antibiotics! you name it, all going the same places—that is, into the water and water borne animals the land and its animals (think rats and pigeons that go everywhere!) the air. And guess what, not only up the food chain again but directly right in our drinking water. Just read a study of the Hudson River done (drinking water source to many many people) between Albany and New York City—that's right, prescription drugs galore. Opioids in the mussels in the Puget Sound, just read that too, today, hot off the presses. I eat a lot of mussels. No way devised to filter them out, all these drugs either.

We're all on Prozac—Prozac Nation was literal not to mention every other popular drug.

If you really want to get fancy now add in all the nuclear waste the radioactive effluence that comes directly to each and every one of our doorsteps, some more than others of course.

Okay now if you have the stomach for more and I'm giving this one its own paragraph with all the foregoing in mind add in this one. Where does all the chemically-laden poisoned water from oil drilling and fracking go? well you probably have already heard it gets injected into the ground and shows up in people's wells at their homes in farm land and such but it is also sold to large scale farms even organic farms to water crops with. You heard that correctly, even on organic farms. I guess the organic designation criteria does not include what is used to water with! This was reported recently as occurring in several agricultural regions in California a state with the strictest of all kinds of environmental standards so you and I can guess it's going on elsewhere many other elsewheres.

All that chemical soup floating around in all of us, it's enough to make you sick! think about dying a horrible death there it is! And wouldn't you want to blame someone! run out in the street screaming STOP! I don't know about you but I dream about death being dead sometimes just dying, to me as one of many many many who have been sickened one way or another by all of this, here's a dream I had just last night what with all this writing about disaster, here it is.

... I'm with my youngest Zoe—and it's her as she is now, and me as now—and we're going somewhere and I get ahead—not unusual for me—and I'm going and there are people sort of marching along and then I'm way ahead and my phone is in my suitcase and I'm still holding onto the handle of the suitcase but somehow can't or don't think of getting into it, it's out of the question somehow, but I want to call her and find out where she is so I can get back to her. But I don't have my phone, no communication. I finally realize I can use someone else's phone because Zoe has hers! One of those pathetic eureka moments of something so simple. Great, what a relief. Why does it

always take me so long to think of the obvious? Like the etymology of some word that is hiding in plain sight and I only grasp one after decades upon decades of life, or like the lyrics to a song I never really absorbed until hearing the song for the millionth time.

I ask around and am handed a phone. But then there's another problem. Some of the buttons don't work, they're kind of rubbery, and then I realize finally. I'm not getting back to Zoe. Ever. I wake up. Awful, awful. So really awful. It takes days maybe weeks to shake the dream of my death. I thought we weren't supposed to be able to do that. Damn it, I found a way. A little, but not very, sneaky way to do so. I can't be the first to "figure" that out.

I keep finding ways. So many dreams, all with the death or really having already died theme. Kind of like knowing that it's over for animal life and I say this including humans and maybe especially humans on this planet, we've done it to ourselves and other animals and we sit and watch almost idly as the numbers get worse not better and we do barely anything and fall way way way short of even close to enough. We are all dead in effect already. Dream on people if you think we'll somehow pull it together while I dream on that I am already dead without somehow recognizing it until it smacks me in the face, can't meaning not ever call Zoe not ever getting back to her or any one/thing else. Not supposed to be able not supposed to be possible. But doctors maybe shouldn't look at me and the others like we're already dead, that might help if they'd stop that. So awful when that happens. As if I have a specimen number tattooed on my forehead ready-made to be a test subject. Never thought of it that way, that the boomers all of us were fed stuff to become subjects. There's a novel, sort of sci-fi/reality kind of thing in this idea for sure. Hollywood should be onto it by now, probably is. Every movie every TV show these days seems to have to have a character with cancer in it. Think *Three Billboards* for example *Bordertown*. I don't think that's just my sensitivity, cancer is everywhere even in art. It's the It thing as I said and rakes in money all over the place and for far-flung recipients, not just for research or treatment. But then there's a joke I was told by an oncologist:

Ten story building all for cancer research, every floor people busy doing very important work to find the cure. There's an announcement from someone on the fifth floor, "I've found the cure for cancer!" she screams. Second announcement (can you guess?): *"Someone has been shot on the fifth floor."*

Too bad there's so much truth to this joke, think not that far back just a few pages ago to the Goldman Sachs quote yeah direct quote no exaggeration no screaming even though I felt like it when I read it the first time.

The institutions—hospitals to put a word on it—are so full of fixed rules, guided by insurance liability, that they're not treating humans anymore. Conditions lesions syndromes but they've forgotten there are real live people attached to those things and it's the people who are forced to undergo ridiculous hoops dangerous hoops for their health in order to have the "conditions" "treated." Oops, there's also a person there we're blasting with radiation in order to get the exact same image we just took with another machine but we've got the toy and we're the only ones who do it's so expensive so use it kind of maneuver. Only facility in the country that has this PET machine right in the OR, well, that doesn't mean use it indiscriminately does it? "No, no we don't do things willy-nilly," they say. Not willy-nilly at all. Just insurance money guided in many respects of that term. Not to mention ordinary things like making very ill immune compromised people sit and wait in public germ-infested decrepit lounges for hours and hours on end just to have a consult. Not even for any actual treatment. Getting so way ahead here.

Some do escape this for a long long time but there's no real telling who in advance. No, there is no escaping it by being good or having good habits or a clean green lifestyle.

Raised in the product appliance purchasing opulence (for some and only so to speak) of the fifties/sixties I was so many were. Stuff everywhere, as I've been saying. New roads to housing developments paved every day new construction new towns practically all these isolated isolating suburban dreams. Dolores Hayden on the making of the American Dream, she got it right don't you think? consumers one and all and then on to being the subjects of the results of all that consumption. Booze as they say tobacco reefer Coke and cocaine mashed potato flakes and Hostess cupcakes Devil Dogs and Oscar Meyer hot dogs Red Hots airplane food for the home in little frozen aluminum compartments burgers from Burger King and the Big Mac Charleston Chews and Yellow #5 Caramel color and aerosol sprays so many sprays—for air freshening for stains hair styles nail polish drying for oven cleaning paint removal sprays sprays sprays all getting into the air earth water food chain pathways and it turns out as toxic and polluting as motorized vehicles—I could go on and on with this lesser lower level list. Did the adults not think there'd be consequences? really didn't give it a thought a wonder a niggling little worry somewhere? just use the miracle thing and toss the remainder the container the packaging? Like a ravine in Bali I saw a deep what was beautiful lush ravine but when I was there and this was about a decade ago it was full to overflowing with refuse! Not exaggerating a speck here this long deep ravine packed with garbage of all sorts. Wasn't the only place in Bali I saw such a monstrosity so shocking against all that natural beauty rice paddies gorgeous colors tropical flowers. Do we really not care beyond our immediate moment? did my parents and their ilk not have any inkling? I've used Drano didn't think about what was in it what it would do downstream from the pipes I was thinking about solving the immediate cloggage and I've used Easy-Off in grossly filthy ovens when I've moved into apartments and wanted them at least to seem clean and wood strippers. All of this probably wasn't good for me but these items and so many more were surely worse for the earth. And that's just stuff that happens after we've got the buildings built the roads paved the tunnels and cement barriers built without enough concern for what was being plowed and scraped and blocked off and dynamited all that life there full of thriving life that was obliterated. Consequences from all of that like a set of dominoes cascading.

The upper echelons of the list of our destructive boom year deeds to come. Like the Nevada test site like DDT Monsanto (glyphosate turning up in Cheerios and Lucky Charms for God's sake! Not to mention a generation raised malnourished on stuff like that and Fruit Loops and Pop Tarts white bread candy corn American cheese) and GE (polluted my area and the fight continues over the cleanup decades later and ironically the stock my grandfather picked to buy a share of just one for me when I was born. Stock split and split and leavened until the day—in my thirties—I discovered I had it and then thirty more years until I cashed it in to give to my doctor for his research, had grown from something like a buck to tens of thousands all on the backs of our poisoning and they want the dump site of the so-called cleanup to be in a thickly populated area as they call it—that's what the road signs say, thickly populated—right alongside the river that they tossed the stuff into in the first place). Good plan that.

Our cousins friends neighbors all inventors of these poisons and then more cousins and friends and aunts and uncles medical researchers to study the impact of it all. On ourselves, and we are of course all dying just some faster and more insidiously than others. Not clear why some and not others but there's a lot of science to be done on that question. Dollars in it too of course, the why of why some things studied and others not. There could be other reasons of course but money is still the first go-to, isn't it? or as a friend of mine insists it's really just because "they" can. Not enough, I say. The "they" is us anyway if you want to be precise about it just to different degrees each of us. I want more of an answer.

As just about me or others but not yet specifically you this isn't so directly painful like a knife right into your heart but the problem—and the pain—is that it is all us boomers, one by one, being offered up. And by ourselves, that's the disorienting part. We did this, some by inventing some by the profit margin and all—yes, that's all of us—by collusion. We signed on for this carnage this destruction of the planet and ourselves, one by one by one, all of us. Each and every one of us thinking we'll escape it or prevent it by eating raw foods juice fasts or moving to the country (next to a toxic dump in rural US of A where the dumpers think no one will protest and for a long long time they were right. Look what the GEs of the world got away with and all over the world). Or those ultra 1%ers who build underground meccas for themselves. Or on a different planet. Billionaires turned survivalist? the Bezos of the world trying to figure out what to do with their millions no sorry billions I meant to say. I'm not used to the numbers we've come to these days for people's—some people's—earnings that is "earnings" while as Bernie showed us in one of his town halls the billions made on the backs of workers full time workers to be clear and yet who can't afford to eat every day or for whom a $400 emergency expense is astronomical and impossible and unthinkable. As one of them said "$400? What about $20 that can turn someone's world inside out." And food prep people airline workers all these millions of people who have no sick leave and go to work with fevers infections coughing and sneezing and then get worse and people who eat the food or get onto the plane they prepped getting ill from them because they have no sick days and even if they have it can't afford to use their health insurance. We know none of this is going anywhere good. And yet we all collude in this in so many ways. As the airline worker at the town hall noted when a plane is late or cancelled or something goes wrong customers scream at her (the person who working more than full time still can't afford to pay her bills or always feed herself or her children or take anyone in her family to a doctor when they need it) hit her she said throw luggage at her. We are all guilty of some form of this. You say, not me, I don't do that stuff but think about it how many times have you gotten impatient testy even with someone not doing something fast enough or well enough for your needs or liking? Hmmmm lots probably. And multiple times and ongoing. Don't you answer the phone rather rudely when you think it's yet another sales call? Well those people need a job and that one signs them up for abuse every call they make practically all the while earning at best a starvation wage. Maybe next time just don't answer or speak in a normal tone of voice and say "No thank you." Yeah it's annoying but come on pretty low level it's just that we're all under a strain well many of us anyway but that's no excuse for bad behavior to strangers. I did a mini study if it could be called that of spreading good will and good feelings on the subway. Would make a point to say something nice or friendly to a person next to me especially if it seemed improbable for me to do so with whomever that turned out to be. Like the young man next to me one day with music blaring out of his earbuds at high enough volume that I could hear more than I cared to but I turned to him and asked what he was listening to and he shared a bud with me and told me about the music and I thanked him and it was a happy exchange felt very good I think for both of us. Definitely had good effect, would watch the person I was kind or encouraging or something to do so to the person to their other side and so on, made a chain of human decency pretty much each time. Like that young man turned to a teenage kid on the other side of him and said something I didn't catch but again what looked like an infectiously friendly interaction. What prevents us from that kind of demeanor rather than our more typical rude nastiness? Don't tell me its human nature, just try acting on some basic human empathy next time you're in a store pick up your phone ride a crowded train stand on a long line or the next time you feel someone is doing less than a stellar job assisting you with whatever. Just try it, probably not going to hurt you or do harm.

We've all colluded with the toxic dousing of the world and the people in it and the plants and animals too. Maybe each and every one of us doesn't own or manage a Dow Chemicals or a Monsanto but drip drip drip we all add in our parts. Even those conscientious ones of us who nevertheless say knowing full well what we're doing and way more often than we'd like to remember, "Just this one time." Just this one picnic or trip or snack cause I'm so hungry I'll use the plastic and I'll just throw it out or I need those packaged wipes for the plane trip so I don't get sick or I'm just so thirsty and forgot my water bottle so I'll buy a Nestle Poland Spring and toss it but I'll try to toss it in a recycling bin (like that's a solution) if I can find one just usually I can't. And that's not to mention people like some actual friends of mine who always everyday every single day eat on plastic plates with plastic cutlery and paper napkins and then toss it all out. *Everyday.*

Or on to bigger and better just this onces. Just this lipstick, this electric can opener, this new car I don't really need cause mine is after all fine but somewhat getting ready to be on its way out this new iPad even these new clothes I don't need. We all do this if we can and at some level to each our own we all can and do. And we do in an ongoing way, the best and greenest intentioned of us all. And this is the small fry stuff but which adds up when you multiply by all the people in the world. Just hold an image in your mind of that Balinese ravine that was filled plastic bottle by plastic bottle one at a time. So it's not just a few greedy men with their "because we can ism" even though they more than anyone with their money and because we can ism try so hard to prove that we or at least they as humans are not animals. With all our great inventions we have proved our superiority and we hold it up to say that men (trying somewhat weakly to mean people for the most part) are definitely not part of the animal *king*dom. Animals are well animals, beasts really. Nevertheless we have largely and singlehandedly killed ourselves and the rest of the animal world with us. Except of course for those who think they'll escape and survive in the bunkers under the earth's crust or up in Mars somewhere. Where ever they can have their spas and pools and bars and Maserati's and whatever I don't even know what. I don't mean to say this with so much bitterness, it's just let's be real and recognize that *they* the Exxons and the Monsanto's and the Amazons didn't do this alone we all did and we all continue to do so when we all know there are things we could change that would help. Each one of us has stuff we could do and don't, each one of us.

Oy! All the boom of the post-war era came busting down didn't it? because we weren't careful didn't think didn't want to think just wanted to enjoy be free and happy and productive and have jobs and buy cars. This is bad bad bad but let's get back to some of the how why where when it all went this way or to correct the passive construction the how why we all led it this way especially the adults all over the world during those boom years. Meaning it's about time wouldn't you say to get back to my parents' story and jumping on ahead and also over part of the country.

EASTWARD WE GO

T HEY WERE LOOKING FORWARD TO being back at Vassar and planned to live in a house on the Vassar farm. Friends of theirs on the faculty were vacating the house to move on and they thought up to U of Chicago and my parents arranged a couple of months before they moved to take it over along with some of the furniture. So all was smooth sailing so far and they were joyfully toasting each other again on this stepping stone.

"I think this'll be fun for a stint and the last step towards our dreams," he said over dinner one last night in Columbus. "A few more publications under my belt maybe a few talks well placed here and there and that's all I'll need to land the big one."

Clinking her glass of milk with his water she agreed, "We'll be off before we know it and me too, I'm looking forward to seeing our old friends again and this time I don't have to be the student at gatherings. I'm an adult now and we have a kid and I've got almost a year's worth of graduate work under my belt. Yes, it'll be good for a year."

"I wish there were somewhere close enough for you to take some courses towards your degree," he said thinking out loud.

"Thanks, I know what you mean but I'll have my hands full with the baby and the politicking I can carry on almost where I left off I mean I know the landscape there and can get moving on some important issues maybe even write some for the *Miscellany* or do some investigative research for them I mean we did get some national recognition when we got picked up by the syndicates. This time I won't have the shackles of the administration on me, what can they do now that I'm not under their thumb?" She said all of this practically rubbing her hands together in glee imagining all the trouble she could stir up.

Knowing her well, he threw in laughing, "You're diabolical!"

"Oh yeah, I'll be busy enough for one year and maybe really only nine months if we leave at the end of the spring semester, that really is a pretty short time." With that she leaned over the table and gave him an energetic kiss. They clinked glasses again and were both full of good thoughts for their future.

As they were finishing their dinner with me already fast asleep in my crib she motioned with a wave of her hands towards the kitchen, "I'm going to get to the rest of the packing, we've got to be ready in another day!"

"I'm going to put some finishing touches on my paper and then I'll help," he responded knowing that he had to send off his paper before they left or it'd be postponed too long and would miss the deadline for the targeted conference and journal.

With that they gave each other a hug and bounced like happy kids off to their separate tasks. Pack she did write he did. Out went the boxes to the moving van off went the paper to the review committee and move they did. To the yellow wood frame house plunk on the edge of the farm a bit away from the campus proper and maybe almost too quiet for them having gotten used to the bustle such as it was of Columbus.

I do remember that house, maybe from pictures but I feel like I really remember it with a porch leading to little steps down to the front and out to the mailbox and the road that heads away from in one direction and towards the fields of the farm in the other and it was dark inside the kitchen where we spent a lot of time and a yard around the back from which it was just a skipping stones' throw to the cow barn that also housed a big certainly from my vantage point pink pig along with the dairy cows. They got fresh milk eggs and produce from the farm in exchange for a very small amount of work, some weeding and such nothing that needed much skill or even time. She did it although not sure how much she liked doing the farm work and I was in tow all the while sitting up when we got there and walking and talking almost as good as those Chatty Cathy dolls a few months later. A more prosaic version of her fantasies of the anthropological explorations we'd do together one day. She could let me roam around since I couldn't really get far without stumbling falling to the ground groping around in the dirt a bit before wailing to be picked up.

All in all it was going to be great for them to be back with faculty friends and family not as far away even though the route to Vassar from the city wasn't then so easy even now it's not a snap but then it was an expedition. Taking the rickety train or driving up the treacherous flooding Taconic either way had its hazards and took hours that seemed longer since the potential for problems en route was large and even an uneventful trip was arduous. Relatives from Brooklyn did make the trek occasionally and so did Omi of course. When my grandmother Aunt June Aunt Ruthie great aunts to me but my mother's aunts and some of her uncles and cousins and probably a few others came up from Sheepshead Bay they did so wearing their best furs on the women and suits on the men that they generally kept in boxes with moth balls and such wielding large pots of homemade soups casseroles gefilte fish and so much definitely kosher food no way my parents could eat it all even doling it out slowly from the freezer still called an ice box in those days. They surely meant well and it was good for my mother to have the support and also to be glad when they had gone reminding her of what she left behind on that day she shakily boarded the Metro North train ride to Vassar with her brother who coached her the whole way how to navigate a *goyish* community what with the different vocabulary and expressions for starters. He was already in his second year at Princeton and had weathered a level of anti-Semitism that had taken him by surprise. Much as he tortured her when they were kids as older brothers do he was fiercely protective of her now. Her stomach churning with anxiety she barely heard his counsel and wanted to bolt the train at every stop. She made it there though on a brisk already autumnish day in 1951 stepping into her new life that she never looked back from not for a second.

Here she was again just a few years later making her way to Vassar with her husband the professor and her baby replete with pram diapers bottles and lots of books including the required Dr. Spock. She was an adult a homemaker and a future and past political rebel. They were welcomed back and parties were had in their honor for a couple of weeks. It was great and jarring to come back as a full fledged adult and she carried it well with all her quips and position statements now having an air of authority or maturity at any rate.

At one of the soirees she got a bit knocked off balance, threw her for a loop as they say. Before I tell it, remember this is the fifties not now. Lots of secrets in those days and so much went unspoken and unknown even when it shouldn't have. In the faculty home of two female professors as so many of the Vassar faculty were female unusually for the times and these two who had been roommates since before her time there as a student. On a crisp cool evening happily in they went meeting some friends on the way along the path. They were all directed to a back room to toss their jackets which turned out to be the bedroom and as she discovered a bit later searching for a bathroom it was the only bedroom with just one bed a double. It took her a few stunned minutes to process the information and then didn't know what to do with it.

"Walt," she said when she got back to him, "did you know about them, you know?"

"Darling, I don't know. Are you having a good time, isn't this great to see everyone all in one place? I've really missed this, I didn't realize how much! Did you hear what Sidney's been up to? Incredible!"

"No, you know, they live here together," she persisted.

"Obviously, they have forever, so?"

"No, I mean together like we do!" Somehow she hadn't understood a lot that had been going on when she was an undergrad and even some stuff said to her from those years, it was all sinking in in an instant. Funny that later on she worked intensively in the gay community in NYC on AIDS issues but that was a lot later. But not so funny I mean it was good work she did but so many adults from the fifties and sixties had to wake up and get over their prejudices and for so many still not a completed process wouldn't you say? Certainly not globally, listen to what the President of Brazil says on the subject if you can stomach it. Maybe you can't but some people I know have to live under that kind of rule, rushed to get married before he took office but still it's not going to be a fun ride there till they get rid of him.

"Quiet, I don't know what you mean, but later. Save it for later, okay? Let me get you a drink." He probably did not know what she was talking about then or for some time coming, I don't know when but by the time they were leaving and home they were tired definitely a little beyond tipsy and had had a good time with that unfinished interchange buried somewhere in their memories under a lot of conversations jokes and stories they had just swapped with friends.

Pretty quickly they began hosting their own soirees and discussion groups. Their home on the farm had the feel of a Parisian salon with a pragmatic American twist in which weighty discussions took place in their small living room crammed full of pipe and cigarette smoking faculty and some wives. There in that old house with low farm house ceilings and small windows meetings were regularly held and far reaching as well as far flung ideas were bandied about. It was great fun and felt important to be debating freely about the crucial demands of the times. More Freud of course Marx Margaret Mead Spinoza Kafka and lots of plays, there was a playwright director amongst them who was very left left of all of them put together who held the hard lines and felt he was keeping them all honest.

Exhilarated both of my parents were after these meetings, the effect would linger in the house for days. They didn't have anything like this in Columbus. They were so clearly tangibly happy to be back east and on familiar ground. Not the dropping to their knees happy of course but that would come later and not that much later. They knew how to enjoy themselves at Vassar, their study group was way beyond full swing and reading all kinds of interesting stuff mostly as I said Freud Freud Freud and plays from which they extracted much to debate about society what's innate what's learned what to do about evil in the world and how to raise the next generation to grow up without aggression in its blood. How to make a just and open political system and what the difference is between equality and equity and between ethics and morality and what difference the differences make. They were back with colleagues they knew and respected and could always have a good discussion with. Some of her friends especially those on the *Miscellany News* were still there and graduating that year. There was never a dull moment if you can believe that I mean in those days Poughkeepsie and Vassar were pretty remote. Like the day the *New York Times* reporter came up to cover the fist fight my father got into with a colleague, something about Plato I never did get the full story. But they were disagreeing about something in a department seminar on Plato's work and it got so heated they hit each other. Actually! right in the large oval tabled august seminar room lodged in one of those imposing stone buildings with a lot of faculty from a few departments. Kind of comical if you could see pictures of the two of them, which the *Times* did print. Both regular boxy pants button-down shirt sort of mid-weightish guys without too many muscles, not being a thing then like it is now almost *de rigeur* to work out. Most liberal arts colleges barely had gyms in those days, and a women's college? not much there but they did have a swimming pool and students did have to know how to dive in order to graduate. Back to the fisticuffs, my father was pretty healthy and walked every day at least a couple of miles but not the strong looking type. Not exactly the Jack La Lane figure. Neither was the other guy although he was bigger and had been on some sort of muscles required team in his day. Just two professors used to sitting most of the day wearing those tweed jackets they were supposed to wear getting all hot and bothered about classical ethics or something. I mean, idealism was pretty strong in those days, not a lot of apathy like today. People held strong beliefs and even tried to act on them. So that was fun. Something was always happening for sure in the study group, had the feel of a life or death importance kind of thing whatever they were reading or discussing, no fluff nothing frivolous that wasn't the time then.

Chocolate pudding. I seemed to eat lots of it I wonder if the food choice experiment had already ended or ceased then and there in a vat of brown gook or if that was part of it. Lots of black and white Kodak pictures of me eating chocolate pudding. Cute bow in the hair. Round face, dark eyes, from the torso up in a high chair with the tasty brown stuff all over the lower half of my face and on my bib, looking pretty pleased. Later all but white chocolate gave me a stomach ache. No one could believe it when I'd say I didn't like chocolate ice cream, got ridiculed about it for being contrary somehow. Oppositional personality they said. It was physical though. Something about my digestive system from the beginning—remember the colic. More on this later surely—especially since it seems to have come back to haunt me bigtime.

Only thing I remember from this dwelling period was being lifted to see through a small, round glass window in a door. Did I forget to tell you that my mother was pregnant again? My father did the lifting. I don't remember what exactly I saw, I just remember whiteness, of the room (and probably of the people). Not a Catholic hospital this time. I don't remember seeing any people, not even my mother or my baby sister (well, they wouldn't have been in the same room together anyway and I only remember one lifting and one window). Just the window and white. Maybe I didn't know what I was supposed to be looking at, maybe my mother was too far away from the door and the little window for me to really see her as her. I don't know. I don't remember. Just a physical sense of being lifted up from around my ribs and all the white. That's presumably why we were there, so I could see my sister Debbie (or, Pesha Leah, her other name. I loved having a Hebrew name, it seemed like such a secret and wonderful thing) who was just born and my mother who had probably been missing already a few days. Probably Omi was staying with us again for this birth but I don't remember if she was there then specifically. She'd braid my hair endlessly, even when I asked for five. Probably if I said six or seven, but I don't remember going that far. She bought me a pink quilt I loved. And a couple of dresses at Altman's—gone from 34th Street, and also just gone. I'd go back there as an adult to remember Omi. Bought a raincoat there in my twenties, still have it love it very classic and well made. She played pinochle. Had that little, round table with the four drawers coming out of the sides at quarter turns of the circumference with rounded drawer faces. Cards and chips and scoring stuff, a board with pegs, maybe.

Omi had friends, some in her building like Suzanne Lieberman from downstairs, the electrolysist, for example, a heavy and breathy and very kind seeming woman. She had whiskers on her chin and upper lip, not so many but dark and thick hairs. I don't know what Omi actually did all day. She made great cold plum soup, I remember that I can conjure up the taste of it right now and the beautiful rich purple color of it. Dora was her real name, but I never called her that. Not once I am sure. She looked old to me but she died pretty young like I and many of us will. The other grandmother was already in the process of dying. Breast cancer, all I remember is her huge edema arm. My grandfather took her everywhere to try to find a cure tried everything they could think of. My mother's sister was going to be next but that took longer and we were already in California by then. That sister Omalia took care of their mother in her final years with my cousin Russell in tow. My grandmother loved Russell and loved spoiling him as it was called, haven't heard that expression in a while outdated now. Anyway a lot of illness on top of the war deaths. Later on both my mother's brothers died of forms of cancer too. So that's another thing, I never ever expected to live beyond childhood. Too much death death death not to mention my mother's death anxiety all around, more later on all this. Like when she tried to read *Charlotte's Web* to my sister and could only get a couple of sentences in before breaking into sobs knowing what was to come in the story. So shocked when I turned 21 that I was still here and breathing while my cousin was horrified that she was so old (also 21). Physically, really viscerally, shocked. Like I shouldn't still be alive and on top of planet earth then, it was disorienting.

Ugh, ugh, ugh. I will try to make this a little lighter (but it's light as opposed to dark, right? So much tendentious if not outright racist metaphor in that. Remember, at this point in my story we're just two years from Rosa Parks being arrested on a bus. Could be light as opposed to heavy, but I think it isn't. Maybe it's both but still. Let's keep an eye on stuff like this) since after all this is my parents' story and it's still the happy-go-lucky wide open any and every thing is possible fifties! Yeah, I know there was plenty of difficulty and nasty politics then not to mention the ever present horrors of the war. It was all going to be fixed people could even get jobs get paid doing the fixing. And could get jobs period, lots of them. And live really live. Without all that fear and dread.

So much wasn't known about all the machinations just under the surface. Literally in many cases, it's 1957 after all, same time when the town of Niagara Falls built the low income housing right up to the Love Canal site. Got the land cheap and could house so many people that the town was bursting with in a rapid expansion period like so much of the decade after the war ended all over the country. Booming booming booming agriculture manufacturing entertainment up up up. Bounty for so many. Our house was in with the trend, happy happy happy. Two kids now, that's a real family. Two girls but I don't think either of them thought that they had wanted a boy, maybe I just didn't pick up on it but kids usually do pick up on things notwithstanding that the only name they originally had for me being a boys' name. My father was in heaven cigars which he did not ever smoke except the time I gave him one for his birthday and he choked trying to enjoy it for me or anyway some equivalent all around the department and lots of pattings on the back kind of thing. Sherry at the department afternoon tea time and everyone talking about theory theory theory and the new baby both on equal footing. He had just finished a translation of *The Trial* with the drama professor in the study group. It had taken them many many months of long nights while my mother was nesting for her second, sewing baby stuff cleaning my old baby clothes making more curtains and singing around the house in this maternity smock I remember as kind of a sixties precursor kind of thing with large pockets all around above the hem. She made me one just like it the next year which I loved would keep all kinds of things in those wonderful deep pockets. Mine was green and blue hers was in oranges and browns. Lots of browns in those fifties which shaded into the bright Marimekko oranges reds pinks just a few years later. She had a wonderful shift she wore all the time in a Marimekko print with huge pink and orange irregular circular shapes. It went straight down to above the knee a little A shaped just the right amount and as I've said she's tall so it worked well on her.

A lot of Hayden playing on our Victrola. And marching music, could that really be correct? Anyway music talking meals cooking lots of meat loaf and pot roast and mashed potatoes and always chocolate cake around for my mother. I don't know if she would bake them but probably. Remember no mixes or instant or fast foods yet and we were on a farm and not exactly near anything bustling or even with a bakery that wasn't a bit of a too far drive away especially with a baby and a toddler to get into the car first. I think the recipes especially for the cake were things her mother would bake for her when she came home from school. That grandmother took homemaking very seriously and would even wash the walls. Wash the walls, let that sink in. Regularly. And make vegetables and such into funny shapes like cars and animals to get her brood of four to eat them and cakes with a large glass of milk for after school. And always a soup to begin dinner in the long cold winter months in the days that the snow would be piled up for months on end and heating meant shoveling coal. And everything made from fresh scratch as was the only option in those days. The gefilte fish the chopped liver of course all the soups and cakes. Not sure about the breads if she bought them. Eggs and milk from a local man who would bring them around door to door on a cart. Fruit was the only thing she bought from a non-kosher vendor being firm that Angelo was the only one who sold reliable fresh fruit.

But back to Niagara Falls for a minute, let's not rush past this doozy. School had already been built right on top of those buried toxic drums. A school for kids. Children! Some of the ground, a huge twenty-five foot area crumbled at the school to expose lots of the drums full of chemicals. The area would clog with water during rainstorms to create large puddles of the chemical brew. The kids loved playing in those sloshy craters. The school shootings we have today are horrific but so was this, they knew what they were doing in that town, Hooker Chemical Company, the very one that laid out those drums under the landfill told them *in advance!* What can we do with this information? Are we getting to the why of these things yet? I feel further away than ever. Who builds a school on top of drums and drums full of toxic stuff. Knowing if and when the clay barrier—a clay barrier? who thought that was enough?—was breached by construction, weather, time. Erosion. For little kids, probably beautiful little kids (usually kids are beautiful for the most part, aren't they?). And let them play in the lethal soup. Why was that necessary or even possible? Knowing, yes fully knowing, what was there. And it took decades to re-uncover the truth or at least some of it. Took not only kids going to school in the neck of this nightmarish situation but people also living there, what a surprise, low income families. Who reported trouble after trouble, disease and odors, for years and years before anything was done. Again, with full disclosure from Hooker Chemical from the beginning— wanted out of liability in exchange for selling the land to the town for a measly dollar, just one dollar. One hundred pennies—so much money saved by the town temporarily at least. Back to the money theme but I'm not doing it on purpose. The because they could thing too I guess. I want more. Ironic that this same site was picked out long long ago to be the perfect spot for an utopian socialist me- tropolis by one King Camp Gillette (yes, as in the razor blades) to house the continent's population, powered for all energy needs by the falls no money no cars all housing with ample light reflected in through glass domes atop the circular inner courtyards.

That vision was penned in 1894! Hydroelectric power for all no fossil fuels, imagine that. Imagine that we had stopped using them way more than one hundred years ago. Let's pause together over this. When exactly do we learn? I mean from Love Canal and many other oil and fracking disasters poisonings of water wells that people drink out of every day—children!—and of having oil sludge emerge on people's properties miles from the rigs and the fracking sites, when do we learn? Well, we don't it seems or maybe we do now at least on the whole for white communities. Like just right now in Weld County Colorado. The predominantly Caucasian populated school nixed an oil and gas drilling fracking development because the (also white) parents sustained a protest. Okay, so let's move it to near another school.

Why near schools? Is that land cheaper? What's the deal? And so they have twenty-four rigs right up next to another school, but this one has Black and Latina students so never mind and by the way we will take extraordinary precautions—and they did, built a wall separating the school grounds from the drilling and fracking! Will buffer the sound and also by the way we're using quiet engines, don't usually do this, see how far we're willing to go to protect the kids? Wow. Parents are protesting here but it's not the same. An elderly neighbor said he thinks "it's wonderful. Everyone is scream- ing. But it's jobs and it's money." Right back to the money theme with racism thrown in to underwrite the whole thing. Really, what when how are we going to do?

I'm going to move on here, back to my parents you might be relieved to read. We'll move on with the story and my family did at this point in time also move. The day had finally come that sunny perfect spanking new California was waiting for them, beckoning every day a little stronger until every box and bag was packed. Me two and Debbie just a baby my father with a post at UC Berkeley and my mother full of ideas about her next efforts. A whole new world to explore new politics new people new ideas and definitely

definitely a new climate wild beauty and just bountiful everything. He had a new research program in mind studying how students study and think and learn and he had the colleagues out there to do it with a fresh approach to higher education and to making it better. He couldn't wait to head north over the Golden Gate and up the famous Route 101 to wine country, he had already been studying the California vineyards which became a lifelong passion for him. He quickly resolved to only drink Californias. Didn't know where it was heading what with the nuclear testing pesticides and hazardous dumping and the fires burning over it all sending the toxics far and wide over the precious vines.

My favorite grim and weird twist and turn story here is the wine story yeah turns out radioactive fallout is useful for dating fine wines and sleuthing out fraud. Remember the completely preventable Fukushima nuclear disaster of 2011? well the radioactive fingerprint of the leak—right into the Pacific sending plumes clear over to California—showed up in California wines and led to a sure-fire method of determining whether the wines have been dated properly for sale. Yay! There's a capitalist use for sequelae of radiation leaks, an authentication process. Could have been averted? what about Chernobyl if we're going down this road? A little injection of science could have stopped that one in '86. Yeah somehow a team of engineers was allowed to conduct an experiment at the nuclear plant without knowledge of nuclear physics or even sound experimental design skills. Oy! and what happened there. Even there horrific as it was including releasing four hundred yes four hundred! times the radioactive material as the bombing of Hiroshima and Nagasaki nevertheless was at worst one-one-hundreth the radioactive release of the weapons testing of the fifties and sixties wow! and the era I am working up to talking about, soon I'll get there. We should all—worldwide—have those potassium iodide pills they're giving out to residents within a ten mile radius of the Indian Point nuclear plant which don't worry has radioactive leaks into the Hudson River and groundwater and is by the way only thirty-six miles from dear old NYC, pretty crazy stuff huh? Not making any of this up yet either disclaimer at the end of the story notwithstanding.

But all that was only to come out to most of us later like even just recently with the horrible Woolsey fire in 2018 burning atop a rocket engine testing site that had breaches undisclosed to the public never cleaned up and only made known once the fire was burning over it. But that's getting so far ahead the fire anyway but it was only one year from where they are now packing to go to California that the missile testing site had a partial meltdown yes that was in 1959. Had a few other nuclear accidents after that contaminating 2,844 acres none of which was revealed to the public until the Woolsey fire burned and burned and not far from downtown LA either. Apparently one of the most toxic sites in the country and no clean-up was ever ever attempted.

Okay, let's try to stick with the story at hand, right now! back to the packing and moving with the two of them totally starry eyed in love with each other with their two tots and with the awesome untamed west coast wide open for their discovery. They were doing it, getting there just like they promised each other and just like they had hoped, plotted, planned and dreamed of.

Jumping on again, no half measures this time, jauntily joyfully leaping over the whole country in one big bound.

WESTWARD-HO!

"WALT, WE'RE HERE!" WITH THAT exclamation my mother dropped her bags on the stair landing getting off the plane and raised her hands to the sky. "We're here we're here, look at us!" She surged over to my father and wrapped her arms around him and Debbie who at that moment was in his arms.

My father chuckled a deep warm chuckle and squeezed back as best he could with Debbie in one arm and a suitcase in the other. He leaned his head on hers and sighed, "It took a while but the wait is over. California, watch out!"

"Breathe in the scent, is that orange blossom? Roses? Look at the palm trees!" my mother was soaking it all in unaware that she was also holding up the deplaning process.

"Come, let's go!" my father said with a jolly grin nudging us all down the stairs and towards the airport building.

They'd had enough of Columbus and of the cold Northeast and had moved on to paradise as they promised each other. Sunny beautiful bountiful California of the fifties. Wow, how stunning and still almost unspoiled it was then! The constant sun the sounds the colors! the temperature the beauty—anyone could grow almost anything, it took no skill there. The smells, everywhere amazing fragrance. The flowers in every possible space citrus growing in every yard and figs and dates and cumquats and blackberries and almonds! Bougainvillea's sunflowers morning glories roses. My father loved all the fruit growing everywhere my mother the pansies.

I loved roses, still do, more much more on roses as we go. The rose garden in Berkeley, always go back to it when I'm anywhere near—its half its original size now. And Cordonices across the street with the long, long slide. Even took my own kids there once. I don't know how impressed they were, or not. Cherries plums apples—oh! I so remember the smell of the apple trees outside of Abe and Ariella's bedroom with the double doors out to an apple tree patio. And their wonderful, beautiful pool beyond the apples. I shit in it once, I was four and I couldn't help it. I don't have much body control now—chemically induced—but I never really did. Would pee in my pants a lot. And dresses. Linda's party and I was wearing my magical white and powder blue dress that Omi had bought for me. There I was sitting on steps watching the party happen—outdoors of course, this was California, everything was outdoors there under the warm bright sun—knowing I had to pee and didn't maybe couldn't move. And then it was all over and I had to move quickly. Happens now for a different reason. I don't know what the reason was then maybe the beginning of some of my weird idiosyncrasies.

My father lifting me again, but not at a window, outside. At a cherry tree—really! We were picking cherries. My father thought California was some kind of miracle. You could pick cherries from a tree. A tree that was right outside our house! Drive a Dodge Dart forever, 200,000 and counting miles on his car, he was quite proud of that.

I've just got to ask again did we really not guess where all the modern miracles were leading? We, I mean, the Everyperson, not the scientists, didn't they have to know something? Big tobacco knew. Big alcohol knows (wine is the It thing now) and knew big oil knew the Exxon's the Getty's the GEs the Monsanto's the Tiger in your Tank knew a lot. DDT was a miracle in its golden years of the fifties with kids running behind spray trucks in the summer getting doused in the hot sun. There we go, kids again soaked in poison. I mean, surely we knew that DDT was a poison, that was the point that it was, so why let kids get soaked in it, literally soaked in the sprays? Doesn't take that much brain power to know that's not a good idea. The big machinery introduced into agriculture, farms big and small all had to have it, all in the fifties. The building of tract housing suburbs electric can openers the nuclear testing all over the damn place with spectators! Really, spectators, Walter Cronkite even declaring how safe it was to be standing there. If you don't believe me, look it up for God's sake, it's true. Don't get me started, so much nuclear testing in the US of A in the fifties (188 is the official count, but weren't there more not included in this count?), like Operation Tea Pot the Nevada fake town to test survival with fourteen blasts in just three months. Spectators too, of course. Later microwaves and we say we're nuking our food when we put stuff into them. I've never used one but so I've heard people say. With radiation leaking out of them and out of our laptops now so that Apple stopped calling them *lap*tops for fear of lawsuits (all that colon cancer in such young people these days! The solution? Screen people younger and younger—money theme playing here— not let's fix the problem just pretend we don't know what it is when we do—why aren't we all protesting, screaming in the streets with big ENOUGH signs all together? Why do we let ourselves get divided, by geography by race by income religion national borders, why? Why do we forget that we are all people?) and radiation from domestic electric transformers right outside so many homes and from dumping hazardous waste that just keeps oozing or sometimes burning even uncontrollably like in Philmont NY for years and years, PCBs, oy! See what I mean, why didn't we and I mean really us, me you your friends cousins aunts uncles grandparents even, en masse, run and shout and protest in the streets that we don't want this? Hostess cupcakes, motor boats, lipstick and nail polish with lead and much worse in it. Endocrine disruptors one and all. Agent Orange on our lawns for kids and dogs to eat. We could say that then the ordinary woman and man didn't know there was something to protest in all that stuff that seemed so great but come on, all that disposable stuff how did the adults not think about where it was going and where it was all leading to? all so intoxicated with the promise of the good life? maybe maybe that's what I want to know but let's just say that's so for now what about today? Today we all us Everypersons do know and we're still not raging in the streets and storming politicians, CEOs offices. I mean some protests yes high school students all over the world speaking out but not just flat-out refusal to go along anymore not happening and why not? and wildlife as we call it to differentiate ourselves, they eat it too the chemicals on the lawns gardens parks forests even. I ate grass stalks, didn't you? Back then, fifties, sixties, beautiful Northern Californians, did we really not suspect or we just didn't want to give in to our doubts with all that glorious paradise and convenience to boot for us? Drive to the beach drive two hours for lunch pop something frozen (inside of three layers of crazy packaging Styrofoam plastic aluminum dyes preservatives bleaches dioxin) into the toaster and ka-bam you can eat and drive on the run and tear your exhaust filter out to get better mileage—how many people did that under the sunny sun? A mechanic told me to do so in the seventies, have you ever torn yours out of your car's exhaust? Same time, different place not all that far away, a different kind of system—a different culture—was setting up in Cuba with Fidel Castro at the helm, but more on this later as it evolved over time and back to the consumer-focused situation on the glorious West Coast US of A and all it offered. Then.

Now of course things are a bit different. San Fran with heat over 100 degrees Fahrenheit, who could imagine that? Used to have to wear a little jacket year round back in the day. I think it was 104 last week, wow! Fires, they do always have fires, but these were worse: Napa, Sonoma could smell the smoke down to Palo Alto almost right away. That's pretty far. Fires through and through British Columbia Washington State all over really with Trump & Co saying it's a forest management problem need to just cut down the damn trees and then they won't burn. There's a weird logic to that of sorts but too bad other things like grasses and so on cause equally horrific fires ones in fact that are burning out of control right now while I am writing this to you. Worse droughts coastal erosion water issues, even more than before. There's more to the list of course but this is getting ahead too. Back in the days of the fifties it all felt magical. I thought so, I'll get to that, me and curly top Debbie out in the garden. Like Shirley Temple, she was, and we had to get home every Sunday in time to watch the *Shirley Temple Show* for her. Don't try watching it now quell the urge so much racism sexism classism just plain ism ism in the show.

Okay, so flash forward a few years to Stanford and in particular the Stanford Hospital for another piece of the pervasive racism of the time. And yet another hospital. The stage is getting set for me it seems already so young. An overnight operation. Abe was supposed to attend so I wouldn't be scared. I don't remember if he did but I didn't particularly trust him. All to "fix"? figure out? the bladder "problem." Did it occur to no one, not Abe even the psychiatrist, I think he might have even been a psychoanalyst, that it was an emotional problem. I mean maybe not, but why not pursue that before hospital stays? Don't remember anyone talking to me about it. Not a lot of adult/kid talking in those days. What if someone had just tried that first? Seems obvious now but these days we are supposed to be constantly talking talking talking to our kids a modern day version of instilling morals.

Lying down on a bed slab of some sort in the OR blowing into a heavy-duty red balloon. And that's it. Cystoscopy over. Nothing learned, nothing changed. But they used to cut out people's—little children's—tonsils with impunity too. Sheila (baby baby sister) escaped that by tripping on a rug on the way in—smart one she is. Anyway, an overnight in the hospital circa 1961. My mother slept on a cot next to my bed, only allowed after she had a fit about it. We held hands all night in case anything happened.

It did. Woken in the middle of the night. Children's ward with lots of beds. Another Stephanie across the way who taught me a card game the next day and we played for hours, so it seemed. I don't know what she was in for, probably didn't then either. Lots of kids in that room, it seemed very big.

Back to the middle of the night. The one child on the ward with sickle cell anemia was put in a chair out in the middle of the room.

The only girl of color in the room, and there were only girls in this ward of course. A group and I do mean a group lots of interns and a doctor in charge circled the girl pointing out all her defects and problems. A teaching hospital (not much teaching in patient care yet in those days, it took my uncle Jay and others to think about the doctor-patient relationship and the idea, doctrine, of informed consent). The whole while the girl was crying, all alone, no parents there and no one thought to comfort her or shield her from the on-slaught. Did they think she couldn't speak English? Did they think?

I had fantasies for many years to come about diabolical doc-tors in their labs and lab coats, white again here too, doing things to patients, so imagine what that girl's dream life afterwards was like. Let's get back to 1957 and the pilgrimage to the Great West. My parents felt they had found Mecca remember. Linda's party was then and there in the Berkeley Hills.

Ducks in a nearby pond, nearby to our house. Which was one single story ranch style house somehow divided in two. One side for our family and the other for Linda's. An accordion door to sepa-rate the households. My father would take me on his shoulders to the ducks. My grandmother, Omi, would take me to feed the ducks outside Gracie Mansion when I would visit her on East 89th Street after she moved from Washington Heights. I visited her alone from California to New York at eight, flying and everything. More about flights in those early sixties days later and all the free alcohol the cigarettes—even for kids! and chicklets. Fast forward to 1985 a Polish Lot Airline plane I was on divided the smoking from the non-smoking sections smack down the aisle, all the way from front to back. Oh well.

But back to the late fifties, okay? Things still booming away and the colleagues in my father's department were welcoming and his research got underway as soon as he arrived. My parents quickly instituted a new and improved version of their study group and joined the California style academic cocktail party circuit. It was glorious all of their fantasies were coming true nothing nothing nothing could be better. And they did get a car, a two-door blimpy looking Chevy, used. One of their first trips was straight up to the wine country. A trek that now one has to wade through tons of traffic but then it was an expedition through unbounded wilderness and raw beauty. Towns like Yountville Geyserville the city Santa Rosa unrecognizable from how they are today. They had a great time tasting going from vineyard to vineyard swirling sniffing sipping and with two babies in tow (me one of them, not really a baby but close enough from the vantage point of wine tasting). The rolling hills with rows of beautiful old vines the reddish earth the purple green and red grapes plump and ripening in triangular clusters it was fall and the harvest season a perfect time to go up for their first visit to such an enchanted area. The ocean practically lapping up to the vineyard hills and orange and lemon groves everywhere gorgeous dirt roads with no need for paving and the vineyard haciendas that hadn't yet become the Disneyesque McMansions they are today. One could just drive up and go in and pick the vintages to try. It was the beginning of my father's self-education in California varieties he didn't have favorites yet or any expertise and was having a great time embarking on this unfolding curriculum. Swirling the bit of wine around in the sampling glass sniffing letting the lush liquid swish in his mouth for an extra-long moment he loved it all and liked discussing the subtleties. She liked it too but didn't quite have the passion for it he did and would get bored after a certain point a few swishes too many not to mention dealing with kids getting restless. For her it was the whole California surround that energized her. She couldn't wait to start delving into local politics with all the lefties hanging out in plain sight there in Berkeley. It was second nature to her since adolescence, telling her father how to vote when she couldn't yet and increasingly radicalizing him as he stopped arguing and began listening and learning from his youngest. Pipsqueak they called her even though she was gangly and getting taller and stronger by the day playing basketball stickball and getting boxing pointers from her uncle.

Back to their first foray into wine country, peering into a white wine glass, my father whispers out dreamily, "What do you think of this one, never tasted a Chardonnay like this, have you?" Not waiting for a response he continued on, "No, never certainly not from France, this is different more substantial the oak the body! I think I'm in love with this one!"

At each stop it was the same drill, begin with the whites in successive order of body depth character and then move on the reds. My father seemed to favor whites though or so it seemed at first. My mother the reds, so they were a good pair as usual, this time in ferreting out which could be their new favorites. The vintners would be ready to make us kids Shirley Temples and I definitely had too many of those bright red maraschinos, once she was more mobile Debbie taught me we could dive straight to the syrupy cherries and bypass the whole drink thing if we wanted but I liked the Ginger Ale so usually didn't follow her on that one. Almost before she could walk she learned how to climb up to the bar seats and charm a bowl of cherries out of the servers.

Drove a little too fast a little too tipsy on the way home one time and were pulled over by a cop saying "you've got kids in the back, slow down" and let us go at that. Nice, just a warning don't know how often if ever that happens these days. Once had a speed trap guy pull me over and seeing it was my birthday from my license said he'd not give me a speeding violation just a tail light out to be fixed notice like he was giving me a birthday present. Since my tail light wasn't out I couldn't get a shop anywhere to sign off on it since it would have been fraud to say they fixed something that wasn't broke, that was a way bigger hassle than the speeding fine thanks a lot! many happy returns to you, officer!

While we were lapping in the paradise and the great boom years went on and on, building, manufacturing, whooping it up with jobs and homes and martinis (again, for some: the visible white nuclear—interesting term in this context isn't it?—family) little pods of seeds of change were being planted all over. Camp Century, for example, far from beautiful California way out in Greenland under ice sheets. The government—ours in the US of A that is—said it was a scientific exploration but it was as you and

I could by now guess a military installation. Cold War sights set on the Soviet Union, a very convenient location. They thought the sheets would last forever —did they really believe that? They pretty soon discovered, just a few years in, that the ice was unstable. Built in 1959 and abandoned already by '67. And not the only military site built by the US of A in Greenland at the time, by the way. It had everything: 2500 miles yes miles of ice tunnels and train tracks a chapel a library a theater infirmary and so on, along with two power plants (one nuclear) 600 nuclear missiles sewage diesel fuel and basically roughly 20,000 liters of chemical waste. What's going to happen now you might be asking, what with climate change and the melting of the ice sheets. All of that released into the water the ground the air. But what potential with the unearthing of this under ice wonderland, a renewed strategic launch site in our refreshed and updated and more scary Cold War.

Linda was a couple of years older than me and had brothers. I thought she was beautiful and wonderful. She probably wasn't really either. One night I had a surreal kind of dream. Linda and her brothers on little foot powered go-carts swishing around our houses and in and out of our side of the house. The next day we woke up to a robbery having happened and our dog Piper quaking in his paws under my parents' bed. It was only dolls—Barbie dolls—that were taken.

That dog would suck on pacifiers and use the toilet. My mother would push him off, wouldn't it have been easier for the dog to just use the toilet? He probably could have learned to flush too. He delicately sucked—no chewing!—on pacifiers thinking he was one of the brood, what was the harm after all? Pacifiers, just think of what the word means and what the function of them is. Okay let's have a little journalism on them, especially for those of you with babies.

Originally made out of rubber—not harmful to suck and suck on until they added lead to make them white. Oh well again. That was right then where we are in the 1950s. Later they were made out of plastics leaching BPA silicone and latex. None of that too good for a newborn or toddler to ingest for hours upon hours a day.

Think about the totality of it—pacifiers teething rings sippy cups and on and on—in a newborn through to old toddler's mouth day in and day out, day and night. Drip drip drip just sucking the estrogenic endocrine disrupting carcinogenic just plain poisonous stuff to keep the baby happy and quiet. Maybe the old-fashioned rum on the gums, whisky in the milk, wasn't so bad after all, relatively speaking.

I had so many pacifiers I would make a line across my pillow with them in a specific order. Another indication something was going on with me but I'm not sure anyone noticed that I was doing that. Didn't give them up until I was around eight. That is getting ahead to when we were in San Francisco and it was so hard to do! Should have looked back on those days when I was in Smoke Enders twenty years later, could have remembered that I could kick a habit, had done it before. Didn't occur to me until right now. Memoirs are useful, diaries I guess better since they're more of an ongoing, reflective kind of thing. Like psychoanalysis so you'd think I'd get it by now.

Onwards. The Berkeley Hills were a dream come true for them. They made fast friends with local professors biologists artists activists. They had lively discussions going once again with an even more left leaning political bend. The inborn/learned debate was raging in academic circles all over the country and they fell right in with it, the group pretty evenly divided on the subject with no one so extreme as to be all one or the other. It was thought to be immensely important which side was right. I mean after all are things like aggression innate? or is it taught? what are the implications either way for society for peace for war for learning environments. Pressing issues of the time. Everyone wanted to know what to do to foster a peaceful productive world to prevent war and famine and dictators.

Many in the group had young children too as you might guess so there were outings every weekend hiking picnics beach trips lots of singing and games and cook outs really great fun for everyone. His work was rewarding and she was getting the lay of the social activist land and also the programs on the UC campus in which she could continue her graduate degree. They even had concocted new what they called California-style oatmeals, a lemony one another with fresh figs one they called almond zip, it was all fun fun fun for them even breakfast! A car a dog two kids good job interesting friends and lots lots lots to do. A house and promotion were coming, they could practically smell it. Things were in more than full swing for them by the end of the winter when my father received a letter from the Chair of the Department back east at Vassar. He was expected as per their original agreement to return for the fall semester, he was missed and needed there. It was a very flattering letter but neither of my parents enjoyed reading it. They had forgotten about that agreement not taking it entirely seriously and felt more kicked in the rear than warm and fuzzy from it.

"Oh God, oh God," is all my father could say over and over. My mother just looked defiantly angry. Kind of like their balloon popped suddenly in their faces. I mean not that they didn't like it at Vassar but they certainly did not want to leave Berkeley either. They had just arrived they were settling in they were happy they had forever plans there. My mother was opposed and said so many times over the next week. However.

Another big dashing leap across. Yes, reluctantly they agreed to a final year at Vassar for him. Needed him to teach two more semesters and it was part of the deal in letting him out of a longer contract to go to Berkeley in the first place. But just one year one more max they swore to each other staring into each other's eyes and then they'd hightail it out of there straight back to California and this time for good and not pivot back again ever.

We packed up yet again and this time I remember proudly carrying my important things in my own green rectangular kids-size suitcase on the plane and out to the car and in every maneuver on that move back. The mood was a bit somber between them I don't think she ever fully agreed that they should honor the commitment, they should just stay and continue putting down the vibrant charged roots in the Eureka State, what could they do put him in jail sue badmouth him?

"I mean, what're they going to do?" she'd say like a broken record while packing, "The whole thing'll blow over and Berkeley will see that they have someone even more valuable than they knew and Vassar'll hire someone else!" As she spoke her Brooklyn accented voice rising not to a yell but loud.

He wouldn't answer feeling he had to hold to his word but also knowing she was probably right and this whole moving thing was arduous another go around what with her being pregnant for the third time and the UC health system and hospital were so great and the weather conditions better since she was due in the winter.

"Well, we're almost all packed and we're going," he would finally say with sadness and apology in his voice and she knew he was sorry and she felt badly for him since the decision really did fall on his shoulders and after all he was an honorable man and that was generally a good thing but just not so great right at that very moment. Her ethical standards were more flexible than his that had been clear from the outset of their dating.

Another plane ride another setting up of a household in the offing and away we went. I was getting older and was going to enter pre-school when we got there and my mother would get a little relief just having the one small kid at home for a couple of hours a day while she was in her third trimester and tired as it was even without the unpacking setting up and having two small kids a husband a dog. At least the community was familiar and they had friends to count on, that was great but they had just made new ones in Berkeley and didn't want to leave what they had there.

"When we go back," my mother said unpacking a stack of dishes after dinner one evening, "no more shared ranch house, we'll have our own even if it's tiny."

My father piped in, "It will be California style with windows and a modern kitchen and a yard maybe small but still with flowers and sunlight and it'll be great."

"Just nine months away really," my mother said wistfully.

Again saying that nine months thing, they both felt the weight of it this time around. And they knew he did have to get hired for another job out there first and that was a bit uncertain even in these boom years. With three kids their expenses would only be on the increase. Neither of them vocalized these nagging thoughts but knew the other was having them too. Anyway, back East we went.

THE GROOVED PATH
EASTWARD

I DON'T REMEMBER WHAT I THOUGHT or felt about all this moving but I'm pretty sure given my general disposition idiosyncrasies as I've so far called them that it was disconcerting not in my nature just the opposite in fact. More on my disposition later, but for now, maybe all the digestive stuff had to do with the switching things up all the time. People changing places changing houses changing my room changing also no wonder I began to cling to the pacifiers and dolls things I could control hang on to keep with me where ever when ever. Wanting to keep things as they are undisturbed consistent. The same the same the same, exactly what I couldn't ever achieve in those days of constant change. I'm guessing I was already what others would describe as shy but it was probably that I was instinctively retreating and not venturing too far in the perceptually chaotic world keeping myself intact by not letting things in or out skin and voice as barriers. The surround kept being unknown unrecognizable. Smells sounds tastes textures temperatures everything really. Always had some kind of sense something was wrong internally and even externally on my face remarked on often by others the face I was unaware of making but still chalked these things up to weird preferences turned out to be more of a tangible diagnosable set of symptoms but that knowledge is for so much later as to not have been able to have an impact on my life or be at least freeing in some way not until I'm so old.

Even our very family members kept changing except my father who was pretty much a constant with the browns plaids glasses accent. Except that he was increasingly gone a lot and at unpredictable intervals as he was being sought out for lectures education reform consulting and such. He was changing the world one educational institution at a time, very progressive ideas. Debbie first didn't exist was tiny and then suddenly was up walking. My mother's body in constant transformation and her accent was not only locational but also situational mood swings being a driving force.

By the time of this move my mother is definitely very visibly pregnant again, I don't remember when I caught on or really if I did but I must have, right? I remember the smell of it. Not good, not a good smell. But anyway, she is, and I'm like 4-ish and Debbie is 2-ish, and baby Sheila Louise (supposed to be middle name forward as Louisiana until they chickened out) is born. I don't remember any windows or being lifted this time. And I don't remember any nursing happening, not surprising really. Ariella had her breasts bound each time she had a baby—three of them, Julian was the youngest. Maybe my mom took the dry up pills. The La Leche League was just a few years old then, probably hadn't reached Poughkeepsie. Even in 1988 when I had my first, they were still and even in ol' NYC considered a bit out there. Crazy, huh? The best thing for mom and baby, and really feels like some kind of weird miracle that food can just pour out of one's body spigots—nothing is ever made up *de novo*, is it? I mean those soda spigots where you put the cup under and press and out it comes, just mechanical breasts and full of the sugar liquid hospitals push instead of the breast spigot.

My mother had probably amassed enough maternity and baby stuff as I've mentioned to you she had sewn baby clothes toddler clothes shifts for her ties for my dad curtains, anyway not a lot of sewing going on this time around. The unpacking stretched on and on not at all like the other moves. My mother was tired from yes her third pregnancy and third trimester of it coming up with the move and my father off to his office a lot long hours to rekindle relationships there and get politicking for the next move west again. Wow! was that really fun for them or was it a hamster wheel? At least they knew what was going on. Maybe the jockeying bartering writing politicking schmoozing did have its moments but they did this a lot of times, aren't you getting tired of hearing about it? I'll just warn you now it never really stopped or sort of did but so much later with kids already out of the house. That was the hard part then the moving with kids and all their special desires to hold onto toys and props and demands like needing to pee at very inconvenient moments and no matter what part of transit they were in, maybe the flux of it all was energizing for them. Anyway they and we marched on and sang in the car and colored on the planes—I always blended colors together, did you or are you partial to solids?—and decorated at least I did with my mother when we'd arrive somewhere.

It was an early fall that year back east with the cold nights creeping into the afternoons with pale winter-like sun when it wasn't raining, so un-California. Two little kids me at least in preschool but that I had to be driven to Debbie too young and too little for much huge with Sheila inside and lots and lots of boxes none labeled too clearly they packed up in such a rush to get going. Right around now my mother was losing sight of the dream and wondering what happened that she was doing this like a crazy déjà vu groundhogs day rolled into one long distorted hall of mirrors. Not that she didn't know she should be and kind of was happy but there was this creeping underlying depressed confusion spreading inside her like the mold growing in some of the food she couldn't bear even the thought of in this phase of her pregnancy. Morning sickness long over somehow the taste thing lingered making it difficult to conjure up the kid food she would have been making for me and Sheila. Lots more bowls of chocolate pudding to come which was fine with us. The singing and dancing went on hold for a while except for times that it seemed just a tad over the top and scary.

My dad would come home at lunch and dinner and tell stories of department antics how his classes were going his students remember all women this is still in the pre-co-education days of Vassar by a couple of decades and where and how they met but this didn't seem to be one of the concerns on anyone's mind they didn't have that sort of relationship and if anyone was going to stray it wouldn't have been him. I think they both were pretty clear on that. Wasn't somehow in his DNA would have sent his already combustible anxiety to the moon. She'd make most of the meals practically all and he would do the dishes and most of the grocery shopping. For the times they were a pretty balanced housework team. He also did all the vacuuming and lots of the dusting kind of stuff and while she was this pregnant and tired he did the mopping too. Window cleaning wasn't really a thought along with other sorts of things her mother did as a matter of course like the wall cleaning thing. That one gets to me I mean if there's dust or spider webs or something I will give a wipe down to a wall but it's not a part of any regular routine I would ever dream up and it's not like my house is dirty or anything.

"You wouldn't believe this guy in seminar today, going on and on about intelligence being innate. Wholly innate! In fact he went further to say that dispositions generally are innate."

"What rock did he climb out from?" my mother asked with a laugh taking a bite of her liverwurst sandwich at the same time.

"Somewhere in the South, um, somewhere in Texas. Austin I think, a pretty sophisticated place, I don't think we can blame his views on UT. And no one questioned him, no one was even going to until I piped up. It was really shocking, and they all sort of left me out there on my own."

"So weird! We'll follow up at our next meeting I hope, find out what was going on. I mean obviously most of us are leaning heavily on learning being the thing." My mother was cutting Debbie's sandwiches into small triangles hoping that would get her to eat more. She had made her a grilled cheese knowing no way Debbie would eat liverwurst. I loved it, so no problem there. Just had to have mayo on the toast first then the liverwurst on top of that. Glasses of milk all around except for my father who drank water.

"I think they were afraid to buck him and his fancy academic lineage. Enough of such nonsense! I tried to have a substantive discussion but it really went nowhere." My father was getting a bit worked up, the nature/nurture thing being really important to him.

My mother too. Chewing she exclaimed, "Lineage schmineage! I mean no one pressed him on the implications? If intelligence is innate then do different people have different amounts of it from birth? If dispositions are inborn then evil is too? Can all we hope for is to suppress it but never eradicate it? Do we not learn it from our experience in the world by mimicking? reacting? Does he think we're doomed to more and more devastating wars, that there's no hope? that our innate intelligence and aggression will afford us more and more powerful bombs and weapons and that some will want to use them? eventually a single detonation will wipe out half the world?" her emotions were rising to a pitch. These questions might seem a bit extreme but they were to occupy some of the best minds for decades until mass extinction from climate change took over. Fast forward to the anti-nuclear movement and the biopsychosocial advocate Margaret Brenman Gibson wanting to find out what caused nuclear scientists to use their intelligence and creativity for such potential for mass destruction. Not going along with innateness theories she sought to find out what in their experience gave rise to their choice of work.

"Something about your munching on a liverwurst sandwich through your tirade is a little comical, sorry," my father said while reaching over to wipe a dab of mayo off her chin. "He restricted his comments to intelligence, didn't touch on the disposition to evil. Since no one else was piping up implications of his line of thought didn't arise."

What no one seemed then while the debate was raging or even now to factor in is that environment also does mean *environment* as in chemicals and such that influence not to mention poison our brains our whole bodies our intellectual capacity our behavior. I think I'm a good example of one way that works out and gives some coherence to my idiosyncracies, but more later, it took me a long

long way too long time to figure it out. Spent an inordinate amount of time just thinking somethings not right kind of off about me or some kind of general damage defect not sure just know something's not like other people kind of experience. Felt ashamed I couldn't somehow break through it and be more like my friends like my sisters some foggy brain experience seemed to prevent it. But I will tell you about it just not right now.

"Were students there? Didn't they have anything to say?"

"No, even Mary Jo who was there was quiet. Maybe she didn't think it was worth it." My father was clearly getting ready to head back to his office and started to get up and take his plate and glass over to the sink.

"She always likes a fight, she's like me, I love her for that!"

"Gotta get back," he said in uncharacteristic slang through his thick German accent while giving us each in turn a peck on the top of the head. "Anything I should get on my way home?" he asked as he was already half way out. Before closing the door behind him he flashed a smile and a kiss in the air at us.

All in all they were doing pretty well even if a bit wobbly and frayed at the edges. They had old friends there the same OB/GYN that she loved from Debbie's birth the house was nice and also large enough and their eyes stayed on the prize of paradise they were not intending to let out of their sites. He had to keep writing she had to keep her cool and do the homemaking thing while she dreamt of her future in California and all the rabble-rousing work she was going to do while pursuing her doctorate in politics. So many active lefties out there also even on the Vassar campus of sorts but she knew she couldn't do much in her present condition but hold it all together. Faculty salaries didn't exactly lend to opulence of any sort but they were still a family wage and they could do okay keep up with most expenses and save a bit for the move even on such a short horizon as they were planning. The department was of course thinking they were there to stay and that he'd go for tenure in a year or so and get firmly rooted. They did play stuff close enough to their vests even with friends but not so close they couldn't send out a feeler or two. Especially at their weekly poker game. Always at their house just like the monthly study group. Their house was the fun one on the block again with faculty members trying to inch their way into one group or the other. The poker game was hot hot hot not that the stakes were high in dollars but people bet stuff they had like art or artifacts or first edition books and they went on till really early hours of the morning and then the guys yeah women played in the game especially since she founded it but for a time she was the only woman and pretty close to the best player but anyway then the guys would have to get straight to their classes and the women had to get to their kids who would already be waking up and the college student babysitter would be out like a light on the couch oblivious to the kitchen havoc being wreaked by the kids under her watch. My mother kept up with the poker game hosting for decades made her feel alive and in touch with her Brooklyn roots. Her accent would become very thick during these games and the slang along with it so much so that nobody really knew what she was talking about. As long as cards were being dealt all was good.

One evening before a game she was making her roasted chicken parts doused in a lot of soy sauce her cooking repertoire having narrowed quite a bit since the move and he was setting up the card table and chairs and putting out the salted peanuts as the staple snack of the game, he said more thinking out loud, "I wonder if we should start going in for some kind of kill soon, I mean we want to know we're going to land a job on one campus or another." He meant Berkeley or Stanford wasn't really even considering anywhere else.

She sighed while giving the parts a baste and mashing the potatoes soaked with milk and butter and salt, "We just got here though still have some boxes."

"It's never too soon and might want to wrap it up by the new year just to know but also to get a jump on people. We're still insiders there just phone calls away and have to keep on top of what's opening up."

"Or, could be made up for you," that was her kind of thinking just create what you want and it was the nature of the times that it wasn't at all crazy to think that way. She did her best to sidle up to him with a warm smile but her volume out front made that a little comical.

"You're right, of course!" he said as though it was the first time he had heard something like that. "I've got to get on it now."

"Give Nevitt a call why don't you, he's the hub. You could do it now before the game begins and before anyone gets here. Hey, kids, come for dinner— mashed favorite here!"

She didn't really need to call out like that since we were right there practically under her feet just like the dog she was always shooing away to get him out from under would say she was going to break her neck tripping over him one day. A toy collie and just small enough to not see under her hugely pregnant belly.

As Debbie and I hopped to the table, he was already on the phone which was stationed right on the kitchen counter dialing Nevitt's number in Berkeley not thinking it's three hours earlier there but Nevitt picked up and soon my father was practically shouting his heavily German accented words into the phone people thinking in those days that that had to be done to be heard such a distance of 3,000 miles away. Much later people thought for a while they had to yell into cell phones too and on trains passengers would be bombarded with multiple loud loud conversations going in every car until the quiet car concept was hatched by some very brilliant commuter. Mobile phones were the final nail in the coffin of privacy but also of decorum and just plain courtesy.

We three were already done with our dinner when my father hung up beaming his huge signature grin practically from ear to ear. "He's on it, can't wait for us to come back somehow didn't think we wanted to come right back. He's making calls for us now!" My father was so excited he forgot to sit down at the table with us and was kind of prancing around the room talking a mile a minute re-canting the conversation.

"Walt, I heard most of it at least your end of it so got the gist, but this is great. Good going, hey kids, sun and beaches for us soon!"

We didn't know what they were talking about but it sounded good or anyway they seemed pretty happy about so we did too. It was definitely something favorable. Even though it was fall in the Northeast with leaves turning color I thought she meant we were going to the beach then and there with darkness streaming into the windows I wasn't too sure about the sun part but didn't question it and was kind of confused when were supposed to get into pjs after dinner and poker players started filtering in. I blipped over the whole misunderstanding as was my habit not lingering too long on meanings a lot of stuff said didn't make any sense to me at all and if every one of those times tripped me up I'd spend all day dwelling on incomprehensible stuff. Okay it was pj time and I wanted to wear my blue and pink horses and wanted Debbie to wear hers too so we could be twins. Debbie was like my little doll who could walk and do things other dolls couldn't. She didn't really talk yet so I did all of that. It balanced out later when she started to talk a lot and me a little. I think we were even by the time we hit puberty for word count and then she surpassed me.

My mother took us to our room for story time while the game was getting set up. Usually we were asleep by the time the players arrived but the phone call and the ensuing excitement delayed the routine. I must admit I was a bit revved from the ambiance but was asleep on cue by the end of the book so that I missed the last couple of pictures I'm sure Debbie didn't miss a thing and maybe even wandered out to the game at some point and got to sit on someone's lap. I never did that but the times we went out there together I'd stare the players down while watching Debbie charm someone into hoisting her up what with her cute curly top and smile not to mention no words, she was an irresistible combination. I definitely wasn't.

As usual there were loud voices card shuffling glasses clinking and a quite smelly room that lingered into the next day with all the smoking and scotch and sodas but none of it woke me up even in that pretty small house. I'm sure my father won a lot that night so on fire he was with his prospects he was doing right for his family and sticking with the pledge they made together that afternoon on the cliffs overlooking the San Francisco Bay. It was like Otis Redding could have been singing his *Dock of the Bay* in the background throughout the game if he had sung it then and there in the fifties. I'm sure lots of thoughts were swirling in both of their heads that night while still fiercely focused on the game they were going to clean up as a good omen as if they had implicitly decided that together over the chicken and masheds.

The house was a pretty simple wood frame one story house with a finished attic making up a study for him. Two bedrooms at the back of the house and one bathroom separating the kitchen and bedrooms. It was considered old I guess which maybe for the US of A it was being maybe fifty or sixty years old. Not as bad as when I was renting a house when my first was born so that's at the end of the eighties and was told it's a very old house, nine years old! What a country. What we could do with all the underused housing would have more than enough for the homeless wouldn't we? Anyway it was a nice enough house built definitely after Vassar was established and up and running. Electricity had to be retrofitted. It had a lot of lead through and through, pipes soldered with it shower and bath pans and such. Not to mention in the paint in food cans in fuel. But none of this was an idea to consider no one was thinking this way not in the consuming public anyway. Remember cigarettes were thought or advertised as good for you! As a stimulant, made you smarter, as a relaxant helped you cope with difficulty. Alcohol used to treat all kinds of conditions too not to mention just general sugar sugar sugar everywhere Coke and colas used to baste roasts with pineapple rings and maraschino cherries atop it was haute cuisine. The times were a popping with opportunity as I've said a few times already and all the expansion availability abundance or anyway future promise of abundance for all was the *zeitgeist* not the what's in this? or what are the side effects of all these wonders?

kind of questions the modern conveniences were miracles of post war inventiveness and ingenuity. It was all great or going to be not like the dark days that had come before and still cast a pall over the western world. A pall that was being peeled away to let the greatness in. What kind of a question would it have been to ask what's in the solder what's in this chicken or beef or potato or strawberry? what's the result of all the antibiotics in animal feed? the chemicals in the produce? No, people were amazed they could even have strawberries use metal for home use products buy things have jobs build homes drive cars build roads own modern convenience appliances that did the work for you build power lines and hydroelectric dams the ones we're tearing down now in shame or some of us in shame anyway. Building building building availability convenience predicated everything else and there were songs written about these themes sung by smart thoughtful people.

Turned out there was beyond a lot of lead in the water in Brooklyn where I was living, Park Slope before it was *The Slope*, a rundown neighborhood then with no services and beautiful brownstones that no one could afford to keep up. We call them beautiful now but they were catalogue ordered homes back in the day. Kind of like the very differently styled home my parents would build in a couple of years when they got back to sunny old California. A builder would come and do a whole block, buyers could choose stuff from a catalogue: doors, molding details, and so forth. Anyway, I was in my third trimester like my mother was the second time back in Poughkeepsie and huge, like 70 pounds of weight gain huge and for some reason I can't remember got the idea to test the water I had been drinking. So much lead in it the testing company thought they had made a mistake and sent me another test, free. Same result. Then they sent me fifteen tests to give out, free again, within a two block radius. I decided to give them to households that had little kids. Almost no one would take them! Free! Important info for their kids! One mother said, "I don't want to know cause if it's bad I'll have to do something"!! Anyway, it turned out that the service pipes, the ones that run

from the water main pipe that runs down the street into the households were solid lead. Almost none had yet needed replacement, so
that's a lot of lead running house after house to the kitchen sink.
Had my milk tested for lead once I gave birth. And that's not even
in Flint. I'm guessing a lot of those service pipes are still in place in
the now glitzy Slope. Sidebar on Flint and all the lead intentionally
put in the water there: not more than a stone's throw away Nestle
bottles pure clean water from another water system and coughs up
a measly two hundred dollars for it per year. Yes, I said that's per
year when that water could be going to the literally lead intoxicated residents of Flint. I bet they'd fork over the $200 in advance.
Instead at best they get to buy that water being bottled practically
in their backyards in teensy little plastic toxin leaching bottles of
water for their kids to drink and for much much more money in
the aggregate. But back to Brooklyn now.

It was really hot that very pregnant spring in Brooklyn, started
being over 100 F in April with seventy extra pounds on me. Going
back and forth to Sloan Kettering that spring and early summer
with my dad in there guinea pigging away. Not that I haven't been
interested in some trials for my condition, but the one they put him
on was brutal and made the short end of his life way more short arduous and painful than it needed to be. He was so afraid. I offered
hypnosis which he resisted and then wanted. Why did he resist
Freud's starting place? Maybe more loss of control when he already
had virtually none. I get that, like me focusing on how much weight
I've gained from the chemotherapy (can't call it chemo the way
people do, like it's some sort of little cute thing—someone called
it therapy recently, I like that a lot better) and trying to lose it. I've
been questioned for that but really come on, there's nothing else
I can even think I can control—no hair and I mean nowhere do
I have a single hair little body control really nausea tiredness inability to practice my profession (and livelihood mind you, practice
gone in weeks, closed it up), even my day-to-day schedule isn't my
own and the what where when of it is not at all predictable. And so

on not complaining just saying maybe I get my father not wanting to be hypnotized.

Back to Poughkeepsie. A name I could spell then, I think that's pretty good, look at how it's said and spelled. I was only four at the time of the spelling and such. I remember back then always having a strep throat and taking penicillin. Ice cold baths (with actual ice cubes floating in the water, really) to bring my frequent 104 degree temperature down. My little body had a habit of getting hot hot hot. And the blue syrup. The red one came later, Triaminicol? I didn't like the red one, but the blue was good. Probably had alcohol in it and I probably drank too much loving that thick blue flavor, telling you this I can taste it even now what more than half a century later. My favorite color was blue for sure, but royal blue, midnight blue, indigo, those blues. Other antibiotics came later, more miracles until doctors not to mention agricultural industry got slap-happy with them and now we humans are antibiotic resistant. My sisters got lots of them for their ear infections. I think for me it was still penicillin pretty much only, being older, I missed the antibiotic craze. My babies were prescribed them quite flippantly, almost never gave them. Just Zoe, she got them a couple of times when I wasn't sure. Scary holding a crying screaming baby in pain with a high fever and not giving them. But fevers do have a purpose, right?

But, you know, antibiotics were already in chicken feed and livestock feed in the fifties. Which means of course we were all ingesting them big time without even realizing it. Like in all those marinated chicken parts my mother would make thinking it was healthy low-fat protein that was the advertising and true but there are always covert factors to consider. Problem is there's hidden meaning the public doesn't have access to until it's way too late. How long did it take for us to figure that out about the antibiotics? In chickens cows milk in our water of course. In fisheries. Purdue cut their routine antibiotics use in just 2014. That took a long time, maybe cause the medical arm of the government finally started thinking about what was going to happen when none of our antibiotics work any more, maybe, or maybe it was a selling point to the "health" crazed ethos. Scare quotes since what habits or anything else have people really changed, health another way to sell magazines gadgets products these days.

All the belly pain, so much gas. I did have colic or so I'm told I don't know what was going on then too young and later I had the urinary problem or anyway the holding onto my pee problem, but always cramps and gas. Was it nerves? I think that's pretty likely in retrospect, given what my general disposition is if that's what we want to call it, normal stuff more stressful for me. My mother would tell me to lie face down on the floor in front of her no matter what guests were over or whatnot was happening and she'd press on my back, I just remember being embarrassed but not if it helped. Must have been a pain for my mother me with the cramps and the peeing and my sister with the constant earaches not to mention she was always stuffing things that no one could get out up her nose. I remember raisins and pussy willows a doctor would have to come and carefully get them out especially the pussy willow that was a diabolical idea, wasn't it? and in the days when doctors came to the house. They'd have to chase Debbie all over before they could get even a peak in her nose. No one looked into the cramps and gas thing and now I certainly do have a big GI problem, so did my dad, maybe not a coincidence. He peed continuously too, and seemed to have digestive problems, and then later died—quickly—of what the intern described so sensitively with a kind of smirk on his face like how could you be so stupid as to have a tumor on his pancreas so large it could be felt and seen even from the outside. Lovely, the training of those people in a helping profession. But before that he had gout, which he thought was so ridiculously hilarious given his diet and lifestyle, probably ate almost no fat or other rich (are there other rich foods that don't have fat in them or is that the definition?) foods, given his second long term partner's (I'll tell you about my parents' foray into the seventies trendy open marriage thing later) cooking and morals, walked a few miles every single day and by this point not high on the alcohol consumption scale, don't know if he ever was martinis notwithstanding, he couldn't tolerate much. A glass of wine would make him more than tipsy. But maybe that's a digestive thing too. Anyway.

Jasper (uncle) and Russell (older cousin) came up from the city and played in the snow with us at this house not sure where it was but not on the Vassar farm this time and Sheila was born in December. Maybe that's why they came, to see the baby. Now my parents had a family of five, wow, maybe that was going to be enough. They were still deep into the study group and general happiness and miraculously had not lost sight of their motorcycle infested vow to each other that day on the precipice of the San Francisco Bay to return and put down roots on that golden sun-kissed soil. While Russell and Jasper were making a snow person (I just can't say snow*man* even though I'm one thousand percent sure that's what we called them then, just can't do it. Not after singing Old MacDonald had a farm … and on the farm she had a … at four in the morning to my babies, et cetera) Jasper was also shouting over to my father who was outside with us but not busy with the snow construction.

"You thinking of building a house out there?" Jasper asked with more than idle curiosity.

"That would be a nice dream to have for now," my father responded kind of wistfully.

"I could help with the design draw up the plans and so on that would save you a bundle, architects having a tendency to be highway robbers with crazy unbuildable plans you know. If I can go to Indonesia to build I can certainly come to California."

Noncommittally my father voiced a gracious thank you and a we'll see. The snow play continued and my father joined in making snowballs and pelting them at Russell who returned the fire double time laughing his wonderful huge smiled yelps in between. And snow angels we five of us made in all sizes and weird shapes, it was a great time.

In the morning with everyone still groggy my father straddled buoyantly over the split rail low wood fence to get to work on to the Vassar campus. Russell and Jasper drove me that morning to pre-school the Poughkeepsie Country Day school where the stout and warm hugging Bea Stone my teacher presided. At the end of that year she wrote that I was very feminine (funny since later I tested out on the masculine side of the scale—likes to play with tools, good at math kind of silly questions that shouldn't allow anyone to think they're getting to anything about gender. It's time now finally to go to one pronoun for all, egalitarian and more correct. Marge Piercy figured it out so long ago what in the seventies? come on already Sweden's adopted it as a national policy. Why do I need to know or really in an old fashioned way try to pinpoint the shape of someone's genitals by a word label on them or their gender self-identification which is of course different from genitalia but still something I don't feel I need to know off the bat or when I go to deposit a check from a bank teller or buy salt hay at the local nursery. Plus if we don't go to one pronoun we're going to have to go to so many that everyone will practically have their own handmade pronoun which is kind of equivalent to just having names and then one pronoun, meaning "human" really, that's it and that's enough and back to Piercy's per for person). People can reserve their personal innermost data for their friends if they want to share, that's different.

Things were still going as swimmingly as they could with two parents and three children all under the age of four. Inside the guts of the house unbeknownst to my parents was of course as we know now lots of toxic stuff lurking around. And none of it goes away and now for some reason even lead and who knows what else are allowed now in all those solar panels we're putting up that over time degrade and leach in all that sun we hope they're productively basking in. I guess lead remains cheap. Lead even in the pacifiers as I said already. In pencils, toys. Asbestos around pipes, on roof shingles, in cigarette filters (imagine! sucking in asbestos all day every day without even being a plumber). The old Vassar farm not likely to have been organic back in the days of DDT, remember we lived right on it in the last round there. Not to mention the other chemicals routinely used on farms and around homes and the spills from car and equipment engine oil changes and gas leaks that no one even noticed or bothered about. Remember the shiny rainbow colored puddles all over? And coal was the heating fuel so what kind of indoor particulates were we breathing in day in and day out not to mention during that restful deep breathing of sleep and throw in the second hand cigar pipe and cigarette smoke and all the chemicals therein. Quite a cocktail wouldn't you say. Well, also add in what was pretty commonplace, the radioactivity flashing in those cute or even beautiful little paintings of flowers and bunnies and such on cribs and other baby furniture, hanging right over the baby, painted to glow with radium in the paint! Emitting, emitting. Not to mention on clock and watch faces. Imagine how it went for the people who painted it on.

We soon made another transcontinental trek, and then later another. It was time to go back to California this time my parents toting three kids, one an infant of course. Not back to Berkeley though, the job my father got was at Stanford at a research institute for human development and more student studies this time of graduate students and it came equipped with a whole research team he'd direct so it was pretty cool. They were both happy clinking glasses and smiling their version of high fives. They were a team again and now my mother saw that maybe he had been right doing the honorable thing, it bought him a certain cachet and this was a way better position, one that could really last forever.

"You did it again, Walt, Congrats."

"We did you mean and we're going and this time we don't have to ping pong ball it back here, we can settle in."

"And our friends in Berkeley aren't so far away, we'll see them too. Pearl and Eleanor and Zack not to mention Nevitt."

"And this time no frantic paper writing, we can pack together."

"And unpack together!" my mother added gleefully imagining how much easier it will be this time. "We won't be rushing and doing and undoing."

So pack we did, fly we did. Five of us this time. On that, by the way, the planes, do any of you remember the four packs of cigarettes they'd give out? Gave 'em to kids as young as me, at four years old, five, eight, until they stopped giving them out altogether. And the little nip bottles, and the teeny packs of chicklets, maybe four in them too but I think maybe there were six of the little brightly colored squares in the gum packs. I would collect them all, and consume them all back home. I might have given some of the cigarette packs to my smoking mother, but I have a feeling I didn't. She could get her own. And we didn't sit together. Debbie would always roam all over the plane just like during the middle of the night poker games at home, talking to people, but in this case to strangers, not me I probably sat stark still. I don't remember, but that's what I'm guessing makes most sense. Looking out the window, I did like the window seat best. Now, I'll take the aisle anytime. Don't like to have to climb over people or keep asking them to get up. But back in those days I probably just sat still staring out and down at the teeny little houses and cars and roads and square patches of colored land in greens and browns and stuff. And the best part for me was when we'd fly through clouds. Magic!

So off to Menlo Park to live not sure how they secured the house but it was a great one I think we all loved it. Packed up me and Debbie to the extent she could pitching in singing the whole time and singing in the car to the airport, coloring and trying to figure out how to play Go Fish for most of the plane ride. Off we went.

WESTWARD TO POMEGRANATE TREES LINING THE DRIVEWAY LIKE IT WAS HEAVEN

T HE DRIVEWAY SEEMED LONG TO me, I mean remember I was five and so my legs were pretty short and it took quite a few steps to get from one end to the other. It took me a while to go the length since I would stop to smell and pick those beautiful fragrant pomegranates right off the bushes that were ours! and lined the driveway. The dangling deep red pomegranate fruit hanging off, lots and lots of them. Seemed they were ripe year round but that can't be correct, can it? California was perfect in those days but that's maybe more perfect than it could have been. My mother and I would walk down the driveway to get the paper in the morning the ol' *SF Chronicle* picking a few beauties along the way while she muttered opening the pages, "This is a paper? Oy!". She'd split the fruit open for me sectioning into quarters or eighths and I'd proceed to make such a wonderful mess with the juice dripping down my chin onto my shirt and whatever else. What a great taste! Intense flavor! Sweet and tart and crunchy with all those seeds I'd just swallow. Had 'em anytime I wanted and never ever got sick of them. Don't know about Debbie I don't think she liked them as much. Even then I don't think she was into messes. My mother would've eaten them too but she was constantly occupied with Sheila and sometimes Debbie and sometimes my father and even Seacrags Piper the collie. Was that when we had the guinea pig? that would have been another set of things for her to do what with cleaning the cage changing the water putting food down. Why are caged animals a thing we like? or fish in bowls? I had always loved watching goldfish swish round until I started thinking too much about that bowl and being trapped in a small space factor solely for our enjoyment. The meaning of that saying about being in a fish bowl finally sank in. She attended to me too of course but I'm not counting that. So sitting down or even standing and taking the time for pomegranates which are a bit labor intensive to eat was just not going to be something she'd do. I wonder if she wanted to?

As it happened the unpacking got off to a slow start between arriving with not a lot of time before everyone's except my mother and Sheila school started which of course neither of them had. Shouldn't necessarily have been an of course for my mother not having school but that was still a ways off and not really much in anyone's mind meaning either of my parents' minds. By now my mother on the one hand had all the packing-unpacking stuff down to a science but she was also tired of it and had only moments in between everything else. I could hear enough to know that she thought my father should do it this time.

"Walt, you have a week before you've absolutely got to begin at the institute, the unpacking and setting up could happen in that amount of time if we set ourselves to it." She didn't go so far as to say he should do it by himself this time as she had done so many times before.

Yes, they knew people in Berkeley who might help—women all of them—but that was a one hour drive from them at minimum and they really didn't know a soul in the Stanford area yet otherwise my mother might have asked someone else and let well enough alone. Even with all their upward and onward mobility hiring people wasn't much of a thing for them to be able to do yet, never was later either.

"I think I've got to get in as soon as possible and start things going, I," my father puffed out his chest and put a fist to it, "am the incoming director and I don't know anyone on the staff yet. We can do it all slowly and prioritize what we need, no? We're here and we can stay and that's what's important. This is a great house too, look at it, with all those trees and flowers outside, our own yard that's already been planted and just feel the sunshine streaming in the floor to ceiling glass not like the old farmhouse is it? We did it! And we did it together! I love you and I love all of us," he said one arm around my mother who was holding Sheila and another around me and Debbie while somehow also patting Piper.

My mother melted and gave him a hug and went to the stove to heat up a double boiler for Sheila's milk. And on they went. My father to the new new new office full of potential studies and findings my mother to the boxes trying to figure out the new house and garden and navigate her way to my and Debbie's school to the closest grocery store to the pediatrician and to meeting some neighbors to start to get a handle on all those practical things. It wasn't an academic community there in Menlo Park being just far enough away from the Stanford campus. The neighbors were mostly long-time residents who had grown up there as had many of their parents and so forth. Mostly Catholic which turned out well for me being taken rather often to Roman Catholic services. For me it was a reprieve from words I could understand, there I just had to sit and let the sounds waft over me. More magic, I thought it was beautiful. And a reprieve from even potentially needing to interact formulate words and such. For my mother it gave her a breather of only two kids in the house.

Charles Schultz was drawing away his Snoopys and Charlie Browns and Lucys right around the corner, before it was *Menlo Park*. Way before and I mean way before the Silicon Valley days. Woodside and Los Altos were gorgeous and wild but not crazy like they are now. Cows and horses and farms and farms and pastures and so much open space. So many birds and so little snow, almost none really. Fine with me. We could go up to Squaw Valley if we wanted to ski. And see Lucy and Ricky and Ethel and Fred there playing bridge in the lodge. Maybe it was poker, I think it was bridge but anyway it was cards. I doubt they skied but maybe. They actually hung out together! I saw it. They weren't filming, just seemed to be having fun, like on the show, when they were having fun and not bickering or feuding or scheming.

So there we were in Menlo Park, California. Let's pause on that a moment. My parents did pause on it over and over standing together watching us play in the back or over a breakfast of a newly invented Menlo Park version of oatmeal, sitting at the table looking out on the flowers. They were happy, we were happy. Sunny. Beautiful. Our house was probably pretty small. Lots of glass like my father noted. Sliding doors, like so many, maybe most, California homes. On a small building lot, I don't know maybe 1/8 of an acre? Don't know how to judge those things but especially from memory that's fifty-eight years old. But the gardens, they really figured it out, those people before us. A back yard with a lawn, of course, it is California obviously. Debbie got a blue and red jungle gym for a birthday—maybe her third?—put out there. She was always climbing. Ha! Like the time Julian had to save her. Well, he didn't have to, he was just a kid himself, maybe five, possibly six, but not older. She climbed out, way out, on a limb of a tree, way high, high high high up in a tree and lurching over a real live deadly drop down far cliff. Beautiful Tilden Park, I still love that park, go back there every time I'm in the Bay Area. Anyway, lots of ledges in the park along the trails. One branch just so enticing, stretching out over that cliff. While the adults were blabbing on amongst themselves. Well not blabbing they were continuing the discussion from the last study group and were deep into the ubiquitous question of inherent versus learned evil. They probably called it aggression or destructiveness but the same general idea of where it comes from and was Freud correct and so forth. No one saw until she was out on this scrawny limb. I didn't either being busy making twig structures and cracking eucalyptus leaves open to release the scent that I still love so much. Didn't have it back east so it was a real treat. She was a small skinny as in light weight kid. She was maybe three, then me and Julian would be five, so that's about right. So there she was, no adult could get anywhere near her without the bough breaking. Quietly and on his own suddenly Julian—also a small kid, maybe even her size even though my age—was up there and going out on the limb. Everyone terrified the branch would break beneath both of them, no one took a breath or said anything all eyes frozen on the point where the branch met the trunk. He coaxed her, back back back slow slow slow to the ground of the path.

The Menlo Park house gardens: calla lilies, pansies—for some reason, I remember dusting the pansies with my mother, but that can't be right, can it? does anyone dust pansies? we were anyway doing something a bit intricate and labor intensive with them— pathways, more flowers. Really wonderful. And the Catholic family with all their kids next door. I don't remember how many there were, but a lot, some so much older than me and Mary and Cathy the two youngest that they seemed like adults. In those days though, think Annette Funicello Ann Margaret Frankie Avalon Debbie Reynolds, sixteen year olds seemed like adults what with their clothes and hair do's and accessories excepting Haley Mills, she seemed like a perpetual kid, a tomboy (there is so much packed into the history of this term even I won't attempt it, but look it up and get a glimpse of what I mean—there's prejudice sexism but also a whole history of just plain raising boys healthier as in feeding them enough at the expense of the girls' plates and letting them out in daylight in the sun in the weather in nature being physical and even a tinge of fostering the growth of the great white race in there into the word apparently)as they called some girls then, the ones that somehow got to wear regular pants and not dainty frilly petal pushers which I however did like and they supposedly could climb trees since they certainly weren't allowed to play even baseball back then. I remember a friend of mine in middle school and this was the later sixties mind you the girls protested until they could wear pants like the boys, just ordinary jeans, nothing crazy and she attended a public school in the so-called liberal northeast Princeton bastion we know prides itself on open-minded thinking.

Mary and Cathy of the famous chip story—I'll tell it (but I really don't know why my kids liked this story so much, they'd have me drag it out to half hour length with different little twists and turns at each telling). I don't think their family provided much relief for my mother their hands full as it was except they took me to church rather often which I guess was some sort of break on Sunday mornings anyway. Can't recall who the neighbor on the other side was so I imagine they weren't much in the neighborliness department or maybe they had older kids grown and such so didn't have much in common with us. As it turned out though there were enough parents and school families to bond with and of course faculty and staff at the institute and later on Stanford campus-wide so things worked out and we all started to get settled. I liked my school with the folk dancing and pottery and teachers I adored, the young assistant teachers would come over for dinner occasionally. The reading thing not so much. I mean I could read a lot already but the reading out loud to my teacher even though it was one on one not classroom-wide was too anxiety provoking. Sitting there with Betty G at one of those little round tables I'd wring my hands under the table I still do that when social engagements have gone on too long for me and I've added the tearing cuticle thing which was not a good development. I'd get so tied up in knots over such a low key low pressure situation that I think she'd let me off the hook more often than not. She'd pick me up and we'd go do something else. One of those days when I was securely in Betty G's arms and our heads were on the same level I whispered in her ear that it was my birthday that day. Oy! At lunch they held an impromptu birthday party for me with cake and lots of little presents each one wrapped. Must have been trying to get me out of my shell. I was mortified and so embarrassed that I was getting all that attention let alone so many presents some thing like on the order of eight little plastic figurines of characters like Snow White—wasn't she beautiful!—and each of the seven dwarfs. No one else in the class got this kind of treatment so they must have thought I needed it and it would help with my anxiety on the contrary it was at a high pitch now. I was beside myself with embarrassment and didn't know what to do but I knew I had to open all the presents each and every one of them. In my panic I exclaimed meaning to say something nice and grateful but said, "I'm going to have to have a garage sale now!" That sentence played over and over in my head for years day after day horrified that I had said in effect that I was going to sell these nice presents they gave me. I may not have gotten over that ever rather it just receded in my consciousness having been paved over with subsequent crimes of that nature that I committed. When nothing worked to quell my evident anxiety over such things as reading aloud playing recorder solo speaking in groups folk dancing if I had to take anything like the lead I'm pretty sure someone relayed it to the school psychologist as really they probably should have I mean what was causing such distress? Only recently have I pieced the strands of my perfect storm together. More later on that one. Debbie on the other hand who had no trouble with the social interaction stuff couldn't tolerate the noise and lack of orderliness so she stayed home that first year with my mother and Sheila, not the plan my mother had for sure. She had stumbled upon the CORE group in Berkeley and all the civil rights activism they had been staging in the Bay Area. She was eager to get going working with them but it was a pretty long drive to any of the meetings even the ones in San Francisco. She could've done it with just a baby but a baby and talking walking very very mobile toddler just wasn't going to work no matter how much she wanted it to.

One night as my parents were lingering in the kitchen my mother suggested, "Why don't we look into having a regular babysitter?"

"We've already hired a few, it seems to be working out."

She barely let my father finish that sentence, saying a little too much in a blurt but those of you who have borne the brunt of child care of the very young understand I'm sure her urgency and it wasn't only over being able to go to meetings but just to be able to go anywhere off alone sometimes just because she wanted to, I know you get it but my father hadn't grasped it yet, not that he was opposed as you'll see, "No, that's not what I mean. I mean re-gu-lar, someone we can count on, hire for so many hours per day or per week, lots of hours, day for me, evening for us!"

"Oh," my father said coming to a short stop.

"You know, Walt, I'd like to do other things sometimes or just be on my own, maybe get involved in things maybe start an analysis like you have," her voice stopped while she was trying to read my father's face. She thought he was going to be opposed that she should like staying home and doing homey kid things, but as you'll see that's not what he was thinking but it is what was nagging at her, that she thought she should want to and have it be enough for now. I mean, she'd tell herself, they just got there, still have a baby and it's all fun and busy so why try to add more just now?

"That's a great idea. My analyst could recommend if you want and yes, why not get out and explore a little? We can do some together the more evening or weekend type of stuff and you can scout around in daylight. There's a lot here!"

They both smiled at each other genuinely from the depths of their hearts, so in tune they were with each other and the world. My mother did find a psychoanalyst for herself and commenced plunging into a four times per week treatment, strategically located in Berkeley where most of the CORE and other civil rights meetings were held. Plus, this was the or at least a right analyst for my mother and a woman which was rather uncommon for certified analysts in those days and even still in some circles hard though that is to believe, a profession in decline and those are usually left to the women.

Okay, back to the chips and their story. Potato chips, the little, kid sized bags. We each got one, me Debbie Mary (older than me) Cathy (between me and Debbie) not Sheila since she was a baby, each of us had our own bag of chips and a glass of grape juice— probably of the Welch's John Birch variety (well someone just wrote in having read this that Welch's grape juice isn't the Welch of the Birchers that I and so many of us thought my entire adult life so I stand corrected if a correction needs to be made)—from my mom in the kitchen. She had a mid-calf length full skirt on, some kind of woven fabric in gray horizontal stripes. And her short, curly hair. Kind of like her college graduation portrait that I had put on wine glasses for her 75th. Now we're up to her 85th, so genes don't tell the whole horrible disease getting story, do they? Her generation didn't have the dousing mine did and I got a pretty good waft of it at the very beginning on that reservation on which the egg and sperm that made me met.

The chips, we took them out to the back steps to eat and slurp. Debbie was looking at her bag, still unopened. "I want to make more," she said slamming the bag on the step.

"Huh?" I asked.

"More, I want more," more slamming on the step.

"But it'll be the same amount in the bag, just bits."

"No, it'll be more—See!"

Piper was there, he probably thought he should get his own bag too.

That's the whole story in its nutshell. Anyway, me and Debbie shared a room that looked out on that back yard. We had twin beds. She had her curly top hair and was so little. I'd wake up just before dawn and open the sliding door of our room. Everything had sliding doors in California as I keep noting I mean it was such a stark change from the bitsy and only seasonal amounts of light we had back east. Floor to ceiling light coming in and it was beautiful. Still in pjs and I'd go to Debbie's bed and get her up too. I'd lead her out into the garden. It was quiet and foggy. The fog and dew just beginning to think about lifting and I'd go floating out into the mist of the garden with Debbie trailing behind me. It was especially glorious when I had a nightgown on that would flow behind me.

"See, Debbie, its magic." That's what I thought, that it was magic and we were wafting about like the swans in *Swan Lake*. Back in Poughkeepsie we saw an outdoor production of *Swan Lake* and it changed my life—I think there are a few dance performances that changed my life, like Min Tanaka at Jacob's Pillow with Cecil Taylor, but that's later. Maybe performances period, like at fourteen seeing *Waiting For Godot* at the Circle and the Square on Sheridan Square with Gil. Circle and the Square long gone now of course, so is Sheridan Square for that matter even though the sign is still on the subway stop, the now called One train then the IRT local. The letter names IRT IND BMT mean nothing now. And of course Ethyl Eichelberger. And Gina Rowlands in *Woman Under the Influence*. Out on a great lawn and a stage flush to the ground in the middle. And the beautiful swan costumes and the music—used to play Tchaikovsky's scores to it every night on my little phonograph. A little red and tan player that closed up into a portable case. Good because we moved a lot as you've seen and I could keep taking it with me, the moving trend not yet concluded which in good time I'll tell you about. I'd have to eventually wake up to take the arm and needle off the record. Not much was automatic in those days certainly not a kiddie phonograph player, as they were called. Think about it we went through LPs, cassettes were next, right? then CDs, then ipods and MP3s (I skipped the ipod and MP3 phases) and now we're back to vinyl which we're convinced—me too—sound much so much better crackles and all.

We'd go wafting out into the cool air most mornings, I don't know what Debbie thought we were doing but she would follow me, she was like my baby or anyway little friend I could tote about (she was actually much more active and adventurous than I, physically anyway, so I don't know why this is how I felt about it. I mean, I would never ever ever have gone out on that limb, learning how to walk over doorway thresholds was a challenge, they seemed to loom there at the end of every room requiring an arduous climb).

Being California things were always happening outside, even the poker games could have practically taken place out of doors on the lawn. Early in the fall my father's institute held a staff and family picnic which was set up behind the building on a nice wide open patio that led out to a rather sizable lawn. So many people so many kids me and Debbie toasted more marshmallows there than at any other picnic and downed more smores than you can probably imagine! My mother was getting to know people by starting political discussions as per her usual and assessing the left or not tenor of the group.

She was deep into it with an older couple when my father joined them. The discussion was over the wall, not Trump's wall of today of course, the Berlin wall. By the time my father got over there having been stopped along the way by others who wanted to have a word with the new director a bit of a crowd had formed with many voices chiming in and it was already pretty heated.

Me and Debbie were busy eating hot dogs off the grill and blowing gigantic bubbles from a wand that had a hoop larger than our heads. The multi-colored globes floated over the whole group sometimes with one grazing someone's head with a pop. People were having a generally good time out there with food and drinks flowing kids playing adults chatting, some like my mother talking about serious matters and others about their tennis game and such.

The university President stopped by and that was my father's cue to put an arm over my mother's shoulder and take her over to say hello to him. As they walked away, she was saying, "It was just getting interesting, the people here are very smart, I think I could learn to really love it here! And they're on all sides of the fence so to speak, I can work with that!"

My father was beginning to respond when they reached the President, so instead with a genuine smile he said, "I'd like you to meet my wife." After some pleasantries about the weather how my parents were settling in and the Stanford campus design including Frederick Law Olmstead's contributions my parents made their way over to the barbeque to eat drink and chat with some of the people on staff at the institute. By this point Debbie and I had definitely eaten plenty and were trying to get the hang of the croquet game going at a corner of the lawn. My favorite part was setting the ball hoops in the ground in a nice path but that had already been done. Hitting the balls strategically with those wooden mallets was another matter entirely. Probably had Debbie been a little bigger she would have aced the game. Off to the side some teenagers were playing the newly invented game of Frisbee. People were decked out in California picnic wear, brightly colored petal pushers with matching sleeveless tops with ruffles at the bottom that just grazed the top of the pants pastel colored dresses with fitted bodices whose skirt opened up into a bell shape down to the knee men in seersucker suits trousers topped with a V-neck cardigan sweater a few even in long shorts. Not only was this casual California attire, all of the people there knew they were the best and the brightest and so could dress pretty much any way they wanted just not as far out as what could be seen on the UC Berkeley campus, that was in a different league of idiosyncratic. My father was wearing his preferred checked pattern short sleeve button down cotton shirt with medium brown trousers and my mother was wearing a solid emerald green dress with a narrow collar and buttons down the front to the waist ending there in a belt and the rest a straight skirt to the knee. I thought she looked quite striking in it. We all went home bouncily happy me and Debbie sugar charged and my parents fired up from some great conversations and their promisingly fabulous new life.

That picnic was great fun for all but every single day seemed pretty special. I'd wear my pink tutu on Debbie's jungle gym, I probably wore it a lot of places imagining myself breaking out into pirouettes and singing where ever I was. My mother said I got married in a *Swan Lake* dress, but really more of a *Sylphides* sort of affair in pink and white chiffon. Strapless, sleeveless, layers and layers of chiffon. Drove the dressmaker crazy who worked out of a little hole in the wall basement shop in a tenement on the Upper West Side when it was still an area one could practically get paid to live in.

Mary and I would pull Cathy and Debbie and Piper in my wagon. It really was a red wagon, very cliché in the stereotype of Freudian lore but I loved it. And I loved that yard, garden, whatever it was, all the flowers and the birds and the one time it snowed, the sparkling flakes coming down and melting as they hit ground—I thought it was more magic in a magical land. But best of all the early morning fog.

I did go to church with them, Mary and Cathy's family—not sure why they took me being clearly Jewish but even Stanford fraternities were pledging Jews that year in defiance of the national frat regs. It was Roman Catholic and all in Latin, no English not a word. That's where I got my plastic Mary and the crucifix. I guess they bought it for me Mary and Cathy's parents or maybe they were free at that church. I loved the not understanding anything, not the words, not the songs, not the odd wafers (I don't think I ever got any). It felt like swimming or floating in just the right temperature where everything is beautiful and fine. The church probably was beautiful itself but I don't remember it except that it seemed very large. I of course hadn't yet seen any cathedrals in Europe. More later on cathedrals and my ceramic studio at Saint John the Divine in NY and the *Hair* troop party at Synod House. Imagine what was coming culturally and otherwise, so many changes afoot for the country there in 1961!

I had other friends Mary Beth for example whose dog Homer was a Dalmatian, her mother was a nurse and father a dentist and her brother's name seemed to be FJ but I always felt unsure of that being not clear on whether that could be someone's name or if that is what I was supposed to call him. Luckily there was never an occasion for me to call him anything. Most of my friends were chosen by whether my parents and theirs were getting along or were probably going to get along and go on family outings together and that sort of thing. That wasn't the case with Mary Beth. She was my best friend and her favorite color was red (mine was blue, but I hated to disagree with her). She wasn't really very nice but I think we were good friends. She eventually got a horse that one day when I was at the stable with her stepped on one of my feet—I don't know why no bones broke, seems impossible or the ground was really really soft or something. Later when we moved to Stanford I used to take the train to her house alone (I was still five turning six, pretty sophisticated, huh?). I don't remember any mishaps or being anxious about the ride just remember having the train schedule and monitoring the time on my watch to not miss the stop which I wouldn't have done since I would keep a look-out outside the window. Staying focused on some often small aspect of the larger picture has definitely been in my disposition not always to such good effect when I miss the macro goings on. Marybeth and her mother were there every time at the dusty station ready to pick me up at the Atherton station.

I have always tried to hang onto friends through all the moves. I still know and love Aviva and Rusty (now Michelle). Josh went crazy in Israel, can't be helped. I used to have to beat him up to keep him from hitting me all the time, he was smaller than me then, boys usually are until a certain age. But that's later too from here but not that much. I hang onto places and kinds of places too, like an orienting device.

Mary Beth with her short pin straight blond hair like her mother's. Her house seemed very antiseptic way beyond neat and clean. And her perfectly flat and straight headbands, I could never be neat like that not even now. I don't mean my house I mean myself. Well, not that I don't dress well when I *Get Dressed* but generally. I was just on the cusp of actually doing better in this regard when I discovered I was ill, now it's a bit hopeless I'm afraid. The short, weird hair hennaed that comes out a distasteful two-tone affair. Oh well, I wish that were my biggest problem. It's going to all fall out soon anyway. Again. For the second time with this illness alone and then a third and a fourth and so on. Takes me a while to stop caring, not that I won't care but I just work around it and that's that. Wore a wig the last time, fifteen years ago. I bought a better one this time, the other one was so bad, but I just can't get myself to put it on. It feels bad, looks crazy even though it's kind of like my hair was (messy, curly, more than half gray). I can't do it, need another option—tattoo or just hats? I'm not a hat person, don't like things on my head. Work around it, I say to myself. Indeed. Not the biggest problem for sure but so visual, so immediate. Makes people uncomfortable, don't want to embarrass my children. Or have the baldness be a constant reminder that I am ill and dying, they know that well enough already. Just when they were becoming so independent in a good way. The time of life to sort of ignore that one has a mother and go off on one's own path for as long as that takes. Took me forever.

There were Lisa and Marc too. Josh was there also even then in pre-school. Marc used to come over to our house in Menlo Park. I remember eating something like baloney and mustard sandwiches with him, I don't remember what we did. I do remember the Playboy Club we all—Mary Beth, Marc, Lisa, me, the beautiful red-haired girl whose name I'm blanking on at the moment but I'll remember, oh! Karen of course. She was beautiful, I thought. Wait let me say something about our teachers and the school. The Peninsula School, it's still there. A Quaker school. Joan Baez used to sing there, Peter, Paul and Mary. It started in pre-K and went through high school. My teachers, two Bettys, Betty M (who my father later dated!) and Betty G (she was like a real Mr. Greenjeans) I loved them both. And they were paying attention. Betty M and her powder blue dress and her yellow outfit. Betty G who would take us to her father's farm for fresh, warm milk from her cows I guess we probably did the milking and home-made, delicious donuts. The milk must have been raw having just come out of the cow. Could never do that now, some parent would sue and the teacher would be fired. They were so different from each other the Bettys and made a great team. Taught us so many things about living and being. Let Josh carry his abacus everywhere and calculate everything with it. I guess it was his blankey or pacifier kind of thing. I thought it was so cool how he could do that.

Back to the Playboy Club. Remember though those were the days in which people—well, not people, men—would display Playboy Magazine out on their coffee tables—great articles inside it would be said like a mantra, never mind the depictions out for all to absorb. News racks in those days too, the meatgrinder cover—in case you don't remember, a nude bombshell going through a meatgrinder. Her legs were already through it if I remember correctly.

Still had her bouncy breasts hanging out. So we kids would go out to the back field—also seemed huge then, and tons of minor's lettuce growing that we would eat. Nostalgically planted some this year, I used to love it so at Peninsula. It was beautiful back there. So, we'd stand in a circle and for example one day, two boys were going to strip or pull down their pants I'm not sure which and Karen too. Before we really got started Betty G came by, she asked what we were doing and we told her what and she said "Oh" and walked on. That would never ever happen now either.

On the count of three, Karen got naked and four of the boys opened pee fire on her, it had been a plan they made secretly. She was soaked, even her long, red hair and she started to cry. Me and Mary Beth and Lisa took her to a bathroom and tried to get her cleaned up or at least dry. I don't remember if Marc was one of the boys but Mary Beth and Marc were "in love" and I hated that for some reason. I remember them in this cabiny thing on the school grounds just looking at each other. It seemed pretty dumb but then inside I was already a pretty angry kid and thought most of my peers were pretty stupid.

Back to my parents this is still their story. For some reason they didn't get the study group or poker games going right away like they had each previous move. It was a way they oriented themselves and ensconced themselves in a community. I guess too much happening at once with three kids one a baby directing a whole institute with a sizable research staff and everything that goes along with that and for the first time not living pretty much right on campus. Don't let me leave out that both of them were in their own separate analyses as I've said. Each on the couch it was the thing to do in those days, how could anyone live without having gone through a psychoanalytic process? It was even an entry requirement for the doctors in the pediatric group we went to. They each were doing it my parents and it led to some weird sounding conversations between them if you ask me, talking about their parents and siblings and such elementary school teachers even as if they were still kids. I didn't know what they were talking about but it sounded odd I knew that. Point being they were very very busy. Not that Menlo Park was remote but the distances to Stanford to my school to shopping and doctors and analysts' offices was enough that it kept them occupied without being able to take much of a breath not to mention as I said no real functionally useful neighbors, that was maybe the biggest blow and something they weren't used to. Pretty quickly as you may have already surmised it turned out that the schlepp to the Berkeley analyst was one of those straws too many on the back of scarce and unpredictable time.

Not just the expectation of functionally useful neighbors in the sense of also having kids and sharing and swapping play times and chores and such but the neighbor thing had been the way my mother would get settled into the politics of the area. In Poughkeepsie she knew what was doing and could dig right into action. In Menlo Park it was a mystery to her and one that she wanted to unscramble locally and not always to have to schlep to the East Bay even with her analysis when it was underway there. I mean a lot was happening, Kennedy President Bay of Pigs the Apollo Program Neil Armstrong the Vietnam War the Cold War and especially the Civil Rights Movement that increasingly captured my mother's attention over the competition with the Red Scare and Communist ideals. She was itching to get going in their community and saw that even the fraternities on campus were getting pretty defiant. She thought the problem was the area that they needed to be closer to the pulse at Stanford thinking there would be hotbeds and political action cells there pushing for justice and equality on campus she could sink her teeth into or start a CORE chapter there even.

"Walt, it's gorgeous here I love this house but I think ultimately we can do better. Let's not think of this as the place and it isn't ours anyway."

"We just got here," my father said one morning over their new concoction of what they called California style oatmeal meaning it had lots of fresh fruit in it even cantaloupe and grapes. "This house is the right size for us and its near enough campus for my daily trips back and forth and the kids are just making friends."

"I can't figure out who it is that's living around here but I know it's not Stanford people and it's not political people and it just seems like there's nothing doing here, I don't know how to get a handle on it."

My father's face lit up as if he just had an idea for the first time saying, "Why don't we have a student live in that spare room? She could help out in exchange for the room and board and then you could be freed up to explore and investigate unencumbered?" He clearly thought that it was not only a brilliant idea but novel as well, he was sure he could feel the tension in the air dissipating.

"A student? They live in dorms and get fed there, that's not going to happen," my mother was sounding irritated.

"No, a graduate student, they're on their own for housing for the most part and end up actually paying for extra rooms like ours. Let's give it a whirl, I'll ask around today about it."

"Ok, ask Marge, she'd know I'm sure maybe tried it herself."

And find one they did. And it was a huge flop so much so I don't even remember her, just my mother's frustration. "Walt, now I have four children," she said one night while we were all playing dominoes and I had just caused a long winding cascade of the tiles. "Christa is useless and I need to take care of her, this isn't working."

"She's only been here a month, let's give her time."

"The precedents have already been set, she is needy and I see why she wasn't doing well living on her own in Palo Alto. I hope there's some kind of campus support for her, but it can't be me."

With that they made the decision to cut Christa loose as soon as possible and also to take a trip to Yosemite during fall break. The trip ended up getting delayed due to Debbie's earache followed by my strep and Sheila's croup. Enough was enough for a while and they just settled into the house the town making friends on campus and making day trips here and there when possible, more to the wine country to the ocean to San Fran it was great fun for all of us.

Spring break we saw Yosemite and stayed in a cabin and made pancakes everyday. It was glorious for my parents and had them reminiscing about their maiden voyage west.

"This is just like the cabin we stayed in before, isn't it Walt! This is great."

"Yes it is but we definitely weren't making pancakes in that one."

"Of course not! Oatmeal forever. In fact do you want some now? We could add in some spring blossoms, I bet they taste great," my mother jumped up as if to go out and pick some flowers immediately and practically squealed out the words at a joyful pitch as she put her arms around my father's shoulders.

"Maybe if I weren't on my second round of these flapjacks," my father responded cutting into a stack of pancakes. He swirled the wedge in a pool of syrup in his plate and raised the forkful over his should in the direction of my mother's mouth, "Want some?" he said to her waving it a bit to make it playfully difficult. Me and Debbie started giggling. "Hey kids do you want oatmeal now or more pancakes anyone? Some silver dollars maybe?"

We opted for the silver dollars, our favorite kind of pancake.

I'm sure it was a better time of year for the trip what with the spring blooms and great weather. And we got to spend the fall and winter such as they are out there exploring more local venues, playgrounds parks vineyards beaches museums. Especially Pebble Beach, we went there a lot and we'd all collect smooth rounded beach rocks and splash at the water's edge. The Redwoods were something else, I knew they weren't just large because I was small and the smells in the forest were unusually wonderful. Everything was going swimmingly on that outing, it really did except for Sheila who wanted to be able to run around and hide behind the crazy big trunks of the trees but after a few steps of trying to hustle along with us she'd stumble to the ground tripping over a protruding roots or dirt clump that was large relative to her size.

"Come on, Debbie," I said moving towards Sheila when she started to howl, "let's carry her with us!" With that I hoisted her up piggy back and instructed Debbie to run along behind me in case Sheila started to slip. That worked and we had peace for quite a few jaunts around trees and through one that had been hollowed out in the middle for cars to drive through.

It didn't take long for my mother to calm down and allow herself to ease into whatever the political scene was there in the Stanford environs together with whatever she could get to in Berkeley. It was enough for now, her aspirations were not slipping by just percolating.

When we were all getting into a groove my parents decided to jumble things up again and start building a house on a cul-de-sac on the Stanford U campus. Just like Jasper predicted but for some reason they didn't ask him for help or advice. That's curious, isn't it I mean he was a celebrated architect and ready and willing as he said. Maybe they didn't want to impose maybe my aunt was already ill my grandmother certainly was ill and had died by then a few years ago already. It was the era of 1950s style out of the catalogue building and my parents had sales reps from a couple of companies come to give their pitch and show off what was special about their components.

"Just look at the styles of Formica we have for your kitchen floor, your bathrooms. I think you are both going to be very happy with our designs, the quality of the work, the process—we make it very very easy for you knowing you both have lots to do besides building your dream house. I assume I'll mostly be talking to the little lady here and you'll have more to say about how you want the kitchen and such but now I want to hear from both of you, what your hopes and dreams are for this forever house you're going to be living in sooner than you can practically blink. I mean, look down the street, we built most of the homes on Casanueva and each one is different. And each lived in by a family that will stay and stay, happy with Stanford of course but equally happy with the home they built. No problems in any of them, ask around. The one you build will have your distinct taste and signature on it. Let me show you some of the layout options for ranches, split levels and even some two stories although not too many of those here. We build them all on an easy to pour concrete slab and they come with built in ready-made heating right in the subflooring, all electric—feels great on those chilly mornings even down here in the Palo Alto area."

The rep took a breath and my mother edged her way in, "Walt, I don't know, maybe we want more of an Eichler kind of thing—more of an open plan, more natural light everywhere, a courtyard in the entrance, you know, like the Aronows built further down the cul-de-sac, don't you think?" Her voice trailed off at the end a bit not sure of the costs involved in Eichlers but people were building them it seemed en masse in the area and they looked so livable. Unbeknownst to her it happened she picked out the only house on that side of the street that this reps company did not build.

The rep quickly dove in, "No, I don't think you want to go that route, for one thing the lasting value hasn't been established, not sure people will want those in a few years. Not that you're moving away so fast, but just protecting your investment and so forth. And the quality isn't like ours, we've been doing this for a long, long time have gotten the bugs out and the value in. Just take a look at what we can do."

A week later, another rep in a longish stream of them appeared with binders crammed full of colors fabrics flooring and sample carpets, finishes and patterns in tow. "I've heard both of your de-scriptions of what you'd like to have in your new home so let's get to brass tacks. We can do it faster cheaper better than anyone else, the three Rs of this business I always say. Let's just take that as a given and let me show you some sample floor plans, some kitchen designs, and so forth so you can begin to envision your home in the flesh. Let's start with the kitchen," he said looking at my mother and taking out some Formica counter top samples, "first of all we do the most modern wall to wall countertops all in Formica—here look at some of the samples of colors and patterns—with appliances fitting in under and over the counters. So, the dishwasher—that's right, no more doing the dishes by hand!—goes underneath just to the right of the sink, the double wall ovens somewhere over on this side where there is also a cooktop set in and then the fridge over here so everything falls into place for your work triangle," he said looking straight into the eyes of my mother.

"Now, the flooring can be in any variety of these up to date Linoleum tiles if you like or whole floor sheets which makes for a neat seamless look," he handed my father some of the samples as my mother was flipping through the counter top options. "Personally I'd go with the sheets, easier to clean, holds up probably literally forever, and the install is a dream."

"What about scuffs and scratches or if some part gets damaged?" my father asked. "I mean, with tiles you just pop out the ones that were harmed, right? With a wall to wall sheet do you have to replace the whole thing?"

"Great question, and yes, if a section gets damaged significantly enough to need to be replaced, depending on what kind of damage and how large an area it might make sense to do a total replacement. Have to say it's never happened since I've been working with this company which is a long time. Linoleum is incredibly durable and can take all kinds of abuse even. Minor scuffs and scratches can usually be restored on the spot without any kind of replacement but even that almost never happens. You'd have to take a blow torch or a hatchet to it or something.

"Moving on the living room, we have some great and also very very durable wall to wall carpeting."

"No, we don't want wall to wall in the living room, we'd like more of a natural feel with wood flooring," my mother quickly interjected.

"Okay then, good you have strong feeling there and know what you want. But you might want to carpet the family den."

"Also, on that, no den, we feel the living room will be a family room," again my mother stepped right in.

"Most unusual. If you visit some of your neighbors' homes you'll see they have a separate den for the whole family tv watching and such and for kids to play with toys and generally wreak the havoc they do and then a more formal living room for the adults, you know for entertaining or sitting and relaxing after a days' work," he said looking at my father hoping for an ally, "you know, without the kid clutter and without the noise I mean you don't want to be trying to hold a conversation over the din of cartoons, do you? We have plenty of economical floor plans that still have a living room and a den if the concern is cost."

My father entered the conversation that was beginning to feel like a dispute, "We are pretty sure we do not want a den separate from a living room. Let's look at some layouts and see what we can rough in that we know we want and need like kitchen, a couple of bathrooms, living room, bedrooms, study for me."

"A garage?" the rep asks now not sure what to take for granted with these two.

"Yes, definitely, if it stays within budget," my mother responded.

And on it went for quite a while, the reps streaming in and out with their samples and catalogues and glossy renditions not to mention contracts they were hoping to get signed on the spot. This took the place of their soirees the poker game and the reading group but they seemed fine with it and were for the most part on the same page about things with some minor bickering here and there when a rep stayed too long or Sheila started crying or needed to be fed. No mention in any of the conversations of the then not publicly known consequences of all that water and stain resistancy flame retardancy on the flooring the carpets the counter tops not to mention on our very pjs as they became flame retardant, those nasty never ever degrading and yet water soluble a deadly combination PFAS discovered in the Manhattan Project where else? Used in fire-fighting foams too now being sprayed all over the country with all the fires torching the earth in this country and all over the world. Water soluble not degradable means in our bellies directly from water food air.

In the end the plans seemed to be made a bit hastily with as it turned out the first rep that came in. A two story, rather flat faced, brown stucco or something like it but maybe it was cement not sure façade with lawn front back and side one car garage no den but definitely a dishwasher a laundry chute that I thought was very cool and often was very very tempted to slide down electric radiant heat in the floors on the ground floor central vac ducts made out of pvc which cut costs automatic sprinkler system right in the ground that would go on and off at set times. Everyone on the block had them and they'd pop on and off. Stanford was very very hot most of the time with the sun baking down relentlessly, I loved that.

The lawn was green green green and my parents were very proud of that. A guy came by to mow and to put down fertilizer that kept it going strong and thick. The front had some tiny redwood saplings planted on either side of the path to the front door, the side was pretty narrow going around the garage to the back and the back yard was small and mostly level until it dropped down sharply to the road behind the house. Across the road were open pastures for horses that went back up a hill and no houses at all over there. The area was still largely undeveloped except for these cul de sac enclosures for faculty and staff even though Stanford U had already existed for well over half a century.

So here we go packing and moving (but stayed at Peninsula my school one more year, so more on that soon). This was a move they were both equally happy about and they did both the packing and the unpacking together.

"With my study upstairs I can work at home some days and help out too," my father said giving the right amount of swirl to a martini concoction as my mother was making dinner.

"And each kid can have their own room and ours will be off to the far side of your study. Kitchen and dining area will be so convenient and real neighbors—we even know some of them already!" my mother chimed in at a gleeful pitch. "A safe street for the kids, no traffic, not that there's much here but we have that corner lot thing which isn't ideal. I do love this house, I will miss it," my mother added clearly having second thoughts sentimentally but also worried about the money it was going to take.

"No, we're doing the right thing," my father swooped in to nip her thoughts in the bud each of them able to read each other's minds, "this is an odd community and we'll be right in the thick of things on Casanueva. You'll be much happier getting involved in all the happenings there."

"And creating some new ones!" my mother added with a grin.

"Yes. It'll be perfect and we'll never need to leave. Not ever."

With this they clinked glasses and he began to set the table while my mother called out to me and Debbie to come in for dinner. Intuiting her worry he added in putting a jug of milk on the table, "The finances will work out they always have plus Stanford is being very generous with the mortgage terms. If we get into trouble which we won't they'll renegotiate the terms favorably for us, they want us to stay prosper and be happy here. It'll be fine don't worry. It's all happening better than we could have imagined, really!" He helped me and Debbie into our seats and went over to give my mother a hug and carried over a steaming pot of mashed potatoes.

ON TO STANFORD

1962, JOHN GLENN ON THE Friendship 7 and all. The Space Race. Sputnik 1 had already happened of course a few years back. I remember my father excitedly talking about taking us all to the moon one day and John Glenn coming back from his orbit mystified in the real sense of the word by human smallness. I can still hear his voice broadcast on my little black transistor radio I kept next to my bed sounding very other worldly like he'll never be the same again. I think Glenn's meaning was only understood on a superficial level of yeah I get what the words mean but. On the other hand I remember getting a sort of kid's version of chills down the spine, more like the hairs on my head standing up all prickly. Something about his delivery commanded attention. When space travel advanced my father actually bought some kind of tickets or placeholders for us. Tickets to go into outer space while building a family home on the mundane earth. Location: Stanford USA. Of course the 1%ers think Mars or somewhere is where they're going to escape to once the earth is sufficiently destroyed or too hot or too dry or too under water or all of the above and they can just have hand-picked people there that they are comfortable with and breed from that stock. Yay. I think we've heard this kind of plan before or some more earthly version of it. What people in the fifties sixties were still escaping and emerging from, those that lived. Would entail a lot of inbreeding the current plot and we do know how that goes. They better take a CRISPR gene splicer along and know how to use it if anyone really does yet or maybe by then. But the by then is getting closer and closer. So okay they'll need at least one scientist a doctor or two nurses and who's going to cook clean build fix? they those Jeff Bezoses are going to actually need a lot of extraneous essential people, aren't they? Would you want to go up with them?

And so we moved to dry town Stanford, which you'd never know from all the drinking that went on there—does not having a liquor store in town really make a difference? Doesn't seem like it especially in the car culture California where driving five miles to a store isn't a big deal. Hell, West Coast people drive hours just one person in the car to have lunch just for fun—I wonder what it was like during the seventies' oil crises I mean I was in New York with the waiting on gas lines to fill up that went for blocks and blocks and hours and hours in New York City. In case the traffic even with the embargo and all that wasn't bad enough then these long lines of cars it was really crazy but didn't seem to deter people from driving that much except some places didn't have gas in the pumps at all I remember that out on Long Island and other more remote places so you could drive there but maybe not back since remember our cars then and now get indecent mileage of the gas consumption per mile variety. I remember during all that with the lines and empty pumps watching images of France (on television back in the day when everyone who had one could just turn it on and get all the channels without paying for this plan or these networks or that cluster of channels like today and the way the internet is going, then they were just channels for all to see) touting their nuclear power and showing everything all lit up 24/7 as we say now like because you have it you can waste energy all the time? it was very very gross and an aspect of French nationalism at its underside—really need to stop doing stuff like just tooling around in a car I mean we really do know better now so is this more of the because I can ism or something even weirder? Like all academic environments, it was most definitely very liberal with the scotches and the ports and such, probably gin. One of my college advisors who was of Stanford vintage and had actually gone there before ending up on the East

Coast and before landing her first job at Princeton where they were so upset at having a female hired *as a professor* that just before she arrived they—the faculty of the department? who else could it have been?—dumped a pile of soiled tampax in her office for her to find on her first day there freshly minted out of graduate school and with her doctorate and all, anyway when I knew her and on this day she was talking to me in particular she was regularly drunk, astutely told me in one drunken fit how badly I was brought up. Oh well. She was probably right in some sense but for the wrong reasons as they say. People often read things correctly about me but for the wrong reasons, how does that happen? Like when my colleague at a conference wanted me to be hanging out with her more and I wasn't responding to her texts as fast as she would have liked called me an aspie said I was on the spectrum. Definitely a pejorative usage that. Thought it was ridiculous and self-serving at the time but in retrospect. Some of my well-worn defenses showing, a lot of aspects do come together I now realize only just now putting it together, the different pieces I never understood before, just thought something was very off about me not good broken not like other people, I knew what I wasn't like not what I was like. A perfect storm I guess of the chaos of the times of the 50s 60s 70s chaos of my family's home and moves and changes and no constants no discipline no structure so I would cling to my own patterns and habits and was duly mesmerized by friends' homes that had regularity and rules. I mean, I hate rules except my own but still. Even down to the toxicity on the Navajo reservation and then ongoing as I've been saying no lack of toxics in the boomer childhoods all lurking there under the hoods lawns carpets faucets fruit loops, first trimester of chemicals called a potential cause. Not all bad to have a label for things. More on this as we go I'm sure, you'll see what I'm talking about.

Of course, money theme playing throughout academia for sure, the Stanford campus looks totally different now, I went back a couple of years ago and even my friend Michelle who spent her entire childhood there got lost because it's so built up and different.

Like so many universities it became about money money money to name one instance when my oldest decided she wanted to go to Princeton and at the info session they said never mind filling out the card documenting that you were here if your parents can't give at least a mil for a building forget it and go home, the head of admissions really said that! to the whole crowd! We happily did leave at that point I was proud of my daughter for being disgusted I mean she was just a kid but she got it and we didn't see anyone else leaving at that juncture.

One of the hills behind our cul-de-sac—Michelle's family lived there too and before us, her father was at Hoover, an expert on what was then called Rhodesia—was preserved for some reason with a walking trail, used to have cows on it. A beautiful, sloping hill with the yellow grass of California in the fall and big old oak and other trees, but not too many. It was a hot hill. Still is. In summer you could fry an egg on the sidewalk and the tar on the road would melt. Hot and dry.

Sun baking down day after day so much of the year. Those roads all those highways and freeways as they call them and so many others—think Arizona, New Mexico, Nevada, Florida (well, that's sinking, maybe not the best choice) could have solar panels on them like other countries are doing—China in a big way. But we say here it can't work while it *is* working already. Oy. Not to mention what if the Sahara Breeder Project—weird name, no?—goes forward, it could power the entire world the entire world all of it with solar and wind power on the Sahara not to mention boosting rainfall there and the vegetation enough so people who are living at starvation level could grow crops and eat and earn a living. It sounds good, is there an underside there too?

Our house was on one side—the left if you're driving in—of the mouth end of the cul-de-sac, Michelle's was down towards the dead end portion on the same side. Sheila, who could barely walk then, I remember her being still a baby or toddler anyway, would sleep walk down to Michelle's house go right in and up the stairs to get into bed with her parents. It was a pretty long walk for a toddler even awake which she was not, like a city block length at least. Ours was going to be one of the few two-story homes on the street, with a balcony off the front of the second floor. I had a room up there on the balcony at the end, then came my father's study next to that, and then my parent's bedroom. I think my sisters had bedrooms on the back of the house, no balcony. I used to sleep out there and also smoke the airplane cigarettes looking out over the street don't think I thought about anyone seeing me but anyway doesn't seem to have happened. Those cute little four packs in so many brands and colors. I remember it being built and the big construction dirt pile I'd sit on top of. Doing that I met Rusty born named Mary turned Michelle. She was really a Rusty then, copper red hair, freckles. When they were in Paris for a sabbatical she became Rusty-Michelle, and then eventually Michelle, who she is now. I always thought she looked like the Botticelli *Birth of Venus*.

That's when I got the powder blue canopy bed that I loved so much. We were really settling in what with new bed sets and Danish furniture for the living room and my parent's bedroom maybe Jasper helped out with selecting those items. I used to assemble and unassemble the canopy part each subsequent move, and yes there were more to come odd as that seems from the early Stanford vantage point. The canopy parts had the cross beams made out of white laminated wood. And then the parts of the arch, probably six of them. The posts and the mattress frame. I loved taking it apart, other things too, clocks for example. Definitely on the so-called masculine scale of things my frilly ruffly bed notwithstanding. Royal blue was my favorite color but powder blue was special too. Those powder blue Monopoly properties were must haves for me and the dark purples, the cheaper properties for sure but my strategy was to own land, build buildings and not worry about having the cash. It did seem to work at least playing with younger sisters it worked. What training that game was, think about it that's the game that Amerikansky kids play or anyway back in the day played and kind of had to master after stepping up from Go Fish. Indoctrination by playing, the best way is to not know it's happening. The mattress was high off the ground and I'd have my pacifiers lined up across the pillow there—yes yes I know I was already about five then but I held onto my 'biers a lot longer than that. Didn't like to play favorites amongst them and I had so many, they each got equal time and in order. I was always fairly methodical and organized, rigid some might say, it was just in me to have an order to things to rank the biers by texture size color and then rotate each in turn. Was also in reaction to my environment, familial and cultural especially as the sixties wore on. Like my dolls they too had a fair and fixed roll call. I would feel bad if I even silently thought I liked one more. The way I remember it, there was a small window on the wall that my bed was alongside, inside the frame of the canopy, so I could look out on the horse pasture. On the opposite wall were sliding glass doors to the balcony. I looked out on the horses and that pasture was across the street behind our house—now a major thoroughfare, with all the honking horns clogged with cars. And the balcony was on the other side, I remember how the light crossed the adjacent wall, the one I faced lying down. Sometimes—especially if my parents or even just my mother, had gone out—I'd watch the light cross the wall, fade (were there streetlights on the cul-de-sac? I don't remember any) and then become light again, slowly, starting somewhere around four AM. Such a real witching hour (okay, I used it but don't get me started on the term witching and all the shades of sex class and probably racism or anyway ethnocentrism involved), the coldest moment of the day/night and everything seems so still. It's when I'd get up to study when I was in college so quiet no people no talking nothing.

We had a carpool to Peninsula from the aptly named Casanueva cul-de-sac. Maeda was one of the drivers and her daughter whose name I forget who had a leg brace and polio. She was a bit older than me, before the vaccine which was too late for her. I remember lining up outside for the sugar cube filled with vaccine serum. A kind of yellow dot inside. It was a long line, it was California after all, everything could happen out of doors. It was hot, I remember that. I was with my mother, don't remember any sisters there, maybe they were too young or maybe they were there but I don't think so. Was she wearing that gray, horizontally striped in natural shades of gray and white, hand-woven skirt? I think so, she wore it a lot. That and a Marimekko pink and orange shift but that came probably a bit later. When we'd come up her porch Ariella would be there spinning yarn that she'd then weave on her big loom. And then they'd make things out of the fabric, like the skirt. People acting like we were waiting for a miracle on that line, that's how it felt. In the days when Pauling would say once we can be vaccinated from everything, we'll live forever. I guess he didn't take in the full weight of the chemical onslaught we were already being soaked in. He thought vitamin C would cure a lot too, have to say I'm getting mega mega infusions of it now with my chemotherapy treatments, the C feels just about as bad going in as anything else. Odd, or at least unexpected, that. I'm thinking today that I'm going to buy one of those Japanese radiation monitors, why not? Be part of the global information stream and be able to detect what's happening radiation wise anywhere I go, moment to moment. Well okay looking back at this passage you see what I mean about how my mind works, it jumps around but that's all part of the chemically created Aspie complex isn't it?

The chemical Armageddon notwithstanding the torture it has wrought, would anyone really want to live forever? Hard to imagine what that would even be like, to be going on with an ever-yielding horizon. Maybe that's okay, kind of how we think anyway until it is painfully clear that that's not what's happening. Would people have kids under those conditions? How would that work, just more and more people and no one leaving through death. We'd really need the space colonies of the Elon Musk variety and then some. He'd have to ditch the idea that the first travelers would likely die en route since they wouldn't.

Which reminds me now. Skulking around Peninsula, swearing to myself I'd never have kids, that it's a mean thing to do to someone. I was very silently angry until I'd explode. Then I wasn't so quiet anymore. They were called tantrums but really I think they weren't unreasonable responses. A lot of craziness whirling around. And for me talking to people or even the thought of it a chore would make me break out in a sweat except sometimes one on one with a friend that could be okay but even then only if I didn't feel tested and with some like Mary Beth I pretty much always did and also like a big clumsy clunky thing next to her agile compact little neat self. Those TV cameras filming at school, I hid under the trees. Mary Beth and Marc and Lisa were jumping up and down in front of them. They were happier kids, I thought they were dumb but probably they just didn't know how to worry that much yet. Dr. Barker, who later was found to be running arms to the Palestinians, was the school psychologist. He suggested I needed therapy, that I seemed depressed. Maybe Betty G had had some input too with the reading and other fiascos of my self-consciousness shyness nervousness she witnessed pretty regularly. Later without fully grasping the meaning I knew my daughters were different from me or me from them. One a team person I would say the other a people person me neither. Being alone quite okay with me, something they don't understand and try to talk me out of. He, Barker, was right, my parents said no. Or, rather, apparently, according to my mother my father said yes and she said no and that was that. Maybe my spectrum dwelling would have been discovered. Not sure if that would have been a good thing, depends what the ideas about it were then in the early sixties. Why would she decline though when she was in therapy herself? That's a mystery, don't you think? His daughters always looked teary eyed to me, I think now they were glassy-eyed probably. Who knows why. But he was right about me and I did need some help. Wish I had gotten it then cause I didn't really ever get it later when I guess I could have on my own. I tried, but I really didn't know how and didn't have the practical sense to figure it out, and also luck wasn't on my side. The therapist I stuck with for five years, three times a week, five years three times a week when it wasn't working or helping or seem to be doing something well it did seem to be doing something I was dreaming a lot and I was realizing things that never ever occurred to me before but the follow through the let's do something with all this didn't happen and that is what a therapist is for to try to nudge stuff in that direction but anyway this therapist in particular was stupid—I know, I should say something softer like unintelligent but she was stupid and badly trained I realized later. Thought I was the problem not her, couldn't tell the diff back then. I was also too distraught and didn't know or find a way out. None of it was in me. Today they'd definitely say I'm on the spectrum but maybe I don't like that whole mentality. I mean, everyone is somewhere on the spectrum and it's also used so pejoratively, an insult. Anything like that in popular parlance loses its substance. Everyone was hypoglycemic for a while, at least somewhere on the spectrum of hypoglycemic—like from zero to full on. But there were things that weren't in me or didn't come naturally and I didn't learn, I think I would have needed help early on about that, something was kind of disconnected and foggy. Didn't know how to interact thought I didn't want or like to but really just couldn't didn't know how to take others into account properly didn't know how to be in the present had to cling stolidly to schedules patterns well-worn paths had that laser-like focus tunnel vision one issue person kind of thing always the play list. I didn't know it was a thing that it melded into a picture of something that could be dealt with except on the edges like learning to try to keep a conversation going without random digressions even when they made sense to me. Psychoanalytic training and seeing patients helped but getting through breast cancer helped more—something in both my mind and body shifted after that, oddly for the better or more human so to speak (except for how I looked physically after and ongoing, like an older and uglier version of myself which I know I shouldn't dwell on but come on its not great to look whatever the way one does and then to look a lot worse and have people react with a startle when they haven't seen me in a while like since before the disease and treatment, of course now it's worse I look lots worse, pretty much like some kind of freak or Ninja turtle). I suddenly needed a normal amount of air water sleep and food and I got people and my relation to them better. Chemical poison treatment antidote for lifelong chemical poisoning. Go figure.

Anyway, new house, Studebaker wagon four doors and all that we took many many trips up to the wine country with three kids a dog. It was all working. My parents were a long way from the days they first were mesmerized by California on that broken-down motorcycle. Everything had more or less gone as planned although they did not foresee the three kid thing beyond the abstraction of yes, we'll have a family or the building of a house thing although of course they envisioned having a home of sorts, also abstract. But here they were and with neighbors they mostly liked and felt they were going to fit in nicely. Reinstated a poker game and faculty from all over the campus came to play opened their salon-like discussions and reading group and were having a really great time practically as soon as they moved in. The readings shifted a bit by then as did the discussions, more focused on education reform and nature versus nurture kinds of themes. Pragmatism was raging and my father like so many others then were called "Dewey eyed." Not to mention Sidney who had studied with Dewey, he would stop by the house whenever he was in the area, sometimes unexpected. Like the time only my mother and I were home. The bell rang and it was Sidney and his wife on the other side of the door.

'Sidney, Ann how great to see you." my mother was in her painting smock and Danskin leggings. We had been in the garage doing some finger painting so she didn't extend her hand in greeting. I think I had paint all over even in my hair. "Come in," she said, opening the door wide.

They came in and took seats in the living room. Sidney chuckled as he took our messiness in with a glance and said, "We were stopping by to check in on you, make sure you are fulfilling your obligations and are a good *balabusta*."

My mother laughed and appreciated hearing Yiddish, a rare occasion out there. They chatted for a while over coffee and some marble pound cake my mother had just made.

Rising, Sidney said, "Well, I am satisfied with my inquiry, your pound cake was excellent, like it had come straight from Brooklyn. I hope to see you and Walt for dinner one evening before we depart," and with that they both left and we went back to the garage.

The poker game banter was different from the study group's, no talk of inborn aggression epistemology or pragmatism mostly it centered on campus politics if not outright gossip. With such a small close-knit community and so many people trying to wedge into the game the gossip thing was touchy. My parents would rake over some of it in the mornings while indulging in their enduring ritual of oatmeal sharing. By then my father had defected some mornings to Special K. When he felt the need for the crunch of the K's he'd have to go through a bit of a rigamarole to hold the peace. I knew before he even stepped over to the cabinet to get out what he used as a cold cereal bowl, something in his demeanor his look he wouldn't hold his head up and face my mother head on as if to beg for forgiveness for the transgression that was about to happen. He loved the oatmeal ritual thing as much as she did, it was their way of starting the day together but sometimes and especially out there in sunny hot California a steaming bowl of anything just didn't work for him. He'd sheepishly take out the box of Special K and put it on the counter near where I was sitting, that was the prelude the hint of what was about to happen. My mother never let on that she was relieved to sometimes also get a break not just from the same warm bowl of greyish stuff but from the constant pressure to invent new formulas new recipes with new names. She loved the ritual too but it was so much better when unforced. On those rare days my mother let my father be the guilty party and then would make her very wet yucky scrambleds with bacon toast jam and sometimes home fries. They would enter into a truce zone each with their own favorite getaway with that inch of separation. Their lives were so intertwined that this kind of free choice seemed radical but not really bothersome just a dance they did. My father eventually caught on to the charade of it.

Back to the gossip. "Did Gladys really mean that Overby is leaving after all that investment and maneuvering to get into his position? Where will they go? I mean who will have them now?"

My father chuckled waving his spoon in the air at my mother's rendition of the situation in the Medical School, "The whole world doesn't know the minutia of what happens here hard as that is to believe!"

"But still, word gets around," my mother's voice drifted as she took another crunch of bacon mixed with egg on toast.

"Who cares really I mean do we? It's not our bed that he made but his own."

"I feel bad for Carol and the kids I mean they'll go down with him, do you think she knew all along or just now as things have played out?"

"You know, let it just be a lesson for us both and I mean you more than me that playing it like a straight arrow isn't only easier it just works out better!" my father was big on lessons to be learned.

"Not always, come on, sometimes I'm right!" my mother said in a light-hearted manner but she meant it too. She wasn't the clean and neat straight arrow type which made her very good at poker.

Breakfast and the conversation were over. My father rose to take his bowl and mug to the sink as he gazed around the open plan living space. They had some very cool modern Danish furniture influenced by my uncle Jasper especially a two couch set a long oval black laminate coffee table with wire legs in a boxy configuration and a couplet of matching high polish cherry dressers in their bedroom. Me with my canopy bed and the balcony I slept on most nights in my blue sleeping bag, I was happy too. I even tolerated the grumpy collie sleeping in my room sometimes until he snapped at me. With this two-story deal when the evening adult events were happening I could barely hear them or smell the smoke especially if I was out on the balcony. Being at the front of the house when they left and drove off I would get woken and I did always really

really hate being woken. Still do, don't even use alarm clocks unless I absolutely have to.

We kids did a lot of playing out on the street with the others. There was already a kid group established ranging in age from about Debbie's age to Michelle's older sibs who were old teens they didn't play with us much but did drive us to the movies and the A&Ws and other drive-ins. We'd go to Palo Alto for fries and root beer floats just us kids in Michelle's family's huge boat of a car cruising down the wide avenues with the radio blaring and all of us singing along as loud as possible. Kick the Can on the street, rounding the circle at the end on our bikes—I had just learned how to ride mine with my mother and father each taking turns holding onto the back until I was steady and letting me go riding off down the street seeing Debbie and Sheila behind me. I wanted to take them too but off I went with the pack. They had the younger kids to play with anyway and mostly we all played together stuff like Hide and Seek Tag and sometimes Marco Polo in the Aronow's pool. Sheila went crashing into a sliding glass door at Michelle's one Hide and Seek round when someone closed it behind their exit to throw us off the trail. Off to the emergency room at the spanking new Stanford Hospital we went all the players packed into the car with Michelle's father claiming she was one of his kids so it could go through on his insurance card. I doubt that would have a shred of hope of working these days he would have gotten sued or put in jail or something like the teacher recently who took a kid to the ER. Game was over for that day.

Things went on pretty well in our new house on the freshly minted street of Casanueva, it was one of so many all over the country new homes new family kids cars lawns landscaping fast food the works! Replicated over and over development after development, in towns off roadways to towns and cities airports becoming a thing big highways fast highways abundance and plenty. Jobs and training. The pieces were coming together in the country. Let's take a look at some of the toxic underside of it, the side effects of all that booming, just a peek at what was to be learned later some known even then by some. In the midst of all that promise for the future well-being prosperity peace time contentment all that growth all that potential for more and more and more, think, and multiply here by the thousands and maybe millions of new construction on quarter acre lots with the circular roads and driveways into two car garages, apartment complexes with garages underneath or on the side, of all that wall to wall in the bedrooms off gassing VOCs not to mention from the new furniture kitchen cabinets made of laminated wood the counter tops and linoleum flooring made from petroleum and the glues that held things together and flat not to mention the gas in the mower and the toxic fertilizers and pesticides used outside the lead and mercury all over the additives being suddenly put into food and drinks willy-nilly antibiotics in everything and not just the chickens. The point was to grow grow grow in all ways possible and profit like never ever before all of us not just the corporations but the regular guy too, it was all coming true. Who knows what was put in the fast food in those days we barely know now even with all the disclosure laws and such not to mention the new-fangled frozen TV dinners in those portioned aluminum trays you could just heat and eat. We had some then back in Stanford but didn't rely on them for sustenance such as it was for a few years. That's just a peek, more later as we go for sure.

We spent a good first year there and my parents were becoming increasingly ensconced. They were pleased exuberant really high with all the luck and success and excitement with what they had accomplished and glad the design building paying settling in phase was ending. There were real things happening in the world and they wanted to get to them. I mean as I've noted there was Cuba and the Missile Crisis for one Vietnam for another Nixon lost in California that was good and lots of people died that year, Eleanor Roosevelt William Faulkner Marilyn Monroe, E.E. Cummings to name some. My mother especially wanted to re-focus her efforts on politics even though they were actually discussing having a fourth child. Seems like a crazy idea since three was clearly over their capabilities already. Okay Michelle's family had six and there was the family of five across the street but most had two or three on the street and in the area. Some had one on campus but most would whisper that obviously something went wrong in those cases. Four was beyond beyond and they didn't do it and it was clear my mother was getting antsy. Anyone could have smelled a change coming already in those early days but I didn't and I don't think my father did either, Debbie and certainly Sheila were too young. In fact, I was surprised every time we made a move or a big change the whole mixing things up thing wasn't in my constitution and I never learned it. Was always like a shocking jolt of some unknown substance like I hadn't been through it a billion times before. New home new people new school new new new different different different. Harder for me than most it turned out and not just that I had an oppositional personality or some other thing that came in and out of vogue with the child psych lingo.

In her itch to get things going, my mother instituted a themed party circuit in which they'd do things like have costumed affairs in which guests were to come dressed as politicians some nights, philosophers other nights and so on, then they'd have debates amongst the characters. Castro versus Eisenhower Dewey versus Descartes versus Hume versus Husserl Rothko would talk to Miro and Klee would talk to Picasso Matisse to the curators at MOMA. Those were definitely good fun for a while, I even got to stay up and dress up for one of them. She tried to organize a radical street theater group with faculty wives but it didn't take so then tried it with students which did but they ousted her as a suspect adult pretty quickly. A bit deflated and frustrated she'd try to make her stay at homeness okay by painting and teaching painting especially to the kids on the block she thought had talent but something was already seeping in. She couldn't handle this life that felt so inert and smug in the success but boredom and stasis of it. I think there was a huge dollop of guilt mixed in there too.

"Walt, Walt, I've got it! A whole new approach to women in sports—of which there are of course so few, I know why! I've cracked it!"

My father was just taking off his raincoat and the front door still open, "Great," he said giving my mother a peck on the cheek and me a squeezy hug, "let me come in the door first! Then we can discuss the revolution," he finished with a warm smile still wrestling with his coat and the galoshes he took to wearing that year. When it rained it came down in buckets rapidly with the water gliding right over most of the dry earth and into the gulleys built along the roadways. Only the lawns with the automatic sprinklers were not parched and could absorb and make use of at least some of the rainwater. Acid rain had long been a phenomenon by then but the term wasn't yet in wide circulation and people were not thinking much about it in those glorious boom years. I had spent a good part of the sudden downpour outside head cocked to the sky mouth wide open seeing how much I could catch. Debbie joined me for a bit but tired of that game and went inside with my father and commenced pulling on my mother's skirt demanding cheese slices and Sheila was banging on the floor with a doll inside of her playpen. It was time to settle the troops down, the brilliant idea would have to wait while dinner started getting on the table. I finally came inside when the rain subsided and didn't think about changing into something dry until it was pj time after dinner.

Bedtimes were becoming very weird and frantic. She'd have us go marching around in line behind her with her hands waving wildly calling out military chants and singing all with a verve or frenzy that was over any top I knew of. Whipped us up more than calmed us down for sleep. Then she'd march us up the stairs after about twenty minutes of that past my father's study to give him a good night hug and pop us each in our rooms saying "Into bed and asleep now" at a high pitch. Don't know what would happen after that except for the times not so frequent yet when I heard bickering in a tone that was new and sure didn't seem fun. Saving grace were the nights when that would begin but people were on their way over or they went out. I think it was the daytime that got to my mother, the idleness of it while being constantly busy with us, with household stuff, with my father coming home for lunch that she'd make. Don't think he ever said he expected her to but she thought she should want to and so it went. She'd be barely getting any portion of her morning going to herself with Sheila napping than he'd be home already. Ditto in the afternoon so even her painting out in the garage was highly disrupted. How much she took on herself how much was social expectations in the air how much my father conditioned unknown the balances there but it was a volatile mix that built out of control. Neither knew how serious it was nor tried to contain it until it felt too late or anyway rapidly became too late with some impulsive behavior from my mother. In retrospect even she thought she should have held her breath and shifted gears but that's not what happened.

A lot of fighting about stuff like toilet seats began to be a common occurrence there on Casanueva. I don't know what happened that they reached their dreams to get back to CA to land him a good job that could last to have her pursue stuff next and in a community of friends and interesting colleagues all that happened in a house they built to their specifications. I mean really what happened that they couldn't figure out the problems that sounded petty? Three kids was maybe too many for them—imagine the four thing!—his mother had three, hers had four but it was too much for them or for her since the responsibility for the kids fell on her for most of the day but then again she didn't have pressure to make money and could do her painting that she did mostly out of the garage and taught all the kids on the block too and she was learning how to play viola with Pearl, I mean was it really so bad? Bad enough to put the brakes on I mean they both had more than their share of quirks but maybe they could have tried to ride things out a bit not just presto pull the plug? Wait until all three of us were in school all day maybe? They hadn't thought through the current plan well enough but what was happening now wasn't a good plan either, it seemed stupid really, I mean fight about something real at least like infidelities or politics. At five I knew it wasn't a good sign if they were fighting about such dumb things. Divorce was becoming very acceptable too almost chichi, lots of my friends' parents were doing it, or so it seemed. California—and that is where we were of course—was the first state in the country to introduce no-fault divorce but that was 1969 and my parents' friends were divorced years before that so we're talking fault here. What was the fault? And whose? I never heard anything about that but probably it wasn't a good story. Except for Josh's parents, I think the grounds were easy there his father being significantly unbalanced would wander off forget where he was and maybe who he was and that he had a job and was supposed to show up and teach courses he'd just go and get on planes and such without even thinking of telling anyone. Is there any other legal contract in the country that you enter into by signing a blank sheet of paper? Have you ever ever encountered one? I doubt it. I mean the parties sign it and can at that point change their names to anything they want anything at all, Minnie Mouse if someone actually wants to but then when you go to dissolve the contract it's up to whatever local judge you go before, it's up to them to say if you can get divorced and what that means. Yeow, that's crazy isn't it? But Ariella did it, Lillian too. My father lots later said those three women—he was including my mother in that mix—were hell bent on ruining our families, everyone's lives, I think he said. Like he had nothing to do with the problems. But he was also war traumatized and that got into the mix, he passed that along to me, more on that later. Trauma, they say now, works down through the generations. I think it must depend on how it's handled, generalizations rarely work in the individual cases. I remember that (particularly dense) therapist saying to me after a few years that it was like I was a child of the holocaust. Had she really not been listening to that extent??? She couldn't keep Clytemnestra straight from Electra either, it was all Greek to her. Wish I hadn't happened on her, might have found a real therapist who could have helped me, I was ready then, very, at 28. And maybe right then and there have unraveled what it is that has been going sideways all these years inside of me that it has a name that I didn't have to feel so guilty all the time for messing up for not being able to carry some basic things off like others. Wish I had known to leave her and move on but I didn't. Wish I had known to leave many people and move on over the years, but I was in the dark about how I worked. Kicking and screaming all the way to not leaving. Not great that trait of mine.

Therapists in general are horribly underequipped for even the most basic of skills and thought capacity to help people. Funny that I became one eventually, but I am getting way way ahead now. Stress isn't good, and I think I was disposed to and trained in stress from the beginning. Maybe that contributed and maybe it didn't. Clearly the chemical drenching is paramount, but all additional factors are, well, additional. They add up.

So my father actually moved out of that new house new family new car new lawn new friends but definitely did not move out of the new job, all after a brief talk in the dining room, me my sisters (Sheila toddling around) my mother my father. My father saying, "Children, your mother and I have decided to have some time apart. I'm going to take a room at the faculty club to give us time to sort things out. I'll be close by and we can see each other as much as we want, it's just a short walk from here." That was it. I typed out, "I'll miss you, Daddy" for which I was never forgiven. Seems like a decent human response.

They didn't even take the time to enjoy their successes together, quite a waste. I mean we hadn't even lived in the house for a year it still had the new house new carpet fresh paint smell. Maybe it was build design move new job new everything achieved your dreams kind of anxiety that they just needed to let settle but didn't. Quite a long ways from the motorcycle days. A waste as I just said. Gotta go slower with some things. I'm sure people said that to them maybe separately at the time.

Still in the dining room my mother piped in, "It'll be fun, we'll get to go visit that faculty club with all those cookies they serve in the afternoons and we go to the club pool all the time anyway we practically live there already!" The whole thing kind of fell on deaf ears I mean we didn't know what was going on or at least I didn't beyond that it sounded like a weirder version of the trips my father was constantly going on, one that didn't require a plane or really any kind of travel more than the walk my father took every day anyway. But a change for sure that much I got.

In that carpool that kept going pre and post separation was Maeda and her daughter with the polio leg brace, Wendy, me, and Mindy. Maybe more but that seems like a lot. Debbie had to go to the Palo Alto public school where kids sat at desks and it was orderly and pretty quiet, the chaos of Peninsula was too much for her—turned out she had a hearing or anyway ear thing. Got tubes in her ears eventually. I didn't believe it at first and would turn down the tv and swore I hadn't when she'd say she needed it turned up. She'd say it was better but maybe she didn't want to make a bigger fuss maybe she thought it should be better cause she trusted me. We'd all drive down to Peninsula from Stanford, that dry campus town. Everyone drinking those martinis pretty heavily is what I remember, just no bars all in private clubs like the faculty club or homes where there's no one to say or like now is required to say, maybe you shouldn't drive home in that condition. That condition was the norm then. I don't think the carpool lasted long cause I remember Charlotte driving me in her VW bug, dancing to the radio music bopping up and down. And it was just me and her no other kids. I knew it wasn't safe the way she drove but I loved her and would have withstood way more than that to be with her. Her favorite color was green and she gave me a poster of van Gogh's *Olive Orchard*. I hung it inside the arc of my canopy. I loved it because I did anyway but also because I loved her. When we moved to San Fran I rehung it exactly where it had been before in that powder blue arc so I could see it all the time. My canopy bed mattress was so elevated that even at eight in San Fran I could sit more or less under it with my friends.

Anyway, one girl with polio, Mindy who had a club foot for which she was relentlessly teased, and Wendy who had some kind of cognitive impairment and maybe resulting but anyway existing emotional disorder. When she would go off I really didn't know what to do. I felt maybe scared maybe more like wary around her. We'd be left alone with her, just kids, and not know what to do.

There was never any information given about what was wrong with her. Not to me anyway. Mindy, of course everyone knew about her foot since, again, it's California and lots of bare feet and swimming and everything outside. I remember trying to protect her in the pool at the Stanford Club where we all had lessons. In those days, the scent of chlorine was so thick it wafted over the whole pool area like a heavy cloud. Esther Williams went blind from chlorine, think about what else it does, good and bad. Gets into one's pores for sure too. In all municipal drinking water, baby formula, etc. Stan would swim laps there with a bathing cap on—I thought that was so funny a man wearing a bathing cap! a really good logician whom I studied with much later and in between my mother probably—might have—had an affair with or something along those lines. He asked me in a graduate school seminar as he was teaching right in the middle of his lecture if I was her daughter. I did ask her about him after that and she said, "Olive skin wavy dark brown hair thick lips tall in the math department I think? No, I don't know him." She wasn't kidding with that answer either. Maybe Stan happened during the separation, I'll never know. Funny and weird, I didn't even think I looked like her in those days but I guess I did enough for Stan anyway. Mindy was a mild kid who probably didn't do anything to anyone, quiet chubby and sad. The other kids were of course mean, that's what they do. I tried to shield her, ineffective I'm sure. My mother swam laps too like Stan. In that pool, at Strawberry Canyon, in the ocean. Being on the shore, she'd become just a small dot. I always felt she wanted to run or swim away from home, getting lost coming home at night, losing her keys, and stuff like that. Probably it was true, not only my fear. Watching the light change across my wall was part of that fear. My mother immediately after my father left started to spend a lot of time in San Francisco I mean a lot especially at night. Turns out she had found political groups there and in the East Bay to join and the meetings were all at night. By day the painting lessons stopped and she was on the phone constantly plotting and planning about this action that maneuver a new invention that was going to make her rich, she started to seem happy and was definitely energized. For a short period my parents kept up the discussion group and the poker game but rather quickly the discussion meetings ended or maybe moved to another location and my father kept going and he dropped out of the poker game that did continue with my mother raking in fun and winnings. Things actually seemed on the upswing and we did see my father an awful lot, I mean as I said I could walk to his institute and the faculty club wasn't much farther. The faculty club as lodging didn't work out for long though, not sure why but it was only a room with a dining hall downstairs, not exactly like the made to spec home he had just left. Unlike my mother he did not seem happier except when I saw him in his office that was clearly working out just fine.

Back to when we were squarely living in Stanford now to say the least, house built. Pre-separation cocktail parties. Women in those dresses and pumps as they were called with the skinny heels men wearing dark suits ties the ties were skinny too, actually drinking things like martinis. I only tried one of those once, was well into my forties probably almost fifty, couldn't do it. Got one sip in, maybe I tried a second taste but I doubt it. Like drinking lighter fluid to me. Not that I don't drink alcohol mind you. Probably never should have for my health, being estrogenic and all. Wish I had understood that a long time ago. Like when I was imitating my mother drinking scotch which I hate. But all that wine, I mean never too much at a time but a slow, constant drip for ages, decades. Another drip drip drip. The wine industry in particular has done a great popularity campaign for wine consumption. I mean think about it have you watched a tv show or a movie lately or ads even that don't include lots of people with the ever-present glass of wine? Everywhere everywhere leads to a happy good life being smart being attractive working hard with that glass next to you or when you've had a hard day or a good day every which way kind of day or event or mood just have the glass there and drink up. Think Mariska glugging it down on *SVU*. Especially my ex realizing how addiction prone I was plying me with the alcohol margaritas Brandy Alexanders Bloody

Mary's trying to get me to take cocaine—that I was afraid of having tried it once or twice, I knew I'd be addicted and dead quickly—stopped my baby sister Sheila from getting it from him such a creep he was going to give it to her too!—and not to mention when I was finally quitting the cigarette habit after eight long years of smoking he'd try to get me to smoke again. That wasn't enough for me to realize I needed to get a divorce? Lots of blaring signs would have been enough for most people, but again something some human thing was missing in me the radar equipment for dangerous people was left out of my kit I certainly proved that over and over and couldn't didn't learn from experience. I often have wondered about that the why I got into such awful situations with men explaining it all away as common women do get themselves into those situations and so many men are that kind of predator it's in our culture but I've recently realized with me it was more than that it was missing access to interpersonal communication of certain sorts stuff people are just born with or can learn but not everyone not me. Anyway the ex in question helped me to think it was my fault and I just had to do better. Statistics, how did I become such a typical female statistic I want to know. It used to give me vertigo that idea of fitting in with the norm of statistics thinking I was such a feminist. How does it happen anyway?

Back to the sixties, Stanford cocktail parties with so many notables. My parents both of them having a genuinely good time. I apparently sat on Tarski's lap at one not Debbie. Maybe that's when the logic bug rubbed off on me. I'd stare down the adults, one of my few talents in those days. I still sort of do it by mistake, I'm not really staring or even really looking at the person I'm probably thinking about something and my eyes look like they're staring. I do it in the infusion room. I catch myself realizing that someone else in there thinks I'm staring at them, I'm not I'm just zoned out trying to hold it together sometimes I do cry but I try not to one day it was unavoidable I was going to cry a lot, some medication was having a very bad effect on me and they let me sit in one of the two private rooms. The nurses are always nice but they were especially nice to me that day. Back then back in the Stanford days I was staring though and I knew it after a point, did it almost on purpose I'd say. I wasn't trying to challenge them, just observing, watching. But it would definitely make adults uncomfortable, and I sensed that much for sure. On the bus too, would just listen and watch people. Everywhere really. The makings of a good therapist? Not sure. I didn't really learn to talk to people until recently was too nervous in college would have to plan out what I wanted to ask or say and then do so after class or in office hours. Even with friends not so much one on one but even then. But dinner parties or parties? Not good, never had a clever or even just ordinary thing to say that was able to come out and would always marvel at people for whom it all seemed so easy and natural. It's not that I wasn't thinking or doing stuff that was at least mildly interesting to someone else it's not that I never had a take on things that might be different au contraire. Just didn't talk couldn't too stressful.

Back to the parties. Not the kind my parents would hold mind you. The men would throw their keys into a pile and fish a new one out after the wives had already gone home (to prep? get into those cute nighties, those short ones? they had a name I can't call back right now, maybe later. *Baby Dolls* think about that name!). Go to the address on the new set and see who was waiting. Seems tame compared with all the details of the sexual harassment charges flying around now. Not saying the party game was harassment just that it's come to crystal clear daylight what people men some men anyway quite a lot of men are thinking about while at work in meetings at home playing sports meaning all the time. Weird stuff. Reminds me of the comments my—our, I did have a co-author— *Get Smart* got from editors, that stuff like that could never happen, does never happen, maybe in the fifties but not the eighties (that's 1980s by the way). What we did was take real live college campus examples and water them down by a huge factor. By the standards of the revelations of #MeToo our content was really really mild. Insidious and worth pointing out but still. First book ever on sexual harassment I might interject here.

This is what the guys dream up to do with their time? And other's unwitting time of course. Let's see if something comes of it in this round. Sure didn't after Anita Hill's testimony even though there was a lot of hope that it was some kind of watershed. Maybe there won't be any guys left standing in their jobs, have to fill the spots somehow and also of course a ready-made excuse not to fill some spots. All those tracks of tenure. Again, not saying the key game was harassment just a bit off.

Lots of stuff a bit off. Like it took no time for news of the separation to spread all over campus and for the late night calls my mother would get from male faculty members, pretty much all married. Or the day the two big beefy police officers were watching my mother sunbathe in our back yard. They could see her from the hill across the street. When they saw her seeing them they came down the hill to our door and knocked. "Just wanted to make sure everything is all right here," one of them said to her when she opened the door still wearing only her bathing suit.

When she said everything was fine, they asked a few more questions. Her anxiety was rising knowing there was something clearly not right in the air. When she was not inviting them in or even opening the door the whole way they did eventually leave. She was shaken after that. She hadn't been afraid of the desperate and cheap phone calls but this was different, they were strangers big strangers with guns and they could have done anything they wanted. I don't know if she ever sunbathed out back alone again but probably not.

September was always hot and me and Rusty and Joyce and maybe Mary Pat would all go down to Tresidder to bowl. Not sure about Mary Pat being a regular with us. She was just enough older that she didn't always hang with us. Rusty was friends with her, and I was definitely jealous of that. Being jealous a lot. We moved so often that I'd leave friends behind for them to find maybe better but anyway more stable friends. It got so hot the tar was all melty on the road. Rusty said it would whiten our teeth if we chewed some. I really liked having my teeth be all pearly.

Along the way one day we dared Joyce to roll in poison ivy knowing how competitive she is and how allergic. To our horror she did it. She wasn't a pretty sight when the allergy kicked in. We're in the era of John Glenn going out into space and orbiting the earth. Also the space race and the building of the Berlin Wall. Those skinny ties and bouffant coifs with hair all teased up. Suddenly out of nowhere Rusty started doing a jumpy dance, spinning around and clapping as we were walking and chewing the tar and in a very low voice calling out "Hey-ya-ho! Hey-ya-ho! I'm going to be a boy for Halloween!" I thought that was weird, or anyway I was vaguely confused, I didn't get it then, the attraction to being a boy or even that there was a costume or something she could put on that would make her a boy for the night. I mean, what was the difference? I don't think I got the difference until very very late. The social difference, the cultural difference, the economic difference. I just didn't see a difference. Funny, me loving those fluffy dresses and ballet and sylphide gowns and roses and pearl earrings and design and sewing. I just didn't see those as something called feminine or female, and why should they be anyway? Didn't dwell on it then or didn't know how, I mean I'm like six at this point. She had her pulse on something there though, Rusty did. In a family with five girls and one boy who played baseball. Mine was all girls as I've said already and when my father left for a stint (spoiler alert!), really all girls. My mother thought she was one of the sisters half the time.

Each house on the cul-de-sac had a lawn front and back. My mother planted some redwood trees in our front lawn as I've mentioned, no one else did that. When we left, the new people ripped them right out, probably first thing they did. I don't think they would have been able to grow to size in that too small space. Maybe though and that would have been pretty magnificent huge redwoods looming not just over the house but over the whole street. And sprinkler systems that would come on and off. Then the water would run off the pitched lawns and into the gulley that ran in front of each house along the street, up the cul-de-sac starting at our house, past the Aronow's to the curved end and up around the end and back down the other side of the street past the Ryan's, the Draskovicz's and so on to the end right across from our house. I'd sit there on the other side of Casanueva when the water was running down the gulley and make little mud houses out of the wet earth, a.k.a. mud. I'd pretty much always have building designs, questions and challenges going in my head. In those days I think the main design question was the slinky house. Outside it looked like a slinky that makes an arch by having both ends flat on the ground next to each other. The outside wasn't the problem, it was the inside. Think of the shapes of the resulting interior, what to do with the space? Don't think I ever resolved that one to my satisfaction. Always always going to be an architect until I changed direction but that wasn't until college and the first ever time my mind woke up such a shocking awakening a jolt into an altered space. My sisters didn't believe me when I started spending all night in the library studying studying in those days people went to the stacks read books did research from books remember no internet then and really so much excitement in those stacks books and books and books of worlds of stuff to read learn think about create. I didn't know any of it existed go figure having grown up on enough college and university campuses somehow had no clue at all.

Back to the mud that I loved playing in so much. I did that by myself. I don't think anyone asked what I was doing. But the mud the water the lawns, what were they fed with? DDT for one thing and many other things for another like 2,4-D an ingredient in Agent Orange no less. Glyphosate in Round Up used everywhere and finally being challenged in the courts, now, decades and decades of harm later in the courts. We'll see what happens with that. Monsanto already has to pay up to the school gardener in California which is good but better is that they're now facing what did I read? 5,200 claims? Good but it should probably be more like 5,200,000 at the very very least. Used it in warfare and then turned that warfare on ourselves, great, smart moves all around. Even only in warfare, it's still going into that potent triumvirate of air, water, soil. And that gets around. Around the world one way and another, so many pathways if you think about it—by air and wind, by imports/exports grown and or made with that water/air/soil and on and on. Ways that us boomers were doused. Not every kid played in lawn run off water but probably a lot did, did you? Anyway, we all played on lawns, chewed the grass from them, jumped in sprinklers on them. Had our houses sprayed inside and out to keep out pests, bugs like carpenter ants and roaches, rodents, squirrels. Now we do stuff like that for ticks too, spray up a whole lawn for the kids to be safe on. Yeah save us from what is being called the first pandemic from climate change, the ticks that is. Endocrine inhibitors carcinogens outright poison all to save us.

Not to mention the lead pipes lead solder lead paint lead in gasoline. I know I've said this already but what about lead in garden hoses did you know that one? even now I recently discovered! Turns out the ones without the lead are cheaper, replaced mine. Lead, back to that pervasive toxin put into the water we drank, the air we breathed, the veggies and fruits, livestock as we call it. Never really thought about that word until now, so antiseptic a label for our imprisoning and breeding living animals. Live stock like the stock of cans on the shelves stock of reams of paper in the cartons stock of cigarettes. Just stock those animals. Awful thought isn't that? I mean like me they're basically considered dead while they are fully alive and breathing and doing the stuff of living animals even if trapped think of all those chickens crammed into small coops that is stock they are literally there on shelves we call perches all crammed in as many per cubic foot as possible just like a Staples store crams in as many cartons of A4 size envelopes on a shelf. More of the idea that we're not them those animals except the humans we treat like animals. Asbestos on pipes in insulation in cigarette filters even. Was it really in tampons too? Let's not leave out Toxic Shock Syndrome that was discovered later.

DEET sprayed all over us to keep mosquitos away every hike beach trip evening outside which in California was always whether or not there were any mosquitos out there just in case don't want to itch which somehow I had plenty plenty of bites anyway that I'd scratch and scratch probably still have some scars around my ankles from doing so much scratching and picking, sunblock slathered over us when we weren't getting burned to a crisp tanning, ingesting flame retardants from our comfy pjs. Pressure treated lumber what a miracle. UFFIs blown in for insulation. We really didn't stand a chance and had no idea. It all seemed great. The spanking new houses and apartment complexes, the drive-throughs not just drive-ins with instant food bowling alleys golf courses swimming pools filled with chemicals to protect us from harm and frozen food in individual portions! You could grow children feeding them those Swanson TV dinners and the chicken pot pies—all straight from the factory to freezer, no muss or fuss in the kitchen. Later you'd just stick 'em in a microwave, have 'em ready in seconds! What could be better, the little compartments of a meat (God knows what was in it—I've been saying that a lot I notice, this God knows thing, what I really mean of course has nothing to do with religion or a supreme being or anything like it, hope I didn't really need to clarify that. Just get a twinge when writing it that I don't know whether to capitalize the god word, brings up a lot of conflict, not about religious validity or sentiment, just the respect to others thing I guess, not sure really what it's about, maybe more later on that) a veggie (usually soggy peas and tiny carrot cubes) applesauce a dessert even maybe a little piece of dry cake (which I used to like, very dry like a good wine like the Drake's Cakes coffee cake, don't make 'em anymore, I miss them in a nostalgic kind of way). I looked for them recently in the throngs of chemotherapy nausea and very very altered taste buds needing bland stuff, definitely not made anymore. All in those little foil heatable trays with the pull-off lids. Aluminum which we still put food in even acidic food that leaches the metals out faster and more efficiently, we know it causes Alzheimer's and other diseases and generally isn't good for you. Still make cookware like pots and pans with it too. Don't heat tomato sauce in 'em if you're still using such things. Go with Stainless, but who knows what we'll learn—from those who already know to be sure—what's in that. Go with glass maybe, but glass has been shown to have lead in it too and not just the leaded crystal—what an idea that is people putting fancy acidic wines and such in elegant etched glass goblets with lead infused into them on purpose! Toss that tray out right away when you or your kid's done with it. And that was before microwaves, imagine how those changed things. Instant frozen meals zappable in seconds to steamy perfection. Radiation leaking from most of them of course but that didn't seem to give too many people pause. Now people with their smart phones as they are called they have attached literally at the hip or breast pocket and sleep next to like a teddy and yet worrying about harm from the water company relaying their meter counts wirelessly. While they are blithely pressing go on the 'ol microwave. Never had one myself. Used one a couple of times at mom's but barely a couple. Or maybe I just watched her turn it on. Getting so way ahead here.

Back to the Stanford campus with its new cul-de-sac developments for faculty, burgeoning institute buildings, my father's operation lodged in one of them. I liked all the books and pencils there. So many pencils. Who uses those anymore? Not even little kids, all have their tablets practically from birth. And the winding staircase upstairs to his office, very glamorous I thought. Definitely Grace Kelly-esque. I passed by it every time I walked to Tresidder. Those soda machines, so cool to just put your cup under and push and out whooshed whatever soda I chose. Dr. Pepper of course! Eventually Diet Dr. Pepper—I won't even go into the ingredients of the low-cal right now. And you could make a mix of whatever sodas you wanted, I do tend to go in for mixtures, why keep it simple? All probably pretty much the same at the base level ingredients. Just the caramel color I'll name that one still used in so many things unnecessarily of course, even in "healthy" Brown Cow yogurt, why?

Probably there was an international faculty population there, but I do remember it as pretty much all white, so unlike living in Chinatown, San Fran next or later the Berkeley flats of the sixties. Peninsula looking back was pretty monotoned also. Certainly the teachers my classmates, that I remember. Lots of blonds too. That Quaker school had a violent undercurrent or not so under. Marybeth and I getting trapped in the auditorium alone with some high school boys saying they were going to rape us (that's all I remember about that) a high school science experiment set up outside in which a live cat was put into boiling water. I swear! The poor cat's scream was chilling, I still can hear it. Who could make these things up? And of course the school psychologist as I mentioned running arms.

Kennedy the first one was shot while I was at school in Peninsula. I remember Betty G. telling us what had happened. Lisa, little blond-haired blue-eyed Lisa with a constantly snively sort of nose started jumping up and down cheering. I guess her parents didn't vote for Kennedy. Betty G. handled it well I think. She didn't shame Lisa but in clear terms told her and the class there was nothing to celebrate about the President—or for that matter anyone—being shot, and to death. Betty G. held it together for us, inside she must have been pretty torn up.

I had my shows already in Stanford: *My Little Margie, Bachelor Father*. But also of course my favorites: *The Twilight Zone* and *The Alfred Hitchcock Hour*. I wasn't just playing in the mud. Oh! of course *The Rocky and Bullwinkle Show*, how could I not mention that one. Natasha, Boris, Nell and Dudley Do-Right. All of my shows soaked us viewers in the culture along with a healthy sense of the weird and ineffable. Later reading *Mad Magazine* cemented the bond in me for the underside of things, the negative I've come to realize of what Debbie saw and sees. I'm oddly optimistic or can be if that's the right word but she's positive. Nell always on the edge of a cliff. Ultimately to be saved by Dudley.

Oh gosh, *The Fugitive* and *The Addams Family!* And Shari Lewis! I loved Lamb Chop. Wasn't so much the days of merchandising like it is now or I would have had a Lamb Chop puppet or maybe I did have one, not sure. I haven't said much about babysitters. Lee was later, across the street on Benvenue. Later became a globe-trotting photographer. I wonder where she is now. In her seventies somewhere. I don't think I particularly liked her, she was very alien, very tall and WASPy. Everything seemed so easy for her in that way that I didn't get at all. Not that there weren't people in my orbit who were waspy—the blond Lisa, Marybeth Marc so many but something about her casual, everything is easy demeanor didn't work for me. Even then—and this is getting so ahead to Berkeley but it holds for Stanford too—things didn't seem easy to me. Things were hard and dismal—except roses and construction and ballet—and bad and just not good. A scared kid. And people were stupid. Some kind of thick semi-transparent wall in my mind separating me from getting to things people ideas clearly. I felt it there all the time and didn't know what it was or how to get rid of it.

Back to babysitters. Barbara. From Palo Alto. With her crooked forefingers—both of them. She'd show them to me so proudly that I wanted them too. And being a determined sort of kid I would daily hold my forefingers to bend in the same way as hers and succeeded, nothing I can do about it now. Very ugly they are. Her father was a United Airlines pilot—a somehow very foreign idea to me to be a pilot. Barbara with her strawberry blond beehive hairdo. The same color as Ann-Margaret's. Everyone wanted to look like Ann-Margaret in *Bye Bye Birdie*. I still have a picture of Barbara's high school graduation portrait. High School students in those days looked like adults, dressed like adults. Compared with now or even when I was in high school. Think Frankie Avalon and Annette Funicello again. All those suits and dresses and hairdos and makeup—wow, what a few more years into the sixties would eventually change! Barbara, she became a stewardess and had to watch her figure, strict weight and dimension requirements for the stewardesses in those days. No pants possible in the uniforms. And no stewards, not then. Later she was sharing an apartment on the Upper East Side in Manhattan with two other stewardesses—I think in the days where I'd win black-and-white milkshakes doing the Rubik's cube thing in under a minute at that basement level soda fountain—and we saw her and she asked, "Are you still having those temper tantrums?" What a blow. I guess I had them. I think I'd hold things in like a lot of people—probably more on the masculine scale again—until I couldn't and would explode. I don't think I knew why I was so beside and beyond. Never really solved it until decades decades and decades later. Anyway, I liked Barbara. She eventually married a pilot herself, settled down in San Jose (before it was *San Jose*) and had kids, a lot of them I think and was able to get heavy for good.

There was a rocking chair in what was my dad's study that became Charlotte's room too briefly as it turned out. I loved her and I thought she was murdered when she disappeared. Crazy, huh? The mind of a five year old maybe. Oh, getting so so far ahead now. But let's back up to Charlotte, an au pair of sorts, maybe a Stanford student or according to my mother she said she was a Stanford student but maybe she really wasn't. (By the way, was no checking done about someone who was going to take care of three little kids? Seems easy enough to find out if someone is a Stanford student or not.) Had a VW bug, don't remember the color but maybe red or maybe blue or green. Her favorite color was definitely green. That's why she had the poster of the van Gogh *Olive Orchard* I think.

Like Omi who I also loved. And yeah Omi came to visit Stanford during the separation which she thought was totally *meshuggenah*. She stayed in the house of course and my father was over a lot then, they didn't try to hide anything from her. Was the beginning of the end of the separation even I could see that. They had a good time together went out and Omi stayed home with us. We had a good time too, Omi maybe wasn't fun like play with us fun but she loved us and cooked all our favorites and as I said did our hair and would try to teach us stuff mostly morals in her less than subtle way and anyway I'd overhear her talking on the phone to people back east about my parents and how nuts she thought they were probably especially my mother but really it was clear she loved both of them.

Back to Charlotte bouncing up and down while driving me to school, or sitting in the rocking chair all quiet in her dark room. How was it dark in sunny California? I guess it was later in the afternoon or evening or something and maybe the front of the house faced East? Anyway I remember it being dark. And I remember talking to her. A lot. In her room. And then one day I came home from school—I don't know how I got there without her—and Charlotte was gone, her room was empty. And I screamed at my mother that she made her leave, that she hated her. There I was sobbing on the curved, spirally end of the otherwise straight bannister. I'm sure I felt like Grace Kelly having descended a sweeping staircase in a white gown diamond stud earrings platinum hair perfect and that complexion! it was that dramatic. It was old style cinematic. All of me was convulsing, "No, she didn't just leave, you made her go," gasping, "or—" I stopped there unable to go on.

Food, what about food? The foods of the period. I loved liverwurst probably Oskar Meyer definitely Oskar Meyer on white bread that indestructible Wonder Bread in the plastic bag with blue and red bubbles on it and with mayo: Hellman's. Baloney too (pre-sliced) and salami (also) yellow bright yellow mustard and cheddar sandwiches (or was it pre-sliced and individually wrapped American Cheese—was that just corn syrup and coloring?). I think it was only Debbie who ate the sliced, individually wrapped American cheese for me it was cheddar I'm sure. So so good. I liked my school lunches. I think I liked milk too, I did later anyway by eighth grade with Nadine mostly Nestle chocolate powder mixed in and then lettuce and mayo sandwiches on white bread. And she had cooks! Would make amazing dinners, but that was the after school snack we chose, sometimes, usually more than one sandwich and more than one glass of chocolate milk. Nadine could handle it being around 6' but me at a measly 5'3"? Maybe shorter still then. I eventually got to 5'4" but now I'm also shorter. Don't even want an accurate measurement now too depressing. Breakfast in Stanford I don't remember I do remember sitting down for dinner at that table but I don't remember at all what we had. I just remember the lunches. And beef jerky but I think that was later too when I had candy spending money and would buy the Bazooka 1 cent bubble gums and the Charleston Chews the Paydays (what a name) and the Reeses and the jerky and in San Fran the Tomo-Ame rice paper covered ginger chews with the little toys in the box and chocolate covered ants.

I was pretty upset when Marilyn Monroe died like the rest of the world. Now we're still in 1962 for that. And already had a pretty close connection with death lots of death all the time. Both my mother's parents already dead my grandmother from breast cancer. I remember her huge edema arm I guess they removed nodes under that one. Baby Sheila was named after both of them. My mother's sister was going to die in a few years also breast cancer. An aunt was going to kill herself jump from the 11th floor a few years after that and of course my father full of anxiety from the Holocaust, death and fear all around that one. I don't think he had said anything directly to me about it yet, but maybe, and soon enough anyway he started flowing books and nightmares my way. Sheila's summer camp and she was really young like eight or probably younger actually waking them in the night telling them the Nazis were after them and they needed to run. What was the thinking there? Good thing for the camp the liability industry wasn't booming yet.

Just don't feel fear, that was one way I reacted to the whole death environment, the air I breathed, not to mention dragging my petrified mother for mammograms from a young age. To think death was okay. Have to say it probably never did me any good that façade that I believed but at this diagnosis I'm living under it went out the window. Never was so terrified at the high holy days with someone breathing on me stuff that sounded pretty Catholic to me that it was the day of judgement coming would my name be written in the book of life—go to *shul!* A real one. Not me saying this, but a friend. I tried to apologize to everyone I could think of. Most were a little mystified and I stopped short of my full list. Never never felt fear like that making up for sixty years with little of it. And I was having a scan the day before Yom Kippur.

My father was a bit of a clean or neat freak. When the faculty club didn't work out he moved to a singles complex in Redwood City, a high rise—also before it was *Redwood City*. He had a one bedroom apartment with a balcony we have some weird holiday card pics from—the only holiday pictures we ever sent out, I guess he slipped that in while they were separated since it would never have flown when they were together—one bathroom and a kitchen that had a pass through to the living room, no dining area but I think there was a small table in the kitchen. Yeah, definitely a small, round Formica table. Anyway, that's where he'd make the mashed potato flakes and steak and peanuts for snacks, Planter's salted, and there was a swimming pool. But before we would leave to go home (his apartment was never ever called our home or even his home, not by him and not by us and certainly not by my mother) we'd have to clean and erase any trace of our having been there fold up the cots clean the coffee table—the fancy long black oval 1950s designer thing that my parents had bought together like the Danish matching dresser drawers that each of them took one of put away every and any thing. Our living room looked a little weird without that large oval, a big empty space where it had been. They certainly acted like the separation was real, did they each think it was? I am not so sure. Maybe he did when he started dating but maybe she didn't she did have a lot of bluster factor going on always. I remember the powder blue set of Freuds on his shelf. Children weren't supposed to be there and the swinging singles would hate us in the pool. The women with their very very very low-cut bathing suits and all the make-up. I don't remember the men. But we would always get in the pool and stay in a long time, it was clear we were not wanted there. The garage was under the building and my father would let us ride on the roof of his Dodge Dart—that had now over 200,000 miles on it, he was very proud of that—or on the hood. Crazy by today's standards but were there even seat belts then? Maybe but I don't think anyone used them.

Oy, the separation dragged on even when the impression I started to get from my mother was that really it was over. I mean they saw each other more and more and my mother was always making comments about the singles' club my father lived in as she called it. She was antsy again and drew him in to her activities in San Francisco some political activities some just fun nights out at jazz clubs or readings by Ferlinghetti and other poets in North Beach at the City Lights. They included some of their friends from Berkeley sometimes on these outings sometimes new political comrades of my mother and even occasionally some of the Stanford group though that was rarer. They were back to themselves and knew it.

"We just got a bit off-course wouldn't you say, Walt?" my mother said one night during a break between sets at that night's venue. "I mean the quiet Stanford thing just isn't us never was never will be."

"But I love my job my institute the research I'm doing it is everything I could have concocted for myself. I get to set the agenda get to design the studies have a really great team of researchers what more could I ask for?"

"But that doesn't mean we have to do that life there, does it?"

"What's so bad, we built the house our kids have friends are safe are happy good schools we have friends and the group is pretty interesting," my father was rattling off the positives without taking a breath as fast as he could since he knew he'd be interrupted, they did still know each other inside out and could have mouthed the other's words before they were said.

"But it's deadly there! The biggest excitement on campus is when they built the new swimming pool or fixed the faculty club lounge it's like their heads are all so deep in the sand they don't know what's happening in the world and maybe don't care unless it involves a longitudinal research study. My biggest excitement is teaching painting to kids out of our garage! I can't do it, Walt, I can't," she said almost screeching to a pitch then and there as the musicians were gearing up to start again. She did have a dramatic flair which served her well in politics.

"What are you saying what are you proposing?" my father was feeling confused and a bit scared.

"Let's move. Let's move here to the city where there's life and troubles and activism. I mean Oakland would be even better but this would be good enough even with all the pastels and the genteel stuff I don't quite get there's a lot going on I could really sink my teeth into and already have! We need to be together on this, please Walt, I'm dying there on Casanueva. I love you and I love our dream but that wasn't I mean it isn't it, we took a wrong turn without realizing it!"

"We just built the house. I like the house it works for us, what are you saying? And the mortgage? Another move? And I'll have such a commute and we'll need two cars in a city and I don't like cities! You know I don't, they scare me so much potential for harm in them."

"Calm down, it's not much of a city probably never will be and we won't need two cars and someone some new fancy faculty hire will jump to move into our house come on you know that's true its brand new and its very nice and a great cul-de-sac—no," she put up a hand to shush my father, knowing what he was about to say, "I'm not convincing myself to stay, just saying it's an attractive buy for the right family and it won't take long I'm sure. We never worried about the money part before and Stanford is generous that way it'll probably even pay our moving expenses. Let's rent let's never own a house again it's not us. Never will be."

"Maybe we could give Casanueva a little more time?" my father was weakening in a weak position and they both knew it.

"I think we gave it too much time and it almost ruined us, look we're separated, how crazy is that? Even Dora knew it was nuts and she's never been all that wild about me let's face it."

"What do you mean, my mother loves you and loves our kids but yes she did keep shaking her head on this visit."

And so it went the debate continued on for a while but as was predictable she won out or her reasoning such as it was won out and move we did again crazy though this one seems to San Fran. Kissed the designer home and Casanueva goodbye and off the five of us went sans dog who had run away some months ago which I forgot to mention here, it was awful all the searching we did for him driving around calling out his name but to no avail.

ON TO A VIEW OF
ALCATRAZ PRISON

THE CORNER OF UNION AND Taylor in the heart of Chinatown, verging on the Italians of North Beach and the topless go-go establishments like the Carol Doda, still there I think. Funny to think that's an attraction, paying money to go into a crowded dark room and watch someone bounce around grotesquely super inflated breasts. Some fantasy about being a nursing infant again when the breasts really were that large relative to the baby's small body? next stop back to the womb? Think about the movies then too like *Goldfinger* which came out that year replete with Pussy Galore yeah that was really her name! and spray painting a nude curvy large breasted (a woman of course, think Guerrilla Girls poster about nudes in the Met virtually all female) body with gold. Juxtapose that with Julie Andrews as Mary Poppins, same year. Okay a lot to take in for a little kid especially a girl. Not such a big city really, at eight years old I would walk all over. Barbara the babysitter turned stewardess had a grandmother who lived in a beautiful home on one of the hills of San Fran maybe Nob, anyway with a beautiful really beautiful rose garden in the back. So manicured and symmetrical. That really appealed to me, order. Two long rows of roses with grass in the middle and little brick borders going the length so you could walk down and smell and look and look and smell.

Funny to think of that serene and static garden against the backdrop of all that was happening that year a year of disorder (I don't know if there are any years of order, try to find one and let me know). It was the year of Beatlemania after all—throngs of screaming teenagers the *Ed Sullivan Show* with the Beatles and the really great shoe that Ed put on that night for seventy-three mil viewers. That's a lot even by today's internet standards! Everything was Beatles the haircuts the music considered scandalous then—*I Want to Hold Your Hand*, was that one of the shocking ones? Also the year Johnson signed the Civil Rights Act while Mandela was sentenced to life on Robben Island. Vietnam. Protests and arrests at UC Berkeley already then. 1964 not yet '68 or '67 even. Stuff that would never ever happen now like Che Guevara addressing the General Assembly at the UN. The year the gorgeous Cassius became Muhammad Ali I remember that and remember not understanding I don't know what I didn't understand but I didn't.

So, why did we move to San Fran? Well, my father was unhappily ensconced in that singles' high-rise as I've said definitely not a good fit for him. Not that he wasn't dating he was including some of my teachers and friend's mothers and such and as I've said Stanford was eroding my mother's state of mind and purpose and with the separation it was hell for her men married faculty members friends of the fam would hit on her campus cops would hit on her, as I've alluded to before especially the scary scene with the two cops coming right up to the door when they knew she was home alone. When they parted ways inexplicably really in the macro sense I mean they were like soul mates and knew it, they both did. Still in her impulsive way no sooner had they separated then she was packing us all up in her mind to a city somewhere she could dig in to something meaningful. That mental picture oddly included my father. Time told that image was correct. In San Fran there was plenty of politicking to do for her lots of anti-poverty work lots of protesting against urban renewal and she was quickly in with Marxist leftist circles and felt better. Her urgency meant leaving the dream house still unsold and that did take a while as it turned out. They made a beeline for an apartment in the middle of Chinatown, that is where we landed with a loud kerplunk. My father learned to be comfortable parking his car on those steep San Fran hills and he drove back and forth to work day in and day out with no more coming home for lunch. He really missed that and I think my mother did not. One less thing to do during a day that she had already begun to pack with meetings and recon stuff. Sheila must have gone with her at least until we found a baby sitter and later Marta whom we made room for by having Debbie and Sheila share and my mother and father in what was supposed to be a living room and certainly no study for anyone no even thought of the den we didn't build into the Casanueva house, I wonder if that was why it wasn't selling I mean people wanted dens in those days probably still do. And maybe a two car garage? It was California after all no snow to shovel or brush off the car but still heat and sun and hard winter rains. Not to mention the fires now but a garage wouldn't protect against that anyway just the opposite.

And move and live we did in an apartment building that other than us housed Chinese people who were mostly Chinese-only speaking. I couldn't even properly hear the sounds made in that language let alone try to reproduce them. I went to the Sara B. Cooper Public School on Filbert Street, still there, for about half of third grade. Mrs. Walker was the teacher and she loved to talk about how good she was for having adopted two children. Julian and Johnna and Janey were in the class, the rest were kids who spoke different dialects of Chinese and virtually no English. Mrs. Walker therefore decided to teach Mandarin to have a common language going in the room. I can still count to ten but that's about it long time ago though. Nevertheless she still had to teach the standard curriculum which included spelling—in English—so she picked simple words and I had so many gold stars next to my name on this big board hanging in the room with everyone's name on it. I couldn't spell and had a miniscule vocabulary but that I could do. Probably the only third grade situation to be found in which I'd get high marks for spelling. Week after week of gold stars. Recess we played Chinese jump rope which consisted of doing contortions with an elastic loop banded around two kids' ankles to make a long rectangle.

It's the first time I became aware of the whole bomb shelter thing. First time I was in a school with desks in rows we were supposed to sit at all day. Crazy idea for kids, always was always will be. We'd be drilled for air raids and getting under our desks. The duck and cover thing. What was that going to help anyway, those little plywood or whatever laminate desks? Crouching under Formica was going to save us from attack? News reels of people building bomb shelters in their backyards—really, to protect them from nuclear fallout? But that's what President Kennedy advised just a few years back. Build 'em, stock 'em. Have a two-week supply— two weeks? Really? Okay. I recently read scores of interviews with nuclear scientists at Livermore Labs in Berkeley taken in the eighties—taken by one Margaret Brenman Gibson and stored in the nuclear room of her New England home. She'd go and interview these nuclear scientists and she did it for five years and then go over to Tiburon and talk it over with the Eriksons, Erik and Joan that is, all tape recorded recorded badly I couldn't make out a lot of it but very very interesting stuff and just one of the many major projects she undertook not to mention her anti-nuclear activism and lucky me I had access to all of her papers most of them quite astounding and full of the hard laborious labor she put into everything she did. It took me four years just to sift through organize and read all her papers let alone do anything with them—they were about the whys of putting so much creativity into destruction. Hoping to find a biopsychosocial model of it all. Didn't get much in the way of answers on that one but some of them had crazy sounding plans for saving themselves. One scientist had devised a retractable one-hundred-foot straw that he was going to shove through the nuclear snow from his bunker and breathe! That was from one of the world's geniuses?

That's when I discovered the wonderful Tomo-Ame, the rice paper covered ginger candy not to mention chocolate covered ants.

I could roam around after school as much as I wanted or do things with my bunch, although in reality I was mostly wandering alone and sometimes with either Johnna or Janey or maybe both and with Julian when our two families were together. They had moved from Woodside and left the Peninsula School, Julian had two older sisters Julie and Thelma, for divorce and a Coit Tower apartment-ish place. Ish because it was a bit or maybe not just a bit odd and we rarely went inside. Ariella had of course first put her husband—their father—through medical school by working as a waitress and then through psychiatric residency and then analytic training. That is a lot of plate slinging for a very very long time. Abe married the beautiful Bethany with her long auburn hair after the divorce and grew a beard. Now they lived in the house in Woodside without Ariella without the kids. Julian didn't like the beard at all. He'd talk about it a lot while making his very complex ship and sail boat drawings. I wonder if Julian has a beard now?

Ariella always said she wasn't a good mother (isn't that what mothers are helped to think pretty much all the time?) and I re-member her telling me this after my first was born and about how her breasts were bound after each birth by the nurses in the hospital so that they wouldn't fill with milk and sag. She eventually moved to Connecticut alone and out in the woods cut her hair off and I remember thinking she was a lesbian. She dropped out of sight and our lives for a few maybe many years. Back in the San Fran days, no before on her porch in Woodside spinning wool and then in San Fran hanging in jazz clubs but I don't know what she did for work. My mother was always political and active that way, Ariella wasn't I'm pretty sure. Oh yeah, in Woodside, we'd all play the spanking game. Julian's sisters made that one up. Just remember Julian get-ting spanked by his sisters who seemed to be enjoying that a lot spanking the only boy and their brushing and brushing me and my sister's hair. Abe with his pancakes that had corn kernels in them, I found them very yucky I mean corn kernels in pancakes what kind of an idea is that? I think I still would be a bit repulsed by them now.

I'd go to the movies alone too. I think there was a theater down the hill somewhere, anyway I'd walk to it. Without fail some man would sit down near me, reveal himself, and masturbate for the length of the movie. And movies used to be longer then so that was for a long time, so much rubbing. And I'd just sit there, I think watching the movie. But, really, come on, next to a messy eight year old girl? Why was that fun? Why was that a thing to do? Do you understand it?

I don't know why I went to the movies alone, it seems a little weird. More like a family kind of thing at that age. Where was everyone else? No idea. That's when Amy worked for us, coming over after school type hours before the adults got home. I don't remember what she did except iron and cuss me out for what Johnna (Chinese) and Janey (first generation Irish American) were saying. Racist stuff in general and specifically about Amy and how I couldn't like her, I argued against but I don't think Amy heard my part in it. I think I liked Amy but I don't remember why or really anything about her except how she looked. I think she wore some kind of uniform, like those white or maybe blue dresses with aprons, but that doesn't make sense probably her clothes just looked sort of like that. Very heavy and very dark skinned. Climbing up the stairs to our apartment—what floor? maybe the third?—couldn't have been fun for her. Later Marta Quiroga moved in from Bolivia to take care of us. She was early twenties, maybe younger, dark honey colored skin— more on her skin soon—and very beautiful. She moved with us to Berkeley at the end of the year too. Yes, we kept on moving on and on. Her sister Tuki also got a job in San Fran at the same time. Also beautiful and very nice but neither as much as Marta. Tuki quickly got married Marta did not.

When she arrived in the US, Marta came toting alpaca ponchos for us and we loved them and wore them probably until they finally wore out years and years even to Berkeley and then the Oakland border and then New York via a short very short a month maybe stint in Connecticut. That last move east was a real blow to the fam as you'll hear about later in the midst of the height of the protest years yup 1968 from one frying pan into another. She came camping with us on the beach and everywhere really. It was over campfires that Marta showed me how she would burn the hair off her arms (for beauty). Once my dad wanted to speak with her privately and took her into her room in our apartment and closed the door. My mother to this day makes a huge deal over how traumatic that was for Marta. I'm not so sure, she didn't seem upset.

"That's not done in Bolivia, a woman alone in a room with a man," my mother said over and over. Not sure there isn't some kind of subtle paternalistic so to speak racism in this but that's what my mother said admonishing my father for his horrible act. "We could lose her over such insensitivity!" she bellowed when Marta was out.

There was a fireplace in what was intended as a living room but was my parents' bedroom. I would make a lot of fires in there, also alone. How did I have all this alone time, I don't know. Yeah, an old-fashioned apartment, the kind people would maybe kill for literally in New York now. Maybe more so in crazy sky-rocketed super wealthy and super poor San Fran of today. The living room had bay windows looking out at something. To the right of that room was the kitchen which could fit a small table. Small but I guess big enough to be functional for us. Those two rooms were at the end of a long-ish hallway. Next to my mother's room was mine, decked out with my canopy bed I wasn't going to let go of any time soon. I would take myself to the movies and around town but across my pillow were almost a couple dozen pacifiers, all in use at the time. Below my pillow was a flank of dolls—I didn't allow myself to have favorites, not a favorite pacifier, not a favorite doll. Couldn't even think it. Next to my room was the one Debbie and Sheila shared with bunkbeds. Those two were always getting ear infections and given antibiotics by the dumpster full. I got off easier with high fevers, ice baths, strep throat and penicillin by the carton full. I don't remember my mother getting sick, she must have but also of course mothers can't get sick, what would happen then? Then, back to the hall, at the end, Marta's room. So that was one side of the hall, on the other side of the hall after Marta's room was the door to get out and then midway down the hall were two halves of a bathroom. One, the first one, closest to the outer door was a toilet, that's it. On the back of the door was a huge poster of a Humphrey Bogart portrait. Head on, hands on table, cigarette in one hand and the pack in front of his hands. Chesterfields maybe not sure. His stare was positioned to be looking straight at you wherever you were in the room. In this case that was easy since it was a small, narrow room just wide and long enough to fit a toilet. Next to that room was another only slightly larger room with a tub/shower and a sink. It was kind of convenient to have it divided up that way. Weird there was no even tiny sink in with the toilet though. But we didn't know about washing hands then anyway.

I used to walk to Saint Peter and Paul Church on Union Square a lot. I don't know if I ever went in but maybe. I don't know if I knew you could do that then, just walk in. That still feels disrespectful to me, going into a church I have no intention of worshipping or anything else religious in. Lots of pigeons in the square. And old people and homeless people. I don't know if I realized then that they were homeless. I don't know what I thought—again my thinking as a kid was pretty foggy and sometimes even as an adult my mind just fogs over and I'll get this uncomfortable feeling I remember an extreme time that happened at my cousin Carol's in Sheepshead Bay. When I came back to San Fran over a decade later as a logician of all things so many homeless people on Market Street, so many. Well-dressed people bustling around by then—late seventies—but a clear, huge problem in the city. The Bay Area being a relatively good place to be homeless, if there is such a thing, given the climate and all but still and especially with all the crazy scale wealth there now. If all the tech dot-commers would just give a dollar for every thousand they earn (earn?) that could probably go a good distance to helping the people around them every day who barely have anything, wouldn't you say? I remember running in the Berkeley Hills up into Tilden Park and so many people popping up out of the bushes, and this was early, like 5:30 a.m. type of time. Funny, I thought of those people as homeless and didn't totally recognize that I was on so many levels. Eventually moved into my window-less miniscule office round the clock sleeping in a sleeping bag I had since I was five on the Casanueva balcony on the tiny amount of floor space but also homeless on a deeper level that I have really always been. An internal kind of permanent exile from a life that's a bit more grounded. A theme throughout and always but still getting so way ahead again.

I think I was walking on Green Street when Monkey Face accosted me. From behind, put his hand over my mouth and said something but I don't remember what any more. Maybe he wanted money, I don't remember that part. All the kids knew he was out and about, but kind of like the Loch Ness monster I never saw him, didn't know anyone who had seen him, knew of lots of people who claimed to have seen him. But there he was, grabbing me from behind. Much bigger than me. He was what then was just called retarded so I don't know what was actually wrong with him. He was kind of pudgy and had a whisky bunch of hairs on his upper lip, not quite a mustache. His speech was low and breathy and his words sounded like they had to be propelled out. I think he did want money, he probably didn't know what he wanted but maybe he did. Anyway, I was scared I just bit him I think on a finger and ran and it worked. I don't know if the pain stunned him or I could run faster (not so likely, I was a non-athletic eight year old and much shorter than him) or neither and once I scooted away he forgot about me. I don't know why I didn't tell the police officers Monkey Face was Chinese, I think it's because I was ashamed to say that to a Chinese officer or that's how it felt, like I would be embarrassed to tell him that. My mother didn't have any idea it was well known that he was wandering around the neighborhood but she was mostly angry at me that I didn't give the full information. That I pretended not to see color. Why wasn't that a good thing? Not the pretending part. Not sure if my father ever knew about the incident, by the time he got home it had probably already blown over and was out of my mother's mind.

That was the year my cousin Susie, my age and we were nine then, had to have a lump removed from a breast. Susie was always reading the *Nancy Drew* books and the *Bobbsey Twins*. I didn't get the attraction much preferring *Island of the Blue Dolphins* and *Keep Your Courage Up Sarah Noble*. She was a DES baby. My aunt (by marriage to one of my father's brothers not by blood) died of breast cancer and it was said it was from the DES, a synthetic estrogen. There's been a lot of trouble with giving synthetic hormones to people. The DES babies have had a hard and diseased time, the girl DES babies anyway. The boys got off easier. So anyway that was 1955 or '56 that my aunty took it but they already knew in 1953 that it was an ineffective drug (at preventing premature births and mis-carriages) but kept on doling it out to pregnant women clear until 1971. Eighteen years later! How do you figure that? Did they make enough money on it by then and suddenly "discover" that it causes harm? Both of my female cousins from that family both DES babies got breast cancer as adults, their brother nothing.

That was all on the East coast, back in San Fran Rusty and I would go down to Fisherman's Wharf not at all the way it is now (so not at all!) and buy a loaf of sourdough (unsliced of course, sliced bread is an abomination if you ask me) and a big, hard shell crab. I don't know, don't have any idea how we knew to do that at eight and then nine years old but we did. And, how did we have that much money I don't know either. I'd go down there to the Bay beach and watch the Polar Bears swim, it was so cold! Bare chested. Of course, I'd go in too, just didn't even think of swimming out to Alcatraz, then a prison and kind of mysterious. The Polar Bears would do it, out and back. I don't know how far that is but it's far. And now quite toxic that San Fran Bay is lots of spills and dumpings and just general garbage later.

That year in San Fran we had a Seder in our apartment and my father led it—by then my mother was in an urban planning mas-ter's program at UC Berkeley with a Sears Roebuck fellowship but sexism still reigned, didn't it, I mean it was only the early sixties.

Around that small kitchen table but it worked and all the dishes and Seder platter and accompaniments fit well enough for us. After the meal I don't know where my sisters went—maybe watching TV—but my parents stayed at the table and talked and talked and talked for a long long time. They were having a great time reminiscing about Seders in Sheepshead Bay about their zooming off on their wheels after their wedding as fast as they could and about funny family stories on both sides. I kept coming into the kitchen to pour myself a little more wine, I was allowed to have it as part of the Seder but I also am guessing I had some organic issue with either alcohol or sugar or both. I poured a little more and then a little more and more and was drunk. Whoa, that felt bad! No one noticed any of it, I am quite sure. A pattern was born or bloomed depending on how you think about it. It's almost worse if someone did notice and didn't do anything. That's a habit I kept with a lot of things, a little and a little more and a bit more, and on and on. Bad habit except that I think there was some internal draw that got triggered young.

That summer we six including Marta moved to Berkeley, went to Hawaii without Marta, and to the Cape also without Marta? Seems a little improbable all of that and also where was Marta? We didn't have much money which makes the whole thing very unlikely although we did finally manage to sell the Casanueva house that helped some but most of it was mortgage backed anyway. Wait a minute, back up, midyear I switched out of Sarah B Cooper to a private school in Marin, Marin Country Day School for the second half of third grade and had a Walker-like teacher there too. The first half of fourth grade I was there too with Ms. Bogardus, I liked her. A lot of playing of four square at that school and horses, the game on foot that is, pretending to gallop around. Well not pretending to gallop just pretending to be horses. So maybe we still lived in San Fran then I remember the bus driver, her name was Betty Donner and always talked about descending from the Donner clan on the Donner trail (didn't they all die?). That must have been the year I got my white patent leather go-go boots. I wore them all the time, walking around the town, to the Haight and the Golden Gate Panhandle, past the Italian cafes to the Wharf, Knob Hill, Lombard Street, I roamed around a lot in those cool boots feeling very avant-garde. Got garter straps around then too and the nylons to go with them, no panty hose in those days. Do any of you remember or know how they stayed on? They attached to these four straps hanging down from the garter belt, two for each leg one front one back, and the nylon was snagged by a metal hoop that forced the fragile fabric over a little button, crazy huh? I mean who would do that? So many women and for so long, think about it. I loved my nylons. They certainly weren't the most comfortable clothing contraption ever made I must confess and the nylon would pull out of the holders pretty easily if one moved too much.

The second half of fourth grade to the Walden School in Berkeley and taking many public transit buses—three at least—to get there, me and Julian did it together most of the time. We must have moved to Benvenue Street in Berkeley after fourth grade. So Benvenue and Walden and those guys who lived upstairs, maybe college students? And Lila who lived maybe next door for fifth grade and Webster Street, Patty, and Walden for sixth. So what happened to my father's commute you might wonder? Okay, with that question now let's back up a little.

After third grade, that summer, we went to Hawaii with Josh's family. Josh my age, and has become fervently right-wing in Israel now, Daniel roughly Debbie's age and Aubrey who I remember as a baby in Berkeley so she must be a few years younger than Sheila at least. Things haven't turned out well for her. And we rented little bungalows in Hanalei from an old Hawaiian man who taught us how to cut open an aloe leaf and slather the gel onto our sunburns. It really worked. There wasn't much in Hanalei then but there was the Ching Young store and one bar and my mother and Lillian would go to it at night. My father hadn't come along on that trip since he was in the final throws of one of his studies and took the opportunity to stay at the faculty club again at Stanford while we were away to work round the clock putting the finishing touches on the report having graduate students check and recheck the numbers and fine tooth comb the galleys with his red pencil.

We chewed a lot of sugar cane on that trip and picked pineapples, I had never seen one growing before or had any idea where the sugar in those C&H boxes came from. These days one is cautioned not to chew on cane stalks, too many chemicals on and in them but then no one thought much about that stuff outside of Adelle Davis, and did she or was that not her focus the chemicals, I'm not sure. I mean all the powders she recommended downing for example in her pep-up drink, I don't know if her concern was chemicals in them. I think so, I remember one line from her about a drip and a drip and you've got a whole flood. Have to look back at her books, she was right about so much.

I took my daughters to Hanalei remembering its beauty. The Ching Young store was still there but of course a lot had been built up in the decades in between. Still beautiful with gorgeous hikes and luaus. We went to one touristy luau which actually was great, the food was great and through a dance show it told the history or some version of it of Hawaii. The other was more authentic. While we were there a protest was going on against mainlanders coming in and buying up land homes and properties. There were many bed sheets with spray paint hung all over the place saying things like "Mainlanders go home."

It seems not that likely but I'm pretty sure we also went to the Cape that same summer also with Lillian's family this time sharing a little two story house in Truro and another long couplet of plane flights. Josh was always singing Rolling Stones songs and Daniel was looking for hermit crabs, there seemed to be something wrong with Daniel. Always marching around screaming hee-uw, it seemed weird. I remember Lillian's leather pocketbook she wore over one shoulder had a cool metal latch on the front. When we all moved to New York someone cut the shoulder straps when she wasn't looking seated on a bus and took the bag with everything in it of course. Josh was very musical and a math whiz (remember how in Kindergarten at Peninsula he was always toting an abacus around?)

and a chess master of sorts. He froze at competitions though. Later he played trombone but that was stolen out of his arms in New York also. We all moved in '68 and those were rough years in New York right through the seventies. Lindsey's Fun City years but still.

Anyway, the Cape. My uncle Josh and family must have been there too but I don't remember them and you'd think I would since me and Holly are basically the same age. So maybe they weren't there but I think we probably went because they were. Josh always gave us Steiff stuffed animals, a really cool brand, his family or maybe just he liked them a lot. They were beautiful and soft. Anyway, ours would disappear, every one of them. And I have always been someone who does not lose anything, not umbrellas, not earrings, not pacifiers, nothing probably ever. So many decades later my mother told me my father would take them away, the Steiffs, throw them out I guess, having been made in Germany. Wouldn't let anything German in the house, not for a second. Wouldn't speak the—his native—language either. There was a store there in Truro that was there forever that we'd go to called Scoony Younguns or at least that's what I remember it was called don't know about the spelling but now it's a fancy fancy expensive take-out called Jams, the way so many things have gone or went in the eighties nineties, now just a lot of empty storefronts all over in cities towns and tiny backwaters even. The Briar Lane jams and jellies shack is still there in Truro on Route 6 that has really been there forever and one of the few that has remained how it once was.

We're talking early to mid-sixties here with the German ban although my father stayed with it longer. It felt like the war had just happened and the wounds were all open, with a lot of traumatized refugees that no one knew how to help and often didn't even try. Another result of the boom years of post war, women moved back into homemaker positions, and if they were lucky enough shipped out to the isolated spanking new suburbs without jobs but with babies babies babies and diapers and bottles and new-fangled gadgets of all sorts to take up time (supposed to be time saving though, right, again my favorite example seems to be the electric can opener, come on, really did we ever need that?? We had one, avocado green it was, I remember using it thinking it was just a thing one has not something to notice or think about the whys of. So many things like that then, they were great because we could have them, conspicuous consumption was a good thing. Recently read about a family in Los Angeles, the city proper, so on a very small plot of land that is completely off the grid and does not use the solar power it generates for anything inessential, like can openers, like grinding things, like a lot of stuff many people take for granted using electricity for. And on this little speck in LA they grow enough produce to feed themselves and sell the rest to local restaurants. Collect rain water when it rains, planted pots in the ground to hold and slowly seep out the water and lots of cool stuff like that, we should all be imitating them).

It was the era of help wanted notices being written thus: help-wanted-men or help-wanted-women. Two different columns. Right in the newspapers. Couldn't do that so blatantly now. Is that better? I know I'm not supposed to ask. Plentiful and varied jobs around for the men for the asking, for some men anyway, like some men I know some of my advisors later, just walked on campus and got tenured jobs in all kinds of departments without publishing without having done really anything yet—unheard of now, there'll be no more tenure soon enough—and building, building, building. And selling. Selling people on suburban tracts, gadgets, appliances, cars, gasoline—remember the little 76 balls for the car antenna? We don't have antennae like that anymore on cars or the little balls and we know how dirty and destructive gas is even though we keep on guzzling it. We just don't think about putting tigers in our tanks anymore, we do it at least with a little guilt sometimes but mostly with a lot of rationalization. The American Dream did have to do with the war. And the war permeated so many homes, ours or at least me. Just read a study that trauma can be passed through sperm. Wow! I think I got a double dose. I got soaked in the war horror and became a bit numb to it on the surface. In retrospect, acting out the trauma in so many ways and for so long blind to the whole thing. Part of the internal exile too, I'm sure. I mean my father was a literal exile, passport revoked, citizenship revoked, fear of torture and death, language even revoked and that includes a whole conceptual scheme, a whole way of thinking and being—it's not just words, it encapsulates a way of life. Different languages lead to different ways of thinking, even within the same family of languages. Let's face it. My father was an exile and I think as a result of his example and direct teaching amongst other significant factors (maybe his sperm) later I was an emotional exile, an internal exile, homeless in my body and self. More later. I did always have some sort of cut-off valve. Just something a little cut out or missing or something like being a lot in a fog, not processing somehow in a timely or even ever sort of way. Some connector thing that wasn't there. A lot of after the factness but more than that a sort of never-ness and inability to grasp and feel certain things. Maybe more so-called masculine of me. Probably had I been a male it would have read different inside and out and been played differently. There was always some lacking thing, some difference, some alone-ness like an exile from birth, that seems like the right way to put it.

It was third grade when I flew to New York alone to visit my grandmother, Omi, and also stayed at my cousin Holly's house. I remember feeding ducks with my grandmother at some pond or something near Gracie Mansion and going to Saks in Westchester with my aunt Rochelle and Holly, it's where Rochelle's mother Ma Rose worked as a sales person behind one of those counters. Maybe it was Lord and Taylor, that sounds more correct. I bought black and also white nail polish there, probably really Rochelle bought it but maybe I did, I saved money always to spend at special times like that. Painted checkerboards on my nails with it. Later, just all black nails by fourth grade (ahead of my time, eh? Black jeans too, always black and tight tight. I'd have to take a long time shimmying the pants up my legs and over my hips, skin tight and beyond that was my look. Black pants, black nails and the red and white striped T-shirt that Russell gave me, it had been his and I almost never took it off), I remember that on my visit to Walden mid-fourth grade and also not talking at all, they couldn't figure anything out about me not by design just by fact. I think I started going there the next week or maybe even the next day.

On that trip Omi took me to Radio City Music Hall and we saw the Rockettes and *The Unsinkable Molly Brown* starring Debbie Reynolds! We went to Altman's and that's when I got the green dress outfit. All this sounds like Omi was wealthy, she was anything but. I think in Zwickau they were well off enough, my grandfather was some kind of businessman, I don't know what Omi did. She did have three sons. She showed me which of her jewelry she'd give me when I was older and Orit and her husband were visiting from Israel and came over and we talked to Suzanne Lieberman downstairs, the electrolycist and Omi's friend. When she died, Omi did leave me some of her jewelry and I think some for Debbie and Sheila but my father held onto all of it saying we were too young (I was nine) even though I never never lose anything as I said and didn't as a kid either, ever. Anyway he said it was all stolen, but in retrospect I think he got rid of it somehow because it was German even though it was his mother's and she had given it to me not him! It went the way of the Steiffs. A lot of stuff didn't make sense in those days and his story about the theft was amongst them. Said he put it all in his green, Samsonite suitcase on the move across the country—getting ahead here too—and the movers just took the suitcase. Well, who puts a small suitcase with jewelry in it that might have looked valuable even though it probably wasn't and gives it to movers? Didn't make sense at all, I knew that, just didn't understand what the truth was. I don't know if I've ever learned to be suspicious, just too literal minded. Even with his visceral migraines and nightmares about the war and giving me all those books about anti-Semitism the war and I don't know what else.

Back at Stanford, in his office in that beautiful building up the winding staircase, he showed me page proofs. Back to my father, that is. Not like today via some kind of edit doc file online but the actual paper galleys, long sheets on yellowish or ivory anyway paper and mark-ups by hand. In pencil. I didn't really get what it was all about, but I liked it. These little snippets somehow became meaningful in my thick seemingly somewhat impenetrable psyche. Like when he was making pancakes, I'm sure from a mix who knows why but in those days everything was from a mix or frozen or both, and he started telling me about negative numbers. I was probably seven. Like something exploded inside my head. It didn't really have anywhere to go then but I think the explosion kind of thing sat there waiting. The whole negative number concept was intriguing. Later he'd send me his publications, books, papers. So did his brother Jay at some point too, maybe after my father died. Young but maybe not as young as I will, we'll see. Pollyanna pops up in me every now and then. Been having more dreams and wake up wondering whether they mean I'm going to live or I'm going to die. They're ambiguous. At least I think they are, you might not. Not so much the one from last night:

On the corner of 86th and Broadway with my two daughters, not sure their ages, maybe a bit younger like adolescents. Zoe—again Zoe principal in the dream, why is that?—disappears and I go down to the subway station there looking for lockers—lockers? And I ask if girls disappear at that corner there on Broadway to someone with their back turned and she just silently and slowly nods her head. I don't find "lockers" and that's it.

Had that one the night after I signed, finally signed real versions of my documents except not a living will. Couldn't figure that one out or maybe I did but certainly everything else. Some choices I just think shouldn't be the person's, in this case me, but rather the survivors. Like the dying and dead shouldn't determine the funeral or not funeral and all those questions. And maybe not the pulling the plug kind of thing, shouldn't that be up to whoever is living? Other things too just can't or don't want to think about them right now. Enough that it took a year and two different law firms and too much money paid to finally get the documents in shape.

Found myself wondering, debating really whether it's the Jews or the Christians who are right. I mean after death is there nothing or something? Am I going to just slowly or not since maybe I'll be ashes rot underground or somewhere above it or is my spirit soul or whatever we want to call it going to watch over what's happening on earth? Decided I'm going crazy when I caught myself at that. Sort of a middle of the night can't sleep kind of thing. Happily that has stopped rumbling around inside my head. I think I'd rather think about other unanswerable questions than that one.

I should be still on San Fran, what else about San Fran? I'm sure there's so much. It was small then and low to the ground and pastel. And the ticky-tacky on the hillside as I said as Petula Clark sang it. And Golden Gate Park and all the statues they kept uncovering, hidden under growth and vines and such. And the panhandle and Haight-Ashbury but not quite yet when we lived there and the Castro where I moved a lot later. All those streets up and down the hills with cement stairs and of course Lombard Street. Some people like some plants just can't keep being transplanted it doesn't work because they need the stability of the same soil even if it isn't the best, it's the stability factor. I think I was—am!—one of those kinds of people. I had enough trouble with the foggy brain not talking thing I had going. If you've got something a little off like I might have or maybe I developed it as a result of all the transplanting and other things but in any case it didn't work for me. Maybe if I had grown up in just one or two places. The yearly or every other yearly sometimes moving and changing friends and schools and orienting locations like where to sniff roses or where to buy candy, the switching it up all the time with no center of gravity, well it just didn't work for me. Not that everything would have been good if only but just that it and I could have been less crazy-ish clueless or whatever the correct term is.

I'm blanking on more of the San Fran of the mid-sixties but in any case we moved on to Berkeley. My mother was still in the urban planning program and my father seeing the writing on the wall applied and lobbied heavily to open an institute like his for UC Berkeley and it worked. None of it made much sense since my mother's thesis was studying urban renewal in San Fran so she was there all the time but hey I think you can tell that my parents' decision-making skills were alternative. I mean so much was alternative leaning then anyway we're getting into the second half of the sixties and things are literally up in flames in the US of A and wherever else the country was setting flames around the globe. Mid-year fourth grade I did switch to the Walden School. That year they had divided the class into a girls' section, fourth, fifth and sixth graders and a boys' section fourth, fifth and sixth graders. Ann with her MG convertible sports car I think it was actually red like sports cars are supposed to be, taught the girls and Barry taught the boys. Fifth and sixth grades were mixed and Barry taught us both years, he really liked us quite a lot and couldn't let go. Started a boarding high school up North in way northern California so we could continue. Aviva got to go, I really wanted to go. Went out for a visit from New York with my mother saying I could decide but when I did it turned out I had answered wrong. Why did she think I wouldn't come back with that answer, my friends there, Barry there, the kids built their own residences after all my dream come true in those days, maybe I'd build a version of the slinky! it smelled so good there I can still remember the scent in the early morning walking down the path to the main school building it was so calm and really great.

The day I visited Walden and yes now I'm sure I started going there the next day Ann was trying to describe the female reproductive system, periods, sex, pregnancy. The girls in that group were mostly on the older end, like Jenny and Kita. I think Reva was already there and she was my age, maybe Allison not sure. Tansi was there, she was eleven and that spring she ran away to Reno or Las Vegas I don't remember which and played whore, not sure what the played part meant at the time since she did it, we knew because it turned out quite soon after that she was pregnant and also was already a little crazy but then did go crazier and did a horrifying song and strip show outside in front of the whole school until someone took her away, to where I don't know. She didn't come back. Before that and before the running away, oh yeah Aida was in the class, older than me for sure but we became friends and we went together to Tansi's sleep-over birthday party. It was very scary, I think her parents or anyway some adults around were clearly high on something and there was just generally a lot of not understandable crazy stuff happening and we were in our sleeping bags outside and it was also kind of cold as I remember it, Aida and I decided we were too scared to stay and called but no one answered at my house. Maybe we called Aida's house too, but somehow I knew Pearl's number, or got it from 411 that used to exist in those days and just like you could call a number for the time and another for the weather, I used to love to call those numbers, and Pearl in her VW bug—yeah, another VW bug this one definitely was green—came and got us and took us to her house for the night in the Berkeley Hills. Remember in those days phones were landlines and that's it. So if you weren't near the phone and didn't hear the ring like you had water running doing dishes in the kitchen or running a bath or whatever, that was it. Answering machines weren't even a thing then. So you could dial, literally dial the number on a rotary dial that had all the numbers go from one counter clockwise around the circular dial to nine and then zero, probably the most important number. Zero actually got you to a person, an operator. If your number wasn't going through for whatever reason, you called the operator and she, usually a she, maybe always then, help-wanted-female, put you through. If you kept getting a busy signal, well, call the operator and she'd try to get through with her operator magic, that was their job. Had a friend from college who became a physicist for Bell Labs and she'd always say when meeting people at a bar or somewhere like that that she worked for the phone company. The assumption always was that she was an operator because what else could she be? so even decades later there were still rotary phones and operators. We still say we're dialing a number, even kids say it who never ever saw a rotary phone. Now we're punching in numbers to the extent that we don't just use our speed dials, clicking on an image of someone's face or something. And don't get me started on digital clocks, kids even twenty-somethings these days maybe thirty-somethings by now can't read an analog clock! what does this mean how can someone—an adult—not know how to do that?

Back to Pearl, I guess I haven't mentioned her yet. We had already known her for years. She had been in my parents' circle for a while. A biochemist who was often off on trips skiing surfing to meet guys she really wanted or seemed to want or thought she wanted to get married. She'd send us postcards with pictures of her in a bikini with guys posing with her, more than one, and she brought us salt water taffy annually when she went to Atlantic City. Somehow I did know to call her and luckily she was home and heard her phone and came to get us, that was great such a relief. I don't know what was happening at that party and probably didn't really know then either but it wasn't good. Anyway, we were very glad she came and retrieved us in the darkest part of the night and got us away from whatever it was that was going on. I wonder if Aida remembers this?

For a little cultural/historical context, remember this is the year that the Supreme Court ruled that married people could use birth control. How did this get to be a decision of the government?? How is this a matter for public scrutiny? But it was. Five years after oral contraceptives came. Legalizing abortion—why is this anyone but the woman's business?—came almost a decade later and of course is in jeopardy now, being chiseled away at bit by chunk. One gyn called my then husband in when I wanted an abortion and when he saw we were both in agreement he consented to do the procedure (giving me a general in the process, how crazy and harmful) but said he wouldn't do another, that was it, his max and final offer. Like he was confused and thought it was his choice. Gross gross gross. And that was 1980, *1980!*

We in the US of A had already been spraying Agent Orange and bombing and had Secret Operations and naming people the Viet Cong in Vietnam for years and sending multiples of ten thousand troops per month by '65. More of course on this later as the protests and the war unfold into the late sixties and first half of the seventies but the draft card burning had already blossomed at the then radical UC Berkeley. To see it now, the UC B is unrecognizable as is the town itself.

The Beatles and Rock'n'Roll were well underway by now. '65 was the year of Nader's *Unsafe at Any Speed* and later to form Nader's Raiders. Went to his museum of Tort Law in Windsor CT his hometown not too long ago and looked at all the documentation of *Unsafe* and his other path-breaking work. Bought a T-shirt. Carson's *Silent Spring* was also published just a few years before this and it continues to be an ever new reality check for us today. Odd that, isn't it?

To the South in Los Angeles this was the year of the Watts Riots, any of you remember? And the year Johnson signed the Social Security Act launching Medicare and Medicaid—Trump and his gang trying to dismantle them now along with any meager environmental protection we have in place. Like it's an Oedipal thing or something driving him to undo or redo what Obama did, I should say the little Obama got done for the environment or social welfare or other stuff that might have done some good for the 99%ers not to mention the rest of the world with all the effects our mega consumerism has on everything everywhere.

Pearl is in a nursing home now in Maryland. Older than my mother by years. My mother had me her first young even for then at twenty-three. Right out of college, a coed who married her professor—how many of those are there? So many of my profs married their undergrad students, the other ones were chasing me—and I presume others—around the classroom (and I mean that quite literally in the case of one Mark Krusmeyer) trying to get me to sleep with them, sometimes marry them, so lonely they were and getting older, only contact with women—no female colleagues, they made sure of that—was with their students and very young students since we were rarely allowed to get to grad school and then were certainly fodder for lonely or just predator profs. Getting so way ahead here. And Harvey Weinstein handcuffed in 2018, wow! He only had to plunk down a million?

So the second half of fourth grade at the pacifist-anarchist school called Walden. By the way from the beginning of third grade to the end of fourth, three schools. And then a move. But first a summer camp for two weeks with Rusty and Debbie went too. There were all kinds of activities archery and riflery both of which Debbie was very good at. Even though we were in different groups by age I could see her shooting those bull's eyes one after another, she was tiny but so focused. Sheila must've stayed home since she was probably only five if I was nine which I was. Camp over, we had probably moved. I remember the packing cause I always packed up my own stuff. I had a lot to pack, but not my pacifiers, I gave them up between third and fourth grade I know it was a big big deal. It wasn't easy at all. We had a party over it. Pretty old to be sucking on pacifiers, I'm sure I had it down to night time for quite a while before.

TO THE FLATLANDS AND TILDEN PARK FULL OF EUCALYPTUS

THE YEAR *TROUBLE WITH ANGELS* with Haley Mills came out, Rosalind Russell was in it too. I don't know why that film made such an impression on me. I did so like Haley Mills, I must say. And weird combo with *A High Wind in Jamaica* coming out the year before and taking my friends to see it for my birthday. They were freaked out, I remember thinking what babies they were it didn't seem scary to me but the Hell's Angels movies the following year did scare me and should have, I wasn't sure why but I knew it wasn't right that rape in the movies were supposed to be comical. Or maybe I didn't even know that but there was a general tenor of them that was horrifying. Then again *this past year* the very year of 2018 the domestic violence in the *Tonya Harding Story* was portrayed as comedy and the night I went people were actually really laughing. It was very eerie and horrible. People looking at me like what's wrong with me that I look so sour and stuff like that. Twilight Zone-ish.

Benvenue Street. 2619 Benvenue, I've checked the number in recent years. A two story house split into two apartments, one on the first floor where we lived and stairs on the driveway side going up to the second floor with some kind of landing outside on the top of the stairs to the second. Young men lived up there, a few. Maybe students, probably, this is Berkeley right near the UC campus. I don't remember a lot of noise from them. Lila and I baked them a fake cake, fake because we pored a ton of salt into it. I think that was our way of flirting with them. They were really nice guys who didn't want to hurt little kids' feelings so they told us it was good. We were perplexed and disappointed.

Our part of the house had a front living room with oak floors I loved to sand with some kind of electric sander and refinish and bay windows and oak window frames and shutters. I thought it was beautiful. It was in Berkeley that I discovered the architect Julia Morgan. She designed a bunch of buildings that UC owned and maybe some homes nearby. I was still a budding architect in my mind anyway. I'm pretty sure I never shared that with anyone until much later until it was almost over. I don't think I was so much solving architectural puzzles in my head anymore but just appreciating structures, like the library near us was definitely in the Frank Lloyd Wright Prairie style and I loved it, and I'd walk to Cordonices, for the slide, but really for the amphitheater style Berkeley Rose Garden. I must have somehow remembered it from when we lived in the hills next to Linda, odd though because I was at most four in the hills on Woodmont.

We also had a round, oak table with many many leaves something like thirteen of them that my mother still has. Yes, as you may have guessed, the poker game continued around this table. People from San Fran came, some old friends from the Berkeley Hills days and even a Stanford person would occasionally pop in. I would sand that table down too and oil it. That was a big job, it must be almost six feet in diameter without any leaves in. I don't know why I did those jobs, I did them alone and in silence and the whole process would take a long time. Should have been a monk but I don't think girls can do that anyway. I'd polish silver too, maybe for Omi? or did we have silver, maybe. I remember doing that polishing often with the pink pungent paste and polishing shoes which is the weirdest of all since especially in Berkeley I didn't almost ever, like really never, wear shoes. If I did it would have been Keds. Yeah I guess the white go-go boots took some polishing. I tried to remain barefoot when we moved to New York, and it lasted a while. Maybe until it got very cold. But that was a very very crazy thing to do there especially in that era of New York—it was filthy. Broken glass trash needles condoms. Yet the girls, seventh grade this is, were more concerned that I wasn't wearing a bra (which I did not need but that's never the point of social control, someone's welfare).

So Benvenue Street and fifth grade, Barry was the teacher of the now recombined boys and girls for one single grade. The school was founded by hardcore pacifist-anarchists and most of the teachers were too. That's where I first heard Miriam Makeba, I found her records in the kindergarten room that I spent a lot of time in reading Dr. Seuss books—yes, I was ten reading them—and listening to Makeba records over and over. A definite trait of mine, I still do it, listen over and over to what I like. Audrey was one of the founders and I would pass by her house often with its majestic sunflowers growing right out front. And she had some kind of flowering vines, maybe clematis, I think the flowers were deep dark blue growing around and over her entry door. I don't think, no I know I never went inside that house or really ever spoke to Audrey but she was a presence. And Denny—Kita's father—another founder. His wife Ida was the dance teacher even though her movement was pretty severely restricted by that point. She seemed very old to me but probably she was in her late thirties or maybe forties. We were doing modern dance of some sort. I remember in one piece being sort of draped on a rope that hung from the ceiling, swinging a little but more like drifting with it, saying the word agony more than once but not exactly over and over. Denny's family like several Walden families moved on to Alaska and some are still there. To me and us kids he was just kind of a big bellied guy who walked around the school sometimes, not clear what he did there. He'd get dressed up in his Texas style hat and silver buckled belt for the school fairs. My mother learned how to do palm readings for that and she'd dress up too. Someone once brought a pony for rides and tacos were had by all. Before Walden Denny was a conscientious objector to World War II. In 1943 he was arrested and was sentenced to prison and eventually served time. Later he was a founder of the public radio station KPFA and the Pacifica Foundation. After Walden he worked for the Sierra Club and co-founded the Alaska Conservation Foundation. A lot of the founders of Walden had back stories like that too.

How did Barry find his way to the school? A New Jersey boy with an MA in Psychology somehow arrived in Berkeley and married Joan and really was my savior. Tap dancing Joan—later had a studio—with her bleached blond hair and phobias or just good common sense about health nevertheless, I mean hair bleach and thinking dish towels are dangerous? He was an unusual guy, very smart and quick and talented with kids. He liked me and that helped. Anyway, Barry taught us fifth grade and then sixth under unusual circumstances. Behind the fifth grade room was a narrow walkway that separated the school grounds from next door and it was full of date trees and the dates would just fall to the ground and get squished. That was a weird wonderful thing about the Berkeley area, lots of food growing all over like the fig trees that were huge weeds really everywhere that would bear marvelous, beautiful colorful, delicious—in other words, I like fresh figs a lot—figs all over town. And almond trees and blackberry vines and kumquats and loquats and lemons and oranges, I mean what is going on when all that food is just out there growing and ignored? I don't get it. Nancy and I used to eat the loquats for sure then and later in graduate school with no money would pick everything I could find and definitely eat it not to mention the free cookies at tea time for the logic group (Group for Logic and Methodology of Science as it was officially called). I made lots of blackberry breads and pies and roasted the almonds and just plain ate the figs. All out there for the free picking, you don't even need to go onto someone's property, a lot of it is just in the open on sidewalks and such. On the small school campus anyway there were date trees.

Fifth grade we did a lot of route making for our camping trips. We'd all get a map and have to try to plot the best route. We'd also make up the packing list of personal stuff plus group food, et cetera, and this was for week long trips mind you with maybe three teachers and fifteen or twenty kids. That's a lot of pancake ingredients and powdered scrambled eggs. We did make both. Suzy's (teacher and also lead singer for the Loading Zone) pancakes were notoriously bad. One fifth grade trip, I have no idea why and maybe didn't then, the boys or some of them especially Jerry (later to Alaska with his family and I think he's still there) decided to entrap and punch out the girls. I was slugged in the stomach and Jerry was strong. Some other boys held me. And then it was over. I don't know where any teachers were or if anything was ever said about it by anyone.

We'd take two or three trips and the last was always towards the end of the school year and often included my birthday. That fifth grade trip we were going to get to Tehachapi the first night and then continue on to Death Valley. I wonder what they do now with not only Trump shrinking the parks—think Bear's Ears! just to name one so beautiful out there—the fires everywhere and Yosemite burning every year Sonoma and Napa and around Sacramento the fires just everywhere. Think all that red Phos-Chek flame retardant being sprayed all over the West kills aquatic life like all of it yet they can say "It's not harmful to humans and other mammals" well if we kill all the fish and frogs and other stuff swimming around and cause algae blooms I'm pretty sure that is harmful to human life not to mention all the other life out there. And this at a time in which ninety percent of the world's the world's fisheries are at or beyond their limits. Not saying we don't have to take serious steps to do something about the fires including maybe Smokey the Bear style we do have to prevent them and most are caused by human action most by a lot which is kind of shocking although I guess it shouldn't be even a fire ranger setting fire to one a while back why cause she was mad at a boyfriend if I'm remembering that right. Burnt his letter.

Back to our trek to Death Valley against all odds it snowed and our big International vans—kind of like today's SUVs that's what we called it the international was that a brand name or what?—got stuck in it. One of them stuck worse than the other. We certainly couldn't camp outside that night but also needed to get to shelter. So we finally got one car out and drove in shifts to a motel not too far away that happened to be empty and also the owners, a couple living there out in what was then the middle of nowhere running this motel, very friendly and nice. I remember talking to the woman owner about the area and about the motel. I think I asked in my blunt way why the furnishings were so ugly, like the curtains in the rooms and the towels, everything? She said and I do remember this so well, "We started out with things looking good and people stole pretty much everything, ashtrays, curtains, you name it it was gone. So we restocked with stuff no one would want." Somewhere in the conversation I must have mentioned that it was my birthday. At dinner time they gave me all these presents, an arrowhead found locally and a primitive hatchet-like tool. A painted stick with an oblong rock tied with a leather strap to one end. The kindness of strangers always shocks me.

By the next day the snow had stopped and we could continue on to Death Valley which was blazing hot on the hiking trails. I took an easy cut in a trail for which Barry affectionately said—"The lazy ones always find the better way." I guess Alice was on that trip, she must have been but maybe not since the trips did cost some money, always very little, as little as possible. I wonder if they wouldn't have let her come anyway if her parents couldn't afford it which I'm sure they couldn't. Don't know how they paid for Walden for that matter, maybe they didn't. Always minimal tuition even for then but still some money.

Alice with her long, red hair and a few freckles across her nose and beautiful face. Her family was from New Zealand, her mother who kind of looked like a very old version of Alice although she couldn't have been too old, I don't know what she did while Alice was at school if she worked at all or what, and Alice's tall, dark haired father with a beard. A graduate student in Psychology at UC Berkeley. For his dissertation he was allowed to interview the kids in fourth grade at Walden. I remember being kind of stunned at how much I told him and also figured he heard a lot more than he was prepared for. I felt guilty about having said so much for years, maybe even decades. I remember how starving they were, I don't know who knew about that. Alice's mother would take her to the Berkeley Coop, fill up their shopping cart and also put stuff inside their sweaters and pants and anywhere they could and go into the bathroom and eat it all. Alice taught me how to steal stuff. The only thing I remember is a long, very long, pen that had segments each of which held a different color ink. I loved it. My mother asked where I got it and I said, "Dad bought it for me," did she wonder if I was lying? did she ask my father? I don't know, what I said was highly plausible. I don't know if that was the extent of my stealing but I know it wasn't much. We didn't have a lot of money but I thought we were rich, I guess in comparison with Alice's and other families at Walden. I got an allowance even.

Spent a lot of it on candy. Me and La Reva would walk at "recess" to this candy store—really a little grocery store that happened to have a big candy rack—south a few blocks from the school then over a few. They had lots of candy. And then walk back with our little brown bags stocked full. Along the way were small not so well kept houses and lots and lots of Motown music playing which I loved, especially the Supremes. This was the year Grace Slick started singing with the Jefferson Airplane and recorded one of my faves—*White Rabbit*. Barry lived around there somewhere not too far from the store. I say recess in quotes because we could decide what we wanted to do and when we wanted to do it. Pervs always know where the little kids are. Cars with men masturbating in them would often park at the entrance to the school and when they'd see me or any girl probably walking in alone they'd swing open a door to give a full view of the activity.

We did have Friday taco lunches and I probably spent my allowance on that too. Funny I didn't buy candy at the drug store up from Benvenue on College Ave, I'm sure they had lots of it. But I did buy comic books there, *Archie*, *Betty & Veronica*, *Spiderman*; Debbie liked *Richie Rich*. And, like most drug stores then, they had a little rotating rack of Dime Store novels. All five of us would often walk over to Telegraph making a beeline for Café Wha? for their bubble gum ice cream, used to count how many balls of bubble gum in the scoop to see who won, mouths all multi colored in bright blues, reds, greens and yellows. Sometimes we'd go into Moe's which became an iconic bookstore. I believe it was there that my dad started getting me the holocaust books. I was more into *MAD Magazine* then and had already hardened myself to my father's stories not so much stories really not as coherent as that but let's say anxiety expressions. I became pretty deaf to the holocaust pretty generally maybe already by then. Anyway, Moe's and other good bookstores back then and cafes and free music in the parks, like the Grateful Dead, the Eagles, the Turtles, Joan Baez, Peter, Paul & Mary and so many others. And all the peace signs and the protests not to mention the Black Panthers that Bobby Seale and Huey Newton founded just that year and the Hell's Angels. Not to mention also Patty Hearst and the Symbionese Liberation Army later. Ok, the Hell's Angels. I was definitely scared of them and I was still afraid later on East Third Street in the East Village in New York.

Fifth grade came and ended and I didn't think I was supposed to like school so it wasn't in my vocabulary but I did like it or anyway liked my friends and Barry. We stayed there at Walden for my sixth grade but another move was in the wings for the summer. We'll get there soon. The school had some kind of problem with the sixth grade, I don't remember if they weren't allowed to have sixth grade or what but we had to move off campus to Barry's house. We held school on McKinley in Barry, Joan and Audrey's front room. It was a private home and one can't have a school in such a place. Against the law but this happily was an anarchist school and liability wasn't a big thing then so up went newspaper and brown paper on all the front and side windows so that no one could see in and see what we were doing. We must have gone to Walden the campus so to speak I mean for some things but I don't remember that. I just remember Barry teaching us something about the government (remember again as I've been saying this is an anarchist school) in his dark front room with the paper plastering over the windows.

Crazy stuff from today's vantage point, liability suits wouldn't let someone dare to do such a thing. Insurance of all sorts drives our lives now, even our medical decisions as I know all too well as do many of us who have needed medical care that gets interfered with by insurance bureaucrats following the money or following nothing in particular other than authority. More on this I am sure later.

We also had some kind of assignment about growing mold, I think we were studying about Louis Pasteur. Barry had gotten us these paperbacks with each chapter on a different scientist. We were supposed to read the one about Pasteur AT HOME. I couldn't believe it and told my mother and she complained to Barry knowing very clearly what side my father would be on for that issue. Homework? No. Something like fifty years later parents are catching on to the too much homework is too much and are protesting and even banning homework in some towns, yay, about time. Anyway, we were also supposed to grow mold at home on something which I also didn't do. The day came though and I just reached into our fridge and pulled out a bag of Wonder Bread. I used to love to squish a slice of it into a small clumpy ball and eat its great texture sweet chemical weirdness. Should be indestructible given what is in it, but our kitchen was amazing that way an unnatural wonder and the bread was moldy. Moldy, moldy. So I brought a chunk in. Maybe if it had been in the bread drawer instead of all that candy it wouldn't have molded?

ON TO NEXT DOOR
TO THE KELLY'S
WITH THE POODLES

Y EAH, THOSE BIG POODLES, ALWAYS seemed a bit like alien
creatures to me. And the big fence around the house so all
we could see was the top of the blue-green slide poking out.
But we knew the pool was in there and once Mr. Kelly let us swim
in it, but only once.

We had a cactus garden in the back, it was there when we
moved in but I maintained it or thought that was what I was doing. We outgrew living beneath college students, it wore on my
father's nerves in particular. So after as I remember it a very very
brief debate move we did further south still in the flats to a very
different style of house and it was all ours. I did love that house
on first sight. Kind of bungalow meets Julia Morgan meets Frank
Lloyd Wright or anyway so I thought. Two stories with two very
small kids' rooms on the second floor in the front of the house, one
for each of Debbie and Sheila. Then there was a space in between
the front and the back where the stairs came up and we used to
play games like monopoly, a game we had to play and had to play
to win. Once I beat Debbie merely by bringing an egg timer in and
setting it for five minutes stating I would win by then. It so freaked

her out I did win. Being the oldest isn't always nice. We moved on at some point from Monopoly to Risk, getting money and hotels not being enough we needed to conquer the world. In the back there was an enclosed what seemed like a large porch room for me, glass on three sides and lots of birds around. There were also two little roof segments, very little, off of each side. I used to sit out perched in one of them quite a lot and listen to the birds and just listen, it seemed very quiet.

Downstairs in the back which led out to the small backyard with the cacti there was a large, old fashioned kitchen with a bread drawer and a pantry and stuff like that. We used the bread drawer to stock up on candy. Our bread—Wonder bread in those days, practically but as I said not totally indestructible—was in the fridge. We had a small, round oak table in the kitchen at which we would sit for breakfast—for me, Cocoa Puffs for the most part—and our thirteen vitamin and mineral pills that we had to swallow a la Adelle Davis. Our diets didn't quite align with the pill intent but the intent was in there somewhere. Then in the middle of the first floor was a wood paneled dining room and off of that on one side was a little way too small room that my parents slept in. It was very small, not sure why that was their choice. I guess they wanted some privacy but it was a strange choice. Anyway, in the front was a living room also paneled to some extent—all with old and beautiful oak—and with built-in window seats and wood interior shutters. A really beautiful house that years later when I went by had been cut up to be basically an SRO for UC students. Such a waste to destroy something like that.

Downstairs from a doorway in the kitchen was the basement. It just had mostly mechanicals like the water heater in it. Other stuff down there too but I don't remember what except that it was very dark. I took it on as another architectural problem, what could I do to make it different, usable, nice even? I would sit down at the bottom of the stairs pondering that question. It was never noticed except once when my mother caught me down there and screamed down, "I'm not going to have a depressive on my hands, get upstairs immediately!" No pause to ask what I was doing.

That year on Webster, a lot happened. I was in love with Matthew and he made a necklace for me I still have it. A hand-made copper chain and a tear drop shaped enameled medallion mostly in greens. We went to a movie together at the Elmwood Theater around the corner from our house, a theater that played *A Man and a Woman* forever but that's not what we saw. And it happened that Jesse was visiting from New York when I accidentally tore Matthew's very cool vest when we were playing capture the flag at school. I brought it home and Jesse fixed it beautifully making me promise, "Tell Matthew that a revolutionary fixed it for him." Mid-year Matthew's family just up and moved to Israel and when they returned things were different. I didn't see him by then we had moved to New York.

I heard on the radio—I had a little transistor radio forever that I always kept in my room and would listen to all kinds of stuff—I remember hearing some news item about a girl who was lost in the wild for a long period of time and she forgot how to talk—and by the way *Island of the Blue Dolphins* was one of my favorite books. That seemed like heaven to me and I set out to forget how to talk. I informed my family that one back movement against a chair back was no and two was yes and that was it. Didn't realize I wasn't going to be able to forget how to talk when people were talking around me and I had devised a means of communication however minimal and also went to school where I did talk to my friends. Oh well, I remember how enamored I was of the idea that I might really, truly forget and then not be able to talk.

I used to walk the city/town of Berkeley quite a lot. Being in perpetual exile I guess it's how I'd orient myself. Walking, walking, getting to know things in their particulars this rose that store a way of homemaking I invented, not being at home anywhere including in my own skin. No constants no landmarks or home and people disappearing including those who had already disappeared in the war known and unknown to me individually and those with whom no real human interaction happened and that was everyone including myself. The exile personality (I had it, someone who lacks normal bearings—geographic social community family language culture space/time—and therefore at best makes her own and at worst doesn't. Where one falls on this range and what the created bearings are determined by the degree of functionality of the person. Mine were the building designs, the creation/maintenance/adherence to patterns and habits like pacifiers and organization and vigilance over them and my preservation. Preservation takes precedence over existence in the momentary present. Like maintaining the habits— addictions really—and keeping everything the same, been the same weight/size since I was nineteen and don't forget I'm sixty-three now like sending feelers to keep me oriented, grounded at least as much as possible. Do I need all that now that I'm moving towards the other end of life, meaning death? I was arriving here anyway, to not need these markers in recent years before the illness as I'll politely call it. Was moving in the present there for a while and I liked it. Felt like a person amongst persons) was in a reciprocal relationship with whatever my cut-offness was—what little kid wants to make it official by losing her language and all ability to communicate? Someone for whom communication was unpleasant mystifying stressful and significantly insignificant. Whatever that lack was and is of not being in the present—as a kid encapsulated by thinking I was born in the wrong era, always said that. For some reason I can't understand now I loved Victorian clothes. But also loved 1920s Flapper clothes, not at all similar those two, call me a Gemini.

Walked and walked. Cordonices and the rose garden were a bit of a hike from the current house but I would go anyway. I'd also troll around Shattuck Ave not far from what is now the location for Chez Panisse that everyone knows about but wasn't there yet and on my way discovered a store called Creations'N'things on Oxford. It was the beginning of the pop art movement and I was all in. The Warhol reproductions, the plastic, pillow earrings I bought (yeah, I already had pierced ears, started begging for them around four and got them at five. At around three or four what I really wanted was to have the middle section of my nose pierced so I could wear a bone through it horizontally like I had seen in photos and museums. But under the calming influence of Mary Beth, I opted for ear lobes and launched a campaign. Before my mother gave in I'd glue little plastic pearls to my ear lobes. That looked pretty good I thought but I wanted the real thing). I was deep into pop art and like to think I was in with a lot of current movements—well, then I was only eleven. When we moved to New York the next year I thought the Museum of Contemporary Crafts was the coolest place to hang out with their exhibitions that were all experiential. Like the one with plastic strips hanging thick from the ceiling so there was no visibility as you went through it you encountered stuff, installations without warning. Not describing it very well, but it was great. It's not there anymore not for a long time.

Aviva came to Walden in sixth grade and we've been friends ever since. Went hiking in Big Bend a couple of years ago. With all the fracking and rigs that have been installed in recent years I'm sure it already looks and sounds different now. The Rio Grande still had water in it then, pretty full up. Not this year. We became very close very fast. She was a ballet dancer—later professionally did more avant-garde contemporary and high-profile performance— she'd practice every day after school and was very very disciplined. She had an older sister Leah and they had an old Dalmatian named Dotty. I was there (again from New York that time) when Dotty died. They had thought out dinners in courses. Melon slices first then salad then main course then dessert. Her dad was clearly sup- posed to be the head of household especially at the dinner table. And there was conversation over dinner. After dinner, Aviva took a walk, to walk off the dinner but also to buy candy and then ballet practice. The structure was so great, I had never seen anything like it. And the parents really sat in the living room in the evening and did things like read the paper or talk to each other. My parents tight as they were never did stuff like that.

A commercial strip of College Ave was around the corner from us on Webster and a few blocks down was a beauty salon run by Eunice Lyle. A very skinny tall woman with her frosted hair per- petually done up in a teased bouffant, she was definitely still living in the fifties. We three girls on the other hand were definitely products of the burgeoning sixties wearing our long long hair gnarly. My mother took us there and Eunice scrubbed our scalps practically raw with her long polished and manicured to what seemed like sharp points nails, and conditioned deeply with heat caps over our slathered tresses. From her we learned the technique of putting Wella Cholesterol on our hair and then sitting with an electric heating cap for however long we could stand it—another electric can-opener kind of thing, did we really need an electric heating cap glued to our heads for health but also for the fossil fuel thing (and by the way, don't get me started right here, I haven't even mentioned the oil spills yet dead birds and fish a regular sight on the beaches in CA not to mention Long Island later and just black strips on the sand. Remember the Exxon Valdez, right? Getting ahead here but to the point of the birds fish and black strips of oil 1989 it was ten point eight million gallons of crude oil right into the Prince William Sound hit a reef it did because the radar equipment had been broken for a year—too expensive to fix! known about for a year!—and on and on with the spills in the Gulf of Mex and everywhere in the world. And now they are building a sixty mile spine of seawalls from the Houston area to the Louisiana border to shield the petrochemical facilities from the climate change they deny!! And the oil industry says the federal government should pay for it. Is there no end in sight to this stuff? Had a friend say to me now two years ago it's all over the environmental damage is not going to be fixed enough and we'll be resisting what we need to do all the way down to near and present extinction at our own hands.)

That year my mother bought a 1956 black and silver Jaguar with a running board and wood paneling and pull-down trays in the back seats and leather upholstery. The opposite of my father's Dodge Dart, wouldn't you say? He went a bit ballistic not understanding, "What got into you? Even money aside which I can't imagine how much this cost and where you got it, what got into you?" I heard him say and "I mean the extravagance of it how does that fit with your ideals?" He was pacing back and forth now in front of the car to the side of the car every which way around the car his arms flapping up and down. "Are you going to drive this straight into the Western Addition doing your study? Really, what were you thinking and what are we going to do?"

My mother couldn't have gotten a word in edgewise but I noticed she also wasn't trying. Even I knew we weren't that kind of loaded. She just calmly stood and waited until my father stopped pacing and stopped ranting, his face was quite red. "Walt, why don't you just ask me about the crazy Bezerkeley story behind this? Why not ask first?" Then she sidled up to him mockingly whispering, "I'll tell if you get nicer but anyway it's ours so just take a look and enjoy it."

It was so not my father's style to enjoy that kind of thing so it was difficult for him to even pretend. "Okay, I'm asking, what is this? Why do we have it?"

"It's a Jag, silly!" my mother responded with a giggle. She knew she shouldn't push it much farther and added, "I was on my way in to the Coop and in the parking lot I saw a For Sale sign on it with this crazy price! $150! So I just walked on past figuring it was in really bad shape or was a prank or something wasn't right. When I came out I heard people talking about it and that it was in mint condition, the guy had just fixed everything when he decided the draft is coming and it's time to skip town skip the whole country not sure to where but not taking the car with him. He was just standing there in the lot waiting for someone to buy it so he could take his backpack out of the trunk and skedaddle. Crazy, huh?"

Weakly my father asked, "Did you even bother to have it checked out?"

"There wasn't time, I mean he just wanted a sale on the spot but there were all kinds of guys around checking it out and they all said it looks perfect."

"Oh, great." Then with a sidelong look, he asked, "How did you even have that much money on you?"

A pause. "I, uh, didn't, had to go get it. Don't worry, its fine we'll be fine, come on let's take a drive!"

I went and got Debbie and Sheila from inside and we all piled in and went for a spin around the neighborhood and then impulsively, my mother made a beeline for the highway and took us clear to Angel Island. It was a warm sunny day. When we got there she surprised us with a picnic she had bought at the coop and had stashed in the trunk. It was a great time and even my father was having fun and admitted the car is wildly gorgeous.

It was another thing I loved cleaning and polishing. It was very very beautiful and seemingly in very very good shape to my eleven year old eyes anyway. I don't think we had any trouble with it and it had no scratches or other mars on its complexion. And it's not like it was a German car so my father did drive in it but he really never understood the attraction.

We drove it around every weekend somewhere else. "Come on, Walt, admit it, we've had the car three weeks and it's a lot of fun," my mother said driving with the wind blowing in all the windows on the Jag's first voyage up to Sonoma. I had polished up the exterior so we went cruising along shining the whole way with the metal catching and reflecting the warm rays. It was another clear gorgeous sky blue sun filled day in Northern California and we were going on an expedition and this time I could draw on top of the pull down wooden tables in the back.

My father didn't answer but he looked at my mother and smiled a warm smile and put his hand on her shoulder and patted pat pat pat in that way he meant to be affectionate.

"Hey, kids, sing with me," my mother shouted to the back of the car. We were already playing the license plate game and didn't hear her.

In case this wasn't excitement enough, have I mentioned that there was a pet store there on our strip of College Ave? One day, out in the window went all these puppies and they were so cute. All mixed breeds, mutts. I fell in love with one that clearly had some Dalmatian in her and a big black and brown patch over one eye. I brought her home and named her Patty after the Peanuts Patty. Debbie being the middle child that she was immediately wanted one too and she brought home a beagle-ish puppy she named Snoopy. So we had two puppies, three kids, two adults and a cactus garden. I don't know how it worked but I do remember taking Patty around the block a lot, past Kita's house and sometimes up to Nancy's, a very dark house with drug dealer brother where we'd fry corn tortillas on her stove. But back to Patty and cleaning up lots of puppy shit in our backyard, I guess that's where we left them when we were at school. Patty had an innate aversion to men in uniforms, especially police. Very apt for the times, its 1967 verging on 1968, Berkeley demonstrations, People's Park concerts and protests and just all kinds of stuff happening. She did once actually nip a police officer in New York when I was walking her up 110th Street back from Central Park. When it came time to move, and that's a whole other story how we moved we were supposed to give our dogs away. The Jag wasn't coming with us either. Debbie did, she found a home on a farm somewhere. I did nothing, I wasn't parting with Patty, it didn't even occur to me I had to do that. Well, the afternoon before we had given Patty to the pound and I was sobbing relentlessly all night long, all night and into the day that we were leaving. I couldn't do it. So we went back to the pound where Patty was and broke her loose and to New York she went. There was a problem.

Our apartment that my uncle Josh had found for us on 110th Street—now called Cathedral Parkway to fancy it up—between Columbus and Amsterdam apartment 5C for $165—okay in today's terms that's more like a thousand but still for a classic six?—a month with three bedrooms, a dining room and a living room, one bathroom wasn't getting vacated the way it was supposed to. We arrived in New York theoretically to move in but ended up staying at my Uncle Jasper's on the Wilton/Ridgefield border—another story about how the state took that house that he designed and built himself to be a fisheries and wildlife center—and yet another story about uncle Jasper singing and playing guitar for us and making funny sounds like Frum-frum-frum just as a habit out of his mouth. Had been a real hero in WWII. And also drank too much and put a hand on my leg a lot in a way that wasn't an accident, it was just what was normal really then even though everyone knew it wasn't. Now more people know it isn't but we'll see what actual change happens. Do you recall there being much change after Anita Hill?

Back to the NY move—because the tenants of 5C wouldn't leave. Until they sold all their furniture. So, eventually we had to give them money for stuff we didn't want or need and was probably pretty gross anyway. But in between school was going to begin in Manhattan also on the part of 110th Street that is called Central Park North, what was the school building is now a jail was a YMCA before it was a school but anyway, and we were still in the bowels of Connecticut waiting for the people to get out. So, then what? In the meantime, Patty jumped into the pond just outside Jasper's house and probably could have swum but Jasper jumped in after her and dragged her out thinking she was drowning. She later swam just fine in Mere Lake in Central Park even in those days it was very murky and probably toxic. I swam there too, didn't know I shouldn't.

On to the Oliver Cromwell residential hotel on 72nd near Central Park West to have somewhere to stay. What could have been called a flea bag then now fancied up too. Dogs weren't allowed but we snuck her in and would walk her in the park multiple times a day. It was a different era for CPW in the seventies, run down, had to be paid to live there kind of thing and I guess the people at the desk didn't care as long as we covered the bill. When we were gone we'd put Patty in the bathroom and one day she chewed or broke through the door and that was that, management said she had to go. To Deer Run Kennels around the corner she went and every day I would go break her loose and walk her in the park, but I knew a kennel was not life for Patty, it was awful. At the Cromwell she'd sleep in my bed, we were as inseparable as possible.

Finally we "bought" the damn furniture and moved in to our apartment. I think I should have already posted a caption:

110ᵀᴴ STREET IN TIME
FOR THE COLUMBIA
DEMONSTRATIONS

A SOFT SERVE ICE CREAM TRUCK was always posted somewhere near enough and outside my window on 109th Street
most of the year playing that jingle I still hear in my head
every so often and could hum it for you right now if you want.
As far as I knew it didn't rove around it just stayed parked there
playing the music all night long. Maybe they weren't just selling
ice cream, I didn't think of that then but I don't know what I was
thinking of then. Partly I just don't remember but I think I don't
remember because it was a different kind of process that now just
seems like a dense fog.

Also behind our building probably right near the ice cream
truck was a school building on 109th Street. Almost one hundred
percent Puerto Rican or other Hispanic origin students went there,
the neighborhood was in those days Spanish Harlem. Willy went
there, a neighbor about five years younger than me, yeah a seven
year old boy. I babysat him. I babysat some other kids in the building, one little girl Dolores three years old who certainly acted like a
huge brat when I was there. Like when she cut open—how did she
have access to scissors?—a down pillow and scattered the contents
while jumping up and down on her mother's bed like she was Santa

making it snow. Once she threw up on the couch and she'd never never go to sleep when she was supposed to. I covered the vomit with a pillow and didn't say a word to her mother when she came home. But that's the thing, I don't think it even occurred to me to let her mother know, part of that thick fog thing going. Anyway, Willy was perfectly fine but he really made me not like seven year old boys at all. His father Larry was even often home when I was babysitting after I had picked Willy up at school. Larry was a sculptor and had a chin-up bar in one of the doorways, a lot of people did in those days before fancy gyms and memberships and such became *de rigueur*, not that anyone in our building could have afforded such things. Anyway, Larry, a sort of big bellied overweight guy who seemed old to me but maybe was mid-thirties or something then was trying to do chin ups and the bar came loose, down he went on his back and he couldn't move. There he lay in the doorway flat on his back. I was twelve and it was the beginning of my diagnostic skills. Yeah, I've diagnosed quite a few conditions in my time. I stood over him and peered down and asked a few questions and pronounced that he had cracked some ribs. Five hours later in St. Luke's emergency room that was confirmed. Me, Larry, and Willy all sitting on those very uncomfortable plastic seats just waiting for Larry's turn amidst the gunshot wounds, drug ODs—definitely no Narcon then—and who knows what else. Remember not the days of cell phones so I doubt anyone knew where we were all that time. Otherwise maybe someone would have come to help us?

I really did not like babysitting and soon moved from that to giving pottery lessons to kids. In my bedroom. Russell built us— me and Debbie—I don't know why not Sheila, maybe she was too young? sleeping balconies. Russell and Bruce right at the dawn of their Scientology indoctrination. I loved Russell so much that when he asked me to go to an informational session I did, knowing I thought it was nonsense I just didn't want to hurt his feelings. It was in a large auditorium sort of room, probably rented from some other organization not like now where they own so many buildings everywhere, right on 125th street two buildings side by side for example. I drive by them often now on my way to the Bronx for treatments. This guy up front talked and talked about getting clear and changing your life and afterwards—and mind you I was about 13—he came straight up to me and said he's never seen anyone sit so still that I must have great powers of concentration. The flattery if that's what it was was not working. Anyway, then on into a small room one on one with a guy on the other side of a small table from me and some meter that was turned towards the guy away from me with two wires coming out and a tin can attached to each wire. I think cans were made out of tin in those days still, uncoated inside of course and with lead solder no doubt those for food anyway. Now they're coated but what with? And the top lids often are not coated, so what's the point. Best to not buy canned stuff or stuff in plastic—oy, don't get me started on plastic. My town introduced a single use plastic water bottle ban, passed right away and now some idiots are working hard to repeal it! What is wrong with people? There is enough plastic refuse in the world 87,000 tons and counting in the Pacific garbage patch as it is so politely called covering 618,000 square miles and counting, not to mention the whale found with 18 pounds of plastic in its stomach. Or the whale that died of starvation with eighty-eight pounds of plastic in its belly! What do we think is in our bellies? Dream on if you think there's no plastic there; it's already moved way up the food chain directly to our mouths. He asked me questions and watched the meter and told me about how much I had to gain from getting to clear, at great financial and other cost of course and years of Scientology work. I left unimpressed.

With the sleeping balcony I had room for a pottery wheel. Not the most prudent thing to have in your bedroom health wise, what with all the clay dust and I got into the chemistry of glazes pretty quickly and started to mix them myself from the powdery elements.

Cleave built me the wheel that for me was a way of holding on to California and Berkeley and Walden. Even Peninsula. We always had pottery classes at those two. Cleave, I don't know how I found him with his studio out on Staten Island. I mean I did love riding the ferry but I'd just go out and back, didn't go anywhere on the island actually. Somehow Cleave, probably mid-thirties or maybe forty-ish, tall African-American potter living where he was part of a Communist cell his family had gotten there on the Underground Railroad—there on Staten Island—amongst as he said the Minutemen out practicing their riflery. He built my wheel from odd parts, a kick wheel that I held on to into my college years and brought it with me to the vestibule of a studio I rented on West End Avenue at 101st Street. I'd be taunted by the security guards on every block back on the walk from the Barnard/Columbia campus to my apartment. And they had guns so it was no joke when they called out the gross things they wanted to do to me or have me do to them. Sarah Zauderer owned the building, a nice older woman again I thought she was very old, but who knows, I was only around eighteen then. "I'll move you to a one bedroom when you get married," she'd say, "you'll never have to leave the building and later when you have children we'll move you to a bigger apartment." That all seemed from outer space to me but nice of her just the same. It was a beautiful building and I actually had a stained glass window in my studio. Don't know why I ever left it, but this is getting ahead to college when I'm barely in High School with Cleave. And the maybe not daily but surely more than weekly school bomb scares have not yet begun. Anti-Vietnam protests? General protests? The whole school would empty out onto the sidewalk and wait for the bomb squad to get there and go through the building to inevitably clear it. Later on in the late seventies bombs went off in NY in coffee shops and such places.

He, back to Cleave, wanted me to be his apprentice, he thought I was going to make a great potter. I'd live with his mother down the street from him and work with him every day. He took me to meet an Asian potter in Port Chester, Charlie, who gave us a demonstration of throwing some kind of vessel. And he and Cleave talked about the clay compound they were devising that had the glaze mixed into the clay requiring just one firing. I don't remember how that experiment worked out in the end. I remember being there with Cleave and Charlie and Charlie demonstrating but unable to put any of it into words—and mind you I almost never spoke myself, God knows how limited my vocabulary was then and until college when in the first semester being accidentally thrown into a Philosophy of Language course which changed my life, repeating to myself to try to understand what the hell is being discussed—I knew I was in love though, this was going to change my direction from architecture, from ceramics—oh! I haven't talked about the summer in Canada with Nadine at the Raku course with Hal Reigger yet—and saying to myself silently: a noun is a thing word, a verb is a doing word, sayings from probably something like fourth grade or thereabouts but I didn't have any idea then and there already in college in a graduate level course by some computer sorting error what those sayings actually meant. Yeah, it was Mrs. Walker's class in which she taught us those maxims to help us understand grammar, something I never ever grasped until maybe well into my fifties thanks to learning from my daughters and helping them study for their Latin exams.

Back to Charlie and Cleave and me and my realizing that day with them in Port Chester that I couldn't be a potter, it was just too non-verbal and I didn't know how I'd survive with people who couldn't put things into words. Weird, huh? I was the most non-verbal person I knew and even in my house where there was plenty of vocalization there wasn't a lot of talking like maybe none even, not really.

Living on 110th I could just walk across 110th Street going east to school. I had a bus pass—every month a new one in a different color and the colors weren't bad, very saturated dark colors mostly, I liked them—but still walked most of the time, most often in that first fall barefoot. Not that much happened on my walks except for the fancy looking cars that would cruise slowly alongside me. The back usually dark tinted window would scroll down and a suit jacketed arm would extend out holding a fan of dollar bills, I don't know about the denomination but money. I guess I was supposed to hop in. I probably looked like I could use the money, barefoot and still gnarly haired probably and who knows what kind of tattered-ish clothes I thought looked great. Not to mention my three dollar dresses—okay maybe they'd be twenty bucks now—from Alexanders, I thought they were great, I wore them for years. In a couple of years we discovered that one could go on Saturday mornings cash in hand to the garment district in the twenties and thirties west and go to the buildings where the brand names were made. The elevator men would tell which companies were on which floor. You could go up and buy seconds or sample sizes for really very cheap. I still have a very warm and beautiful plum colored wool coat with a deep plum velvet collar that I bought on one of those floors for twenty-five dollars and it's still in good shape and I still love it and am still roughly the same size.

Have I mentioned yet that my father didn't come with us to New York? He did join us later, but that wasn't in the initial plan. Ever in the vanguard my mother decided that they had done the conventional thing for long enough and it was time for a change not to mention she missed the energy of the East Coast and just couldn't hack it in their promised land. She pitched the idea of an open marriage and my father went with it. He didn't understand at the time that she was then going to up and leave for New York taking us with her. The initial idea was just to have things be more flexible. When they told us it was straight out of a comic book I had read in which there was some kind of lesson about divorce with the dad in the strip saying to the kids, "Your mother and I still love each other very much, don't we kitten?" We had every reason to believe them, there was none of the fighting and bickering of the pre-separation days. After months of surreptitious planning though my mother let my father know that we were going to be staying east. He hadn't meant that wide open, but we all dealt with it and eventually he followed us east with a transfer of his work to SUNY Stonybrook. They never did get divorced even though both found other long term partners. My mother spent quite a lot of time with my father when he was dying in various hospitals, I overheard them reminiscing about the good old days still sounding as much in love as ever.

Ninth grade Nadine came to New Lincoln and moved into the Bishop's residence at St. John the Divine's since that's what her father was. Quite an unusual one at that, if you remember him siding with the squatters across the street, ordaining the first out lesbian woman. He supported and more than that was active in so many progressive movements and causes. He had a lot of kids too. Nadine had eight sibs, nine of them! Being at their house for dinner was like going to a large banquet with lots of conversation going all around the table. Was like being in the company of giants, literally, most over six feet and me a paltry 5'4" looked at each head on at chest height at best. Nadine lived across the street from me and we became close like almost right away. An odd couple since she was about six feet or over, blond and waspily beautiful and I was short and dark and chunky and whatever. Anyway, she joined me in the ceramics thing and we started teaching together out of my bedroom on 110th Street and founded a studio we called 89 Lions, the 89 part was her, the lion part was me. Eventually St. John's gave us a room so we could move the operation out of my bedroom— who moved all that heavy stuff? The fly wheel alone of the wheel was made out of concrete—a whole room for our pottery and glaze mixing and they let us put my kiln in the boiler room and gave us two fourteen year olds access to the boiler room, would never ever happen now again what with the huge liability industry. We'd get up at around 5 AM to turn on the kiln and then sneak out of school to flip switches—it wasn't automatic, just had cone settings and trips for the temperature regulation—at least twice during the day and then in the evening after we had made many lettuce and mayonnaise and white bread sandwiches and chocolate milk glasses later and even maybe dinner or sometimes before we'd shut if off to cool down overnight. One time sneaking back in through the school sidewalk metal hatch to the basement, the hatch closure thing, you know the metal sheets that are supposed to be flush with the sidewalk and never are? Well, I don't know if they're spring loaded or what to open but anyway this one was defective and when I stood on it, it gave way and I went whooshing down to the cement basement floor, good I didn't hit my head I guess but I did bash up an ankle and leg and had to hobble around on crutches for a couple of weeks, the exact couple of weeks leading up to the ninth grade production of *Lysistrata* in which I was playing the starring role. Not good. I have always thought they gave me the part because I didn't talk much and maybe they thought it would help, but in fact I was dramatically okay once I stepped into another person's personality, like in the street theater I was doing. I could put a lot of emotion into it.

But before Nadine and maybe during Cleave there was Abrachef. A Czech definitely really older man, not just my kid perception of older, a ceramicist who for some reason had a studio in the basement level in a building on Columbus just in from 110th Street. Before my kiln, he'd let me bring my pots to glaze and fire in his studio and we'd talk. He'd look disdainfully at my glaze patterns and ask if I was in some kind of design school that taught me to do stuff like that. He'd talk about having survived two revolutions only to come to New York to be in the midst of another—it was around 1968-69 and Columbia and the country was after all in some kind of uproar.

It was with Nadine after ninth grade, that summer, she moved away after that, back to D.C., but we went to a Raku course at Nelson University in British Columbia, flying to Vancouver, staying there in a Y—we were kids, how was that allowed? Fourteen, wouldn't happen now, and then a day or two later to Nelson to get to this place only to find it was for graduate students, mostly from the Chicago Art Institute, and that Riegger the instructor was the real deal and we were going to dig up our own clay, build our own outdoor kilns, mix our own glazes and learn how to make traditional tea ceremony ware. What sounds bad about that? We were miserable! We immediately called Nadine's mother who happened to be at a ranch in Montana to save us. She said wait a week, and we were so mad how could she do that to us? By the end of the week, we were quite happy and loved the place. And hitchhiked with other people in other programs there, like Charlotte from Kamloops who said she had never seen a Jew before and that my nose wasn't all that big, and Rumon—he'd say, like rum'n'coke—an Indian student there who tried repeatedly to prove to me that I could after all keep a beat, and others. We went to Spokane camping along the way because Charlotte knew that if we said we were all Canadian and had lost our way, we'd get put up in a hotel by the Washington police. It was true. I can't imagine what the hotel was actually like. But a lot of beautiful camping weekends and really hard work during the week, it was great. Nadine went home to D.C. after the program and I went on to visit Aviva in Oakland and then Russell in LA before going back to New York. I had my box of tea bowls and such, some of which my mother still has and I think are beautiful, each individually wrapped in newspaper and then tightly and carefully packed into a cardboard box to protect them, with me on each flight. Coming through US customs because I looked like a dirty hippy—kind of like at an anti-Vietnam protest in D.C. with Rusty and some woman on a bus called us dirty hippies and Rusty's mom told us our underwear were probably cleaner than that woman's so what was she talking about—as the officer told me—remember I'm fourteen now and look it—the customs officer decided I was smuggling drugs, which I was very afraid of and only tried once or twice which I'll go into later—and was ferociously menacing and made me open the box and unwrap every single piece of paper and then gave me no time or tape to rewrap anything and pushed me along. I was crying and sure everything would break after that.

But I've gotten a couple of years ahead here. Let's go back to the first weeks in New York back at the Oliver Cromwell and starting school at New Lincoln on 110th Street and Lenox Ave in an old Y building as I said later to turn into a jail and yet with New Lincoln defunct so many students had a reunion by having a tour of the jail, weird, I didn't understand the attraction in that. It was fall, September to begin with, when school started and probably hot enough anyway certainly warm enough to go barefoot as I always had. I remember I had this bright yellow and navy striped horizontally, short sleeved mini dress that I really loved and so wore it to school a lot. One day in the library a swarm of girls circled around me, I remember Mandy and Alix and Debbie (different Debbie) and whoever else, paid no note of my tangled long hair, no note of my bare feet—how was I allowed into school with bare feet every day? Wouldn't be allowed now what with liability and all—and were very disturbed by my lack of a bra. I was twelve and really really didn't need a bra and hadn't even thought about bras. Of course, they were all talking about bras and boys and periods but I wasn't going to be up to any of that for years. They were pretty serious and menacing. They also talked about things like Aruba that I had no idea of, had no idea what even kind of thing they were talking about.

And that first Halloween we went around the neighborhood, probably in reality just a few apartment buildings since they were pretty large buildings. The gargoyle building which I always loved was kind of creepy inside, but it was Halloween. A woman an old woman for sure emerged out of one dark apartment there with apples for us but it was in the days of razor blades in apples so we threw them out right away. Five apples right in the trash. Oh yeah, speaking of trash, it was all over the streets and the air was thick with soot. You wouldn't know it from today's standards in the US of A where the air looks clearer (question: but is it clearer when a reported 95% of the world population lives in unhealthy air? Where is that 5%, is that even realistic that some 5% could sequester themselves in clean or cleaner air?)—but then we export a lot of our trash now without the incinerators allowed, and huge heaps of it pile up all over—like India's trash piles, don't know if any of it is ours but still they're so big that chunks fall off and kill people, recently killed some kids—but then every roof top had thick, black soot and smoke coming out of the incinerator smoke stack. Yeah, every apartment building incinerating its trash and burning who knows what kind of filthy fuel. And out of every car, thick, awful exhaust. It was *de rigueur* to take the filters out of cars after inspection to get better mileage, a practice that probably only increased after the oil crisis as it was called in the seventies. Along with that filth was what came out of every kind of male's mouth and what their hands did in those days on the street to strangers, to kids, to me. Later, much later, Lara at twelve baring her braces to a penis exposer on the subway that he should come closer so she could bite it off. But she was precocious.

I did a study a few years later to see what influenced the gross behavior of males on the street. Nothing it turned out. I dressed all kinds of different ways, including overalls covered with clay, acted all different ways from smiling to practically foaming at the mouth and talking to myself (no cell phone and Bluetooth then, so the crazies were the ones talking out loud with no one else there, can't tell now), and different neighborhoods, and the tabulations showed no differences overall. Ugh. One of my daughters points out that in every iteration I was still white. I don't know what to say about that in this case, probably made a difference but the constancy of the harassment no matter what really no matter what even given that I was (and am) white and young (not any more) was the point.

We ate a lot of frozen food in those days, everyone was doing it being before the days of rampant habitual take-out. These days in New York people use their ovens like they're just more storage space. But now there are microwaves for reheating, there weren't then. Celantano Brothers were the fancy ones, Sara Lee—I'd eat the brownies still frozen, Debbie ate a lot of canned peas, like a whole can at a time, uck makes me sick just thinking of those off color peas swimming around in that milky water in the cans—Swanson TV dinners. You get the idea. Miracle food. And lots of cigarette smoke everywhere not to mention the adults soaked in alcohol as a matter of course. Even cigarette smoke in classrooms, movie theaters, restaurants, thick smoke everywhere from that. When they banned cigarettes from restaurant tables, not the bar mind you even if it was only a couple of feet from the tables, people thought it was ridiculous, no one would go to restaurants and pay money and not be able to smoke. We've got a single use plastic bottle ban going into effect now and not just store owners who profit from the things but just people are against it, that it's a ridiculous solution, let's just improve recycling, let's do something else but come on not that, that's what they're saying now that its past and they forfeited their ability to vote on it. Taking away things we've become accustomed to seems ludicrous until looking back they seem barbaric. I mean, who would go to a restaurant to eat that was filled with smoke? Not too many people. I hope we survive to be able to look back in disgust at all the plastic metal paper petroleum waste we've been up to.

When I went to college at seventeen I started smoking probably already addicted from the second hand smoke and then in withdrawal. Smoking cigarettes, drinking a lot of coffee and mixing Adelle Davis's pep up drink and having liver and onions for breakfast. Of course, liver was very very cheap in those days. I got into college as an anomaly. It was after eleventh grade and I had an almost perfect math SAT score and low low low Verbal score, so as a girl I was like a boy and anyway different from other girl applicants, still called coeds in those days. I applied to Barnard and to Columbia Engineering and got into both. Coming back fresh from the SATs I relayed some of the logic questions to my mother and sisters and they howled with laughter when I told them the answer I picked from the multiple choice. Happily, it turned out I was right I later realized sitting in an introduction to logic class.

It was the early seventies and Barnard admitted three juniors from my high school alone. Desperate times I guess, no one in their right mind was going to send their daughter to Morningside Heights in those crime infested days. New York was in a recession and in what seemed to be a death spiral of disarray. Dirt, soot, buildings collapsing, potholes so big car axils would break daily just driving down the roads and eventually later the West Side Highway itself collapsed. On the other hand, there seemed some room for hope: 1970 inaugurated the first Earth Day and the NRDC and the EPA (don't look at it now with Pruitt Wheeler et al up there doing crazy things) were born, so was Greenpeace a year later, and the Clean Water Act and DDT banned the next year and following that the Endangered Species Act, stuff was on the move. We were doin' it. Making stuff better, it just didn't look better yet. And some stuff did get better that's for sure but you just can't ignore the fact that for some communities stuff didn't get better usually the ones with low income or inhabitants with darker skin. Like the town in Texas right up near Dallas that's populated with mostly African-Americans and with low incomes *have no running water at all* and that's right now! and has been the case for decades, decades! At least three of them and counting as I've had to say to you quite a lot recently on these pages.

As a plus we three were all commuter students and wouldn't take up any precious dorm space. Could have become an engineer if not for the orientation day the Engineering School held for admitted students. There were three females there, counting me and my mother who came with. And the profs didn't look like anyone I could recognize, more like army sergeants or something with crew cuts—remember this is the early seventies in NYC, Columbia to be precise where protests had just been roaring and lots of lefty politics on campus. I bolted, it all looked too scary to me. A shame, I think I would have liked being an engineer. They are certainly needed in every corner of the earth now, for sure for sure.

But back for a moment to 110th Street. I had one sole day in my field hockey career. Got hit in the face by a backward swing of someone's stick and that was that. I retired to folk dancing with Cyrelle and that was magical. That hockey day I was a little slower returning to school from the Central Park field we played on and about five or so girls from the neighborhood obviously not in their own school wielding a large thick tree branch it took three of them to hold up, swung it at me and hit me pretty hard. I returned to the school building eventually, that kind of thing wasn't so unusual, but usually it was boys on boys. Getting out of hockey was easy after that, not that I told anyone about the incident. Didn't even occur to me. It was decided that it counted for gym class that I walked with the gym teachers Bonnie and Norman, Norman who later was revealed to have been selling drugs to the kids right in the school and another gym teacher Stu Ratz, really his last name, who was molesting boys, through Central Park before school in the mornings.

Move again we did.

AMSTERDAM AVENUE, NY
IN A CRISIS

W HEN I RETURNED FROM CANADA via Oakland and LA
I was told to come (still toting my tattered box of Raku
pottery) to another address. First I heard of a move. My
wheel was put in my very very small new room, since Nadine's family moved back to D.C., I couldn't very well use the studio and the
boiler room at St. John the Divine's for just me. My kiln was set up
in the apartment building's basement in one of its boiler rooms, also
would never ever happen now. It was a Mitchell Lama building, buy
the apartment—four bedrooms (three of which really teeny teeny),
all sun and large windows looking to the East—for three thousand
dollars and sell it whenever you do for the same. Had to qualify,
low enough income, to get in and waiting lists of course. There
were many of these high rise not at all attractive Mitchell Lama
buildings in the neighborhood. Eventually all voted through some
loophole to be able to sell at market rates, except for ours being full
of fair minded lefties who decided to do the right thing.

Tenth grade and close friends with Lydia and also Nora whose
mother left her and her brother was a drug dealer who gave us some
psilocybin one day and we both had pretty bad, scary trips out in
the wilds of Manhattan. Her father was an artist and her grandfather owned one of the well-known rare antique book stores—back
when there were bookstores. And when people read books. That

summer, me, Lydia, and Sheila—Debbie stayed home scooping ice cream—went with Holly and later my father to Europe. Holly, the folk singer, renowned in Europe at least if not the US. She, without children herself then, went on a UK tour with us three kids and my father joined us later. She tried to make it fun, but really it was crazy. We went to Scotland, Wales, and parts of England on this pub folk singing tour and then ended up in Aldeburgh for I think a week, right on the water. I'm sure it was very nice. She really was a lunatic. Some things she was clearly correct about but she went about them in such an abrasive manner that she didn't seem right at all. Like when my father was dying himself of pancreatic cancer and in the early diagnosis days, most memorably at Sloan Kettering, she had her ostentatious note pad and tape recorder in the consultation rooms with the doctors. The way she went about it of course they didn't want to say a word assuming she was a suer, and maybe she was, I don't know that. He died an awful death at the hands of advanced medicine. Didn't learn until this year that even back then my doctor was treating people with better success and much less suffering. I wish I had known. Sloan just slapped him on a trial and he was in horrendous amounts of pain even morphine could not sufficiently address. Whoa, way ahead of where we are, that was all in 1988. Within months of my first being born and the best dog I ever lived with, well, maybe neck and neck with Patty, died too.

At a certain point, we went off to Europe to meet my father somewhere and start our driving trek, in Holly's Volvo I'm sure, and she did all the driving, don't remember my father driving once, to what was still then East Germany and to my father's home town Zwickau. And fast she drove with us three kids in the back and always a window at least cracked open on my father's side due to his lingering primitive fear of being gassed. Couldn't be in a room with the windows and doors all closed either, ever. What a trip, lots of fighting, the adults I mean, us kids did fine. We went through Paris and Basel and Chablis and Prague and lots of beautiful places and museums and walks. My architectural mind definitely exploded on that trip. My father hadn't been back to Germany since he left at the age of something like sixteen and needless to say the days in Zwickau were traumatic, probably for all of us but anyway for sure for my father and I think for me. Not to mention our stop in Vienna and the B&B or whatever it was we stayed in, a *pensione*, with the *patrone* telling us if we crossed the border into then Czechoslovakia we'd all be killed instantly. Poor woman, she lived in a very dark house concretely and metaphorically and had the history she lived through to back up her story.

I think I was a pretty hip kid, walking around especially the East Village which wasn't all NYU like it is now then, in my monk's robe. Had a red cape I wore a lot too. Frequenting St. Marks Place back when it was interesting. That thrift store there, pretty sure I bought a floor length black velvet coat with a white fur collar, I loved that coat, I had such a crush on a girl who worked there, I don't know if I ever even spoke to her just remember *Black Magic Woman* playing in the store and her dark soft curly hair. I remember being in the flowing red cape walking up Broadway towards Columbia and getting followed. I'd duck into stores and wait and come out and there he still was, went on a long long time. I was scared but not as scared as I was a couple of years later by the lewd security guards, whose security exactly? Not young female security. As I said before, they had guns and would say disgusting things to me as I walked by them. I wonder now if they could have left their posts or blocks they were guarding, I certainly thought they could. And why not, what would happen to them if they did? Cops do that stuff all the time.

TO COLLEGE AND
TOO MANY APARTMENTS
NOT TO MENTION
THE FRATERNITY

WELL, BEFORE I GET TO all that. Graduated at 17 after 11th grade, hopped in Paul's standard shift I didn't know how to drive and drove clear across the country as I've said already. Coming full circle to my parents' maiden voyage across the country. For me it was the middle of the country both north and south of it that drew me in. The red earth the flatness of the plains the beauty of the mountains.

We stopped in Chicago for Paul to see his grandmother I couldn't meet cause somehow she couldn't know he had a girlfriend? Wasn't that what boys were supposed to have and to sleep with them or have sex anyway. Cat Stevens playing in the car most of the way. Paul liked Cat Stevens a lot, like Nadine liked The Band and Aretha and Debbie liked Janis Joplin. After that back to New York and working for Grove Press owned by Barney, Paul's father, who gave him luggage for every birthday. What was the message in that? I guess it seems pretty clear but weird. I was the entire Permissions & Rights Department, did they not have one before the 17 year old me who had no idea how to compose a business letter happened in the office? Can't be true. Anyway, the guys always going in the screening room at lunch to watch the Evergreen, division of Grove, porno videos. And looking at me with their wide reddened eyes on the way out and at the parties Barney would have at his Hamptons compound, a series of three I think corrugated metal structures, Paul had one to himself. And they had a pool and were pretty close to the beach and Jackson Pollock's house and others. Makes it sound like a horrible place, all the porno and feminists picketing Barney on Houston Street where he lived in a converted industrial building, and shots fired through the skylights one day, right into Paul's room. But it wasn't, it was revolutionary, for anti-censorship, pro-experimental and just good fiction and good writing. If personally he wasn't the most exemplary guy in the room that is often the way it goes with guys—not saying women are so great, just saying the guys live in patterns like grooves in the snow or something like that, trodden paths.

Went to college after that summer and fell in love with math with philosophy of math with studying with the stacks with just thinking, maybe I had never done it before. Well, of course I had, the slinky building and all, but it was a different kind of thinking I was doing hitting the ground running or some phrase like that, it was all new. A new world, crazy since I had grown up on several college and university campuses. Of course thought I was going to be an architect going in and was told to major in math for architecture—seems like kind of a dumb idea in retrospect, but I didn't question it then. But anyway so immediately in love with stuff like the foundations of math and of language and also formal logic and its foundation, wow, I never turned back until I was kicked, well blacklisted—another one of those racist phrases, no? why black for something bad?—out. But that's a story (of greed, corruption, violence—not really, just plain and ordinary sexual harassment and discrimination) that happens later.

1976, my Junior year and Heidegger died and they wouldn't lower the flag that they lowered for absolutely everyone else on campus, the Columbia campus that is. I was incensed, probably the most brilliant and far reaching of all philosophers ever and they wouldn't lower the flag in respect for that. I protested but nothing happened. Had spent eight months in Paris including one college semester studying Heidegger and Husserl's work and roaming around Paris. I spent a lot of time walking everywhere, as per my usual anyway, but this time around Paris, everywhere. I didn't have any money anyhow to stop somewhere like in a café. All my money went to my third of the rent for a tiny studio I shared with Marion (Hampshire College) and Violet (not sure, maybe U Penn?). An improvement over my first attempt at renting a room from an old Parisian woman who turned out quickly to be very very anti-Semitic. And, as per my usual studied a lot, in the rooms at Reid Hall. George was often there too sometimes with Peter, both smoking their pipes and talking about stuff I didn't understand but it sounded interesting.

Once the semester was over I biked with a lot of books in my saddle bags from Milano where Warren and I bought bikes through the then Yugoslavia to Greece and then a boat from Samos over to Izmir. This was 1975 and the height of the Greek/Turkish conflict in Cyprus, it was very dangerous and we were very stupid. Biking in Turkey in now August was very hot, hot hot hot. Well, wait, camping on the beach in Greece was scary was chased by some Greek men while Warren slept, and was yanked off my bike in Yugoslavia quite a few times by men who just wanted too. Warren was miles behind, even though he was a strong wrestler and I was literally a 98 pound weakling. Biking through somewhere towards Greece we ran into several British bikers who told us if we went into Turkey we'd be killed. Nothing could have been farther from the truth, I had such a great time in Turkey. Pick-up trucks would stop us and say we had to get in it being too hot to ride, would take us to their homes, feed us wonderful Turkish food, let us sleep somewhere and then send us on our way, over and over in different kinds of iterations. Istanbul was amazing in those days and I loved the chanting in the early pre-dawn hours.

Back to New York and Barnard/really Columbia since my majors were all across the street at Columbia, always in classes that were all men except for me. Saw so many good movies in those days with George and Peter, independent movie theaters thrived then and bookstores, real ones were everywhere, St. Marks Books, Eighth Street Books, the New Yorker Bookstore, Colosseum, Book Forum, Bruner Maisel, all over the city. It was fun city in so many ways. And publishers, not just Barney even though he really stood out as some kind of maverick genius at picking books that were—are!—truly brilliant that no one else would publish. Beckett, Ionesco, Robbe-Grillet, Kobo Abe and on and on, no one publishing these authors. Experimental, real theater, people trying new things different things all over the place. It wasn't about money yet. Not in the way it became. Was also the era of snuff movies and awful awful skewering of women in so many ways and everywhere, wrote a novel about that but in the eighties, we'll see what happens with that.

Yes, fun city in so many ways but not in terms of the filth pollution poison and the poverty racism sexism classicism all rampant in this city that alongside housed so much creative energy. All that poisoning from the city and from what came before the stuff that gets ingested doused inhaled pre-adolescence I think is the most destructive and all we boomers got literally tons and tons of it day in and day out and everywhere, no location was safe. Look at the results now that we're old or at least older not old enough to die yet we are. Rampant disease rampant cancers in particular. I'm on my second. In the past if I heard someone had not only one cancer but two, I wondered what was that person doing? Blamed the victim. Now healthy lifestyle in hand for over four decades and on a second cancer myself. The story I've been telling you chronicles some but only some of the hows. Think about it, didn't even go into the pipelines and protests like Standing Rock and the pipeline ruptures and boring through pristine forests to lay the pipes, just to cite one big story I didn't weave in but there are more. Some still we in the

public don't even know about yet. Maybe we will before we im-
plode our habitat or too many of us have died either from dreadful
cancers or from the mis-treatment of them when some many even
know better. Money theme plays here as a strand.

It's a really weird sickening sort of feeling to actually know this
thing, this disease is the vehicle by which I am going to die and in
not too long. That seems to be my and so many people's situation,
yup, a cancer type that's difficult to enunciate it's so awful. In case
I wasn't already an exile type of personality this kind of disease
is very isolating even with the kindness of friends and strangers.
Career gone, recognition (if any) goes quickly, work gone (and for
lots of reasons depending on one's kind of work. Being an analyst,
I closed my practice pretty much on the spot rather than have my
patients watch me die. Even aside from that consideration, the
treatment schedule is so arduous and constant and at times and
really most of the time unpredictable trying to keep to any sort of
schedule is folly). Trying to make dates with friends often, usually
fall through, even with my very good friend Aviva who has now
travelled across the country three times and I haven't managed to
see her once. Not complaining here, just relaying the reality of it.

No future it's not only I can't plan into the future but it just
point blank isn't there and not like the present is so great. Well what
does that leave but the past and if you're like me not necessarily left
with the pleasant parts of the past but the difficult the ugly moments the traumatic bits keep replaying like a really broke down
record. Can't say that's much fun, better to have the present/future
ever going on and on farther than the eye can see but that's not an
option. I keep hoping the option will open back up but I know I'll
take that thought to the grave.

In a somewhat different state talking to you at this moment,
almost two years later after diagnosis and because I was lucky
enough to find a genius and brave doctor. I realized pretty quickly
that the standard of care in virtually every hospital in every state
of this vast, huge country for my disease is a death sentence, meaning a quick and very unpleasant arduous death sentence. I would

very very likely be dead now or on my way to dying had I followed that beaten path. Instead, with the help of many, especially an angel I must mention right now since he's stayed with my case—yes he is a doctor too and a brilliant one as well, really tends to the sick and doesn't leave their side when they need him—stayed with me through and through I was saying before I interrupted myself, found my doctor and am actually doing well right now, that is, most of the time feeling pretty good. But that doesn't mean there isn't a serious disease here, it's just not visibly raging at the moment. Some say, oncologists that is, that that kind of state doesn't last, it always re-engages the rage cycle. I am doing most everything I can to stay on the good side of things and certainly my doctor is for me and many others who enter into his chambers, I'd like to actually die old or at least older than this. But that's being greedy, I know, I mean I'm still here more than a year and a half really later and went to one daughter's graduation and then went the other's last September, didn't expect that September '18 sounded very very far away when I first heard the date and had just been diagnosed certainly didn't think I'd get there. But to look at me (except the weird looking face with no eyelashes and scanty eyebrows at best at the moment and bald Yul Brynner style smooth head with a few hairs but apart from those things I look pretty good tanned strong big muscles for an old lady from all that hard physical labor I do and can do partly with crazy person strength and force of will. When my youngest was very little she wanted me to promise to live to 104 and she never forgot it either. Even if that was never going to happen, 63 is a bit too far on the failing side of that. When isn't? that's got to be pushing the boundaries of *hubris* to state a number don't you think? I'm not going there.

If I can keep writing, I can keep shifting the now as we all do. I like that, it would be indecent for my now to end this soon, really indecent even though it has of course happened many many times before. (to get way ahead of myself here and as I started to say just a bit ago, sorry for the spoiler, right now, two years later almost, I measure normal on every dimension measurable. Those dodos in their labs with the backing of those high and mighty hospitals and research centers would say, impossible, kill her now! Thanks to a doctor who follows his own science and his own conscience and is not to mention, brilliant.) But who knows what's coming, I am tainted. I worried about my own, private septic system, what to do, it leaches out near enough to my vegetable garden. Had to find a way of exporting my toxic waste. Will I do this until I just get worse and die? I don't know and no one knows, else I'd ask, well, I have asked anyway but it's a dumb ungrateful question, I know that. I have lots of spoiled brat complaints I mean I could be dead now and I don't like that some medications make me tired some give me a fever and an awful taste in my mouth and I hate the smell of the stuff in the pump I have to wear pumping away overnight more than that for twenty hours and these are my concerns? kind of ridiculous I should look around the treatment room at people who have intensely yellow skin or who are unresponsive and not just dozing off or who are emaciated or who just plain aren't responding to treatment and then get a grip. But depression has sunk in. I warned my sisters that this would eventually happen and here we are. I thought someone should know that my thinking isn't stellar and I've been making some bad judgement calls and just weird behaviors that are so unlike me even if not serious. Not earth shattering but just not me. Not that I don't have anything to be depressed about but I think its chemical. It happened before and faster when I was treated for breast cancer fifteen years ago. But this is awful, I know it's happening and I know my cognitive functioning isn't great and I don't mean the awfully named chemo brain thing I mean real cognitive functioning stuff and really feeling depressed like this isn't worth it kind of stuff.

And now I've lost my hair for the fourth time. Fourth! It is such a pain when hair falls out, it takes a few days at least and it comes out all day long, hairs everywhere, on the sink, the counter, my desk in my mouth everywhere. And each time I've told myself after being upset, okay so you're bald, so what just wear it like it's okay. But it isn't okay and it looks awful unless you're young and gorgeous.

It's like wearing a neon CANCER sign on my head. People—people I know who were friends even—run the other way. And it's not so great in the winter either no matter how warm the hat.

And think about not being able to plan more than a couple of days in advance, that's rougher than you think it's not how the world of adults works. Also can't really make any decisions. It sounds like I'm complaining and I think my doctor is fed up thinking I'm complaining but I'm not it's just the reality of it. And taking now yet another super harsh medication that I may or may not need that flattens me makes me not at all myself haven't been able to write for example for a couple of weeks now. Every night going to sleep— so early, basically when it gets dark, what am I going to do in the winter if this keeps up go to sleep at 4:30? saying tomorrow will be different tomorrow will be different you'll get up and write and do some yoga and do all these other sorts of mundane things and when it keeps not being possible I think it's natural to wonder why I'm doing this. Yes, I can by brute force plan some things like going to my daughters' graduations like going to their performances like talking to them on the phone and that's all great that I'm here to do those things. And today I am clearly writing at least some but I also started taking a yet another heavy duty medication last night so we'll see how it goes once enough of it is in my system, like maybe tomorrow.

I have this sort of sarcastic chorus line I've been saying from day one of this: Good thing I'm not ill or I could never do all these things the medical industrial complex requires. If you think it's easy being ill just from a processing-administrative standpoint, you are as they say dead wrong. Had to make charts for all kinds of things for the medication—including injections—I have to take at home since some are on a two week schedule, some are on a three week schedule some are on a most but not all days schedule and some are just whenever it seems right to my doctor to take them. And I do have to keep track not only of when I have to do it but also that I have done it how much and when. Okay and then charts of symptoms cause once they're not present it's not like they're all stored in my head a few weeks later, I'd be happy to forget them but I also do just forget them. Then I need to schedule things like scans okay not a big deal if the imaging place is functioning even close to efficiently but they never are and also which technicians I won't let touch me like one who had me deep in the MRI tube and started the contrast flowing into my veins and I told him eventually screaming that something is wrong I know how it's supposed to feel on the nth for n large time and this isn't it this hurts A LOT. But Constantine didn't believe me or something wanted to get to his quota I don't know what the problem was except I knew it wasn't going in right. Finally he got me out but by then my muscles were quite infiltrated with the gadolinium definitely not where it was supposed to go and finally a nurse came a very young wisp of a nurse who looked scared stiff. So anyway scheduling I have to say no Constantine and only the nurse Rob and use the Dotarem and so on. Okay not a big deal either. Then there's the scheduling and process consultations with experts "experts" like interventional radiologists for my potential ablation of lesions that are probably empty of cancer one very near my kidney so possible kidney damage comes with the procedure and the other near a lung so possible collapsed lung. Anyway I fax them sixty plus pages of medical records I have for the most part kept pretty organized in spite of the fact that I have hundreds of pages and many categories of things. And I get them the eleven CDs of previous scans and I talk to the medical assistants who rarely know much and are overworked and are difficult to get on the phone and even then to what avail. And then finally maybe I get an appointment with the specialist. And they are either arrogant and know everything or are maybe arrogant or not but know nothing and in any case they don't any two of them agree with each other and how is that possible when I consult with five? Shouldn't be possible but it is. So then what to do with something that is time sensitive and it took months to gather the intel. There's also of course just getting and withstanding the harsh very difficult to take treatment and the nausea and the exhaustion and the fevers and chills and the chemical depressions and the total TOTAL as in everywhere hair loss (you can see this one really bothers me even though I know it's minor in the scheme of things) and not being able to control one's bowel movements either constipated in the extreme or it just running out unpredictably I often feel like a tube of toothpaste on constant squeeze mode or both (I know you wouldn't think both could be possible but it is) and the confused just plain bad thinking and needing nevertheless to stay clear to advocate for oneself. And this is in the best of circumstances in which I have a brilliant and caring doctor and he has a great clinical team and I can pay for the crazy priced medications and the car services when I can't get myself there. Imagine when any one of those things isn't so easy I just can't imagine it because I keep ringing my chorus line over and over every time I marvel at what I have to do while I am being treated with drastic medications for a dire disease and it all seems just overwhelming. Someone asked me what happens to people who go for example to even touted oncologists for the standard of care? They die and a lot faster than they need to. And a lot more painfully. I know too many people who had that fate. They just die and here I am not dead yet though I most likely would have been if I went to one of those *crème de la crèmes.* They weren't interested in me either since my disease was diminishing I was of no use for their trials.

Oh and I haven't even mentioned the insurance layer. How much less insurance covers since they were all allowed to rewrite policies after the Affordable Health Care Act. Yeah I've had the same policy for at least twenty years but after that horrible act—of course we should have single payer but will we?—Medicare truly for all?—Blue Cross was allowed to rewrite my solo practitioner policy because it didn't have pediatric dental care. Pediatric dental care?? No one meaning me surely had any need of that but no matter. It was the loop hole that allowed them to jack up the payments—by me—for pretty much everything while looking like they had lowered premiums. So I pay A LOT more out of pocket than I would have before and also pay for medications "that aren't approved for my condition" but that I need and those ones have particularly crazy prices and I have to deal with what they call specialty pharmacies, no brick and mortar for them. They'd rather spend their overhead having reps call me multiple times a week to confirm a refill that is sent to my doctor's office and is prescribed by my doctor and they keep me on the phone for minimum thirty minutes each time mind you several times a week and they go over the dosage administration doctor's address and so forth and I have to okay everything like I'm the prescribing physician. And it's not like they can call in an efficient way for all or at least several medications at a time no no it's often one at a time and sometimes often really multiple calls for the same one med because of system glitches that didn't recognize a previous set of calls for the same thing. And each time they call the rep says how can I help you? to start off. They are calling me! Other things I go to a physical pharmacy for of course and other things require a superspecial specialty pharmacy. So just keeping track of all of that would really be a mind fuck I don't even attempt.

Turns out hair does serve functions and not just the obvious ones in the nose brows eyelashes. Think arm and leg hair when you feel something like a hair moving, could be telling you there's a tick trolling around looking for a good spot to lunch in you. Hair as beacon, not just aesthetics even though it is odd how alike we baldy ghosts look. Take away the hairs and people don't look so different. Odd that when I'm looking around and see myself in the other inmates. Skin color age weight don't differentiate as much as hair.

Weird sort of indescribable feeling knowing what is going to kill me. I mean, coming back to this again just once more bear with me, we all know we're going to die but it's sort of abstract, a fact but without shape or contours. Once it gets a shape, *this* is going to kill me and in not long at all, that's way way different. A sort of sickening but oddly out of body experience. The world looks different too, I am different, everything is kind of other, even myself, become object to myself and of course slowly or quickly to others as well. Get the documents in order, get the people in place, get everything in place. Have conversations about stuff with immediate family. Get an executor, health care proxy, explain to those that aren't those things (but assumed they would be). Toss papers I don't want found, toss junk others shouldn't have to deal with—I got a dumpster a large dumpster and nearly filled it, and tried to purge some kind of metaphorical dumpster but that didn't or hasn't yet worked, reviewing the unpleasant to tragic bits, only some washed away so to speak. And somehow also keep going as if I don't have that knowledge, or to fight it, to protest with persistence. Talk to everyone who might know something to help, but of course they all pointwise disagree with each other, not established wisdom except the sort that comes with the authority of institutional backing, and they are the most likely to be wrong.

I should know. Can't get too much—maybe a little but really, truly not a lot—cleaner and greener than me and yet, look at me, writhing around trying to keep the now moving forward until it's decent. Twice hit. Blindsided the second time, what's wrong with me? Not just in the genes either, by the way. Fool me once.

I'm going to end the story here, but before I close I will ask a few parting questions and ponder a few things even if by now you've gotten kind of used to me and don't want me to stop just yet. So even this year in *The Lancet*, hardly a hotbed of radical journalism, printed quite a list of health effects of climate change, stuff I've been talking about but to get hit by such a list all at once is arresting. Just some of it, wildfires (yeah, we know how many are ranging at almost any given moment, but in Napa/Sonoma? And then in Napa again, Colorado, New Mexico) and the numbers of the acres burned are hard if even possible to fathom, the square miles of it, floods, yes we know this too and how Manhattan in going to lose twenty feet of shoreline since we seem to be doing nothing about the now certain eventuality in the near future of this, and that's not to mention coastlines like in Florida, and whole islands that will be gone soon, I think one already disappeared last year. Like real islands not just little specks. Okay, back to the list, droughts, yeah even here in the northeast of the USA we've been having real droughts, so imagine elsewhere. Heatwaves, yes we did always have them and cold snaps and such but not like the swings we've got going now. Even in the middle of usually cold New England around the 4th of July, rainy, cold, oy not this year and for weeks really going but such a ferocious central, horrible week of heat, scathing down on the earth the really drier than bone earth. Temperature rise, decreased crop yields, increasing water shortages and contamination, water-borne diseases air-borne diseases respiratory diseases kidney disease dehydration population displacement undernutrition ice sheet collapse lack of mental health impact decreased labor capacity decreased thought capacity (I added this one but it's obvious) and the *Lancet* list continued on and on, this is just a sampling a taste of the thing in a more than respected medical publication not some left wing ideological sort of rant as it might be called. Conservative even, this list is just skimming the surface, the obvious glaring truth of what's already clearly happening and on the rise.

What if and I mean really what if, all the consequences positive and negative 'cause there are both,

we hadn't used DDT ever?

we hadn't used glyphosate?

we hadn't produced large, gas guzzling cars or what if we had switched to the all-electric cars in the 1980s when we had them and they were good and the batteries went for long range?

we didn't use formaldehyde in housing and furniture or put lead in stuff like house paint, gasoline, plumbing?

we didn't incinerate?

there hadn't been electric can-openers and electric pencil-sharpeners?

there were no single use plastics of any kind?

What, if in a possible world all this were taken away, would we still be ourselves?

Well, that's all I've got for now. And just to let you know that any resemblance of characters, events, or locations in this book to persons living or especially dead including corporations, rivers or anything else legally deemed a person these days, actual events or locations is coincidental. No reality to any of this of course.

ABOUT THE AUTHOR

MONTANA KATZ is a psychoanalyst. She has written two novels (*Clytemnestra's Last Day* and *Living Dolls and Other Women*), a play (adapted from *Clytemnestra's Last Day* by the same name), books on psychoanalysis (*Contemporary Psychoanalytic Field Theory: Stories, Dreams and Metaphor* and *Metaphor and Fields: Common Ground, Common Language, and the Future of Psychoanalysis*), and two award-winning books on gender bias (*The Gender Bias Prevention Book* and, with co-author Veronica Vieland, *Get Smart: What You Need To Know But Won't Learn In Class About Sexual Harassment And Sex Discrimination*). Her writing is situated at the confluence of fact, history and the unconscious.

Printed in May 2020
by Gauvin Press,
Gatineau, Québec